RYAN J.CLARK

RYSQO, THE BLACK DRAGON

Ryan James Clark, a first time author and nineteen year old Renaissance man. Born in Philadelphia Pennsylvania November third nineteen eighty five, he has exceeded expectations once again. Those who have known him closely recognize his talents as a martial artist, an artist, and a self taught musician. When he took on the challenge of writing *Rysqo, the Black Dragon*, he was fifteen years old and a sophomore in high school. Four years later, his story is complete.

As the only child to a hard-working single mother, Ryan has long awaited his chance to prove to the world that with hard work and determination, anything can be achieved. He has won numerous awards of recognition and achievement throughout his academic years. He has competed and won in many martial arts tournaments, collecting trophies and congratulations for more than a decade. With all his success in life thus far, he was never satisfied. He knew that there was more he could give to the world, so he authored the ultimate love story.

Ryan James Clark

www.rbddesigns.com

Coming soon:

Pandora's Seduction
A Shattered Mind
A smile is forever
The Theories of RED

RYSQO,

the

BLACK

DRAGON

RYAN JAMES CLARK

A message to the reader:

A few things that are about to be read may disturb some people seriously, and if you are sensitive to your beliefs, or caught up in your ways never open to change, or a different way of thought, I suggest you stop reading and put this book down.

This book is dedicated to anyone who has ever loved, been loved, or lost a loved one.

Author's Note

I wrote this story originally as part of a challenge. In my tenth grade English class, we were studying Mary Shelley's *Frankenstein*. My teacher explained to us how young Ms. Shelley was when she wrote what has turned into a classic. She put up a challenge to the entire class; whoever can write a masterpiece like *Frankenstein* automatically passes the semester. I took her on.

My original version of this story was about ten pages long and had so much loose thought in it, it would take ten scholars to decode it. That was a long four years ago. Now I have finally had the opportunity to publish my story. I can make no guarantee that it will be a success like Mary Shelley's *Frankenstein*, but I will do my best to take your imagination on the ride of its life.

It will ultimately be up to you how successful my story is. If you remember it, then I am successful. If you learn from it, then I am successful. If you encourage others to do the same, then I am successful. I have done many things in my life that I am proud of, but when it comes down to it, never has there been an opportunity to contribute to history and society like this for me.

My story is indeed one of fantasy, and romance. It is mildly graphic, but all for a reason. I have split my story into six parts, or components. These components are what I believe life is made of. Each possesses a different lesson or theme that you should pay close attention to. I wrote my story very loosely, without too much definition. I have done this to encourage you to imagine and think. I also have provided a quote before each chapter. These quotes represent great importance in my story. They represent "the prophecy" you will soon read about. With all great stories though, there remains those questions you will have for the author. While I encourage people to try and figure things out for themselves, I do yearn for feedback and I am eager to assist you in your journey through *Rysqo, the Black Dragon*. Enjoy!

~*Ryan James Clark*

Outline

Rysqo, the Black Dragon
    ~The story is introduced
Rysqo, the Black Dragon, part 2 – The Dark Heart
    ~Secrets are revealed
Rysqo, the Black Dragon, part 3 – The Wheel of Destiny
    ~A path is walked; no one can see the end
Rysqo, the Black Dragon, part 4 – A Foretold Future
    ~New roads are open, only one has an off ramp
Rysqo, the Black Dragon, part 5 – The Shadow
    ~A new force
Rysqo, the Black Dragon, part 6 – The Forbidden
    ~The Ultimate end…

Themes

Life ~ the wonders of existence
Decisions ~ choices you make that open up your paths in life
Self Value ~ looking into yourself searching for an understanding of yourself
Consequence ~ results produced by decisions you did or did not make that affect you
Solemnity ~ finding yourself…by yourself
Death ~ the end of life

Rysqo,

the

Black Dragon

INTRODUCTION

This is a story about life. This story was not written to stimulate human emotions, or cause people to go out and take action. This story has been written to make people aware of life. This story was not written to tell about someone else's hard times, or even allow who ever reads it to take a walk in someone else's shoes. This story has been written to show people life, life's colors, and all of life's wonderful things. What is behind living and what causes life to go on? What causes people to go out into the world day after day and endure all of life's many hardships? What causes people to walk down the wrong path in life, and sometimes find their way out, and still strive, and push themselves past their limits; to go on? Though mankind has discovered and created many things in our world, though mankind has explored outer space, and developed different pictures of the solar system, we are still far behind. We spend so much time on the developing of the luxuries that we can not see living without, that we neglect the most important things that affect us everyday. The smallest, most under appreciated things, that often go unrecognized, are the ones that sometimes carry the most importance.

What drives you day after day? Is it a multimillion dollar mansion, or an average row home? Or even if you live in the worst of all places imaginable, you never know who has it worse. In fact, you could never perceive the thought. Your situation is always the worst. It is all you can ever see or care about. We all share our own perceptions of our selfish living and how we treat others. The importance of the survival of humans as a whole, the securing of the well-being of life past your expiration, might not seem as important as making every meal, or just looking out for yourself. Who is so pure to judge? What human on this Earth is above all damnations others are plagued with? What human on this Earth is above the greatest human fault, being human?

This force is the power, or the inner being which is always talked about in all human beliefs. This force is the drive, the will, the strength, and the knowledge. If you think about it though, what drives you is what drives me, and what drives everyone.

Humans can not find a way to explain our existence today, whether it was chance of science, or some divine higher power. People whom find no need to explain their existence are sometimes cast from the crowd. People whom do not follow a general belief for existence are sometimes cast from the crowd. People whom fall into some form of belief and join together, or those who are influenced by the thoughts of

8

others, they are wild cards in life, played by the first hand they are included in. They never turn their back, or wander from this hand, but it is a path they choose to take.

Though this is one of the most unexplained questions in the universe, people sometimes tend to avoid the answer. They do not want accept evidence due to years of belief, and or faith; and many try to even avoid the questioning of the possibility of another answer to our existence. They fear their fate will change, and bring suffering or unhappiness after death. All cultures have their beliefs and fears. Some of these beliefs and fears conflict with those of opposing cultures, and some allow different possibilities. If you think about it though, there is one belief that all cultures, religions, or social groups, commonly believe in but have yet to explain. This same belief is what drives us to do what we do, to go on day after day. This belief or unexplained force can cause us to inflict damage to ourselves or others in any instance. Though humans are perhaps one of the most intelligent forms of life on this planet, this honor of knowledge damns us. With this knowledge comes the question of more knowledge, such as explanations of emotions. These are things some of Earth's creatures never contemplate. Humans though, we are controlled by it.

I am not a religious person at all, but I see power behind this force, true power. This is the type of power that can not be contained or suppressed, if it takes hold of you, your only hope is to go with it, or it will plague you forever. This unstoppable force, that I have spoke of since the first few lines is, love.

No force on Earth is stronger than that of love.

Those who use someone's love against them, by playing with their emotions, are driven to do this by love. They love to do harm to another's emotions, or they have been hurt in the past and seek revenge. Love, a word so commonly used, and loosely at that. It is spoken inadvertently at times, and it may be the only word that can be used to describe a deep attraction between two things, but is it thus proven that saying this word confirms it.

Love is a word that carries deep meaning behind it. Some fear the word and shiver at its mercy. Love, is a word spoken to describe an unexplainable force of great power. It is a force of attraction; the glue of existence. Why should it have a name though? Why should it be okay to say love if people fear the word God, and dare not to say it hastily and without regret? Is love so meaningless to humans now that they forget its power? If you remember though, wasn't said to be the love of Jesus Christ that saved people? At least that is how it is explained in Christian beliefs. All beliefs seem to intertwine though, for all supreme or superior beings in all beliefs seem to promise some sort of salvation if certain acts of loyalty or devotion are done to please it, him or her.

Love, an emotion said to be shared by mortals and gods alike. What do you see love as though, a mother's caring for a child? Think for a moment, of any instance, in which love has not driven a human to do something, anything. Remember though, love is the foundation for all emotions, without a second part it would not be complete. I will not say that it is exactly equal, though it may be, but there are other emotions. Love brings with it hate, and so forth. The love explained in my story, is the same type of love, the only type. The love in my story is a love worth fighting for, a love worth living and dying for. It is the same love that may bring some people much pain in life, and bring others happiness or pleasure. It is for you to decide what this love means to you though. This book is filled with many hidden meanings, some that deal solemnly with my personal beliefs, others that can be recognized maybe after a second reading of the book.

This book is indeed not just a fantasy story of love and emotion, and until you realize the true meaning behind my words as they are written, until you feel what I feel, you have not succeeded in reading the book.

I do not see my words or beliefs as more important than anyone else's, but they are words of wisdom. I was once told a deep lie, "with age comes wisdom", and this is far from the truth. With age comes experience. Wisdom is what we each hold inside ourselves. We each have our own wisdom, or knowledge, that we hold to ourselves. No one else has access to this unless we give it to them. What we learn adds to our wisdom, thus age is no factor. Knowledge is indeed a source of power, and a source of power that can be easily accessed.

Heed to my words, though they may not seem to affect you at first, I am sure that in some way they relate to you. It is all about opening your mind and going for the ride.

I will let you see what I see, feel what I feel, but I will restrict you to nothing. Though these options are at your disposal, you have your own feelings, and could never possibly feel what I feel, unless what you feel is, love. Is love what I feel though? It is for you to decide. All I ask is that you enjoy the book, and share it with others.

The greatest disrespect to the living is not to live. The greatest disrespect to the dead is not to live. The greatest disrespect to the unborn is to live a life of nothing. Please let my words, my thoughts, affect you. I wish to live knowing that I have touched someone, something, in a way that they will always remember and share.

PROLOGUE

The man walked with his son through the crowd of people. He waited in line for his check to be cashed, as he saw the bank teller look behind him over his shoulder.

"Excuse me sir, hold on."

"Not a problem", he said.

The man turned around to see a middle aged man walking to the teller station next to him. He eyed him, he looked strange. The man turned to look at him. Their eyes met and locked momentarily. The man's teller asked the suspicious looking man,

"Can I help you with something sir, that teller is on a break?" He looked at her, and walked closer.

"Yeah, fill this bag up now", he commanded. The man pulled out a semi-automatic weapon. The man next to him saw the weapon and shielded his son.

"Get back Rysqo." the boy's father whispered. The gunman said,

"Empty it now!" Rysqo's father raised his hands up and walked closer to the man. Rysqo looked on as if confused by what was taking place in front of his eyes.

"Don't do this." his father pleaded. The gunman pointed the gun at him,

"Shut up." Rysqo's father continued to try and talk him out of it.

"Look my friend, it really is not worth…," he was interrupted.

"I said shut up", the gunman barked. Rysqo's father continued to talk. The gunman was filled with frustration and he pulled the trigger. Rounds entered the chest of Rysqo's father. He stumbled back, into the counter. He slowly slid down to the ground. The gunman looked at Rysqo, who was in shock. They stared into each other's eyes. The gunman rolled his eyes. He then looked at the teller,

"I said fill up my bag". The teller agreed. The worker whom was on a break had called authorities when the shots were fired, but the criminal had gotten away, unscathed. Rysqo was very upset, but he did not cry, he just got a pale blank look on his face.

Chapter 1: The Collective's Preferred

In the beginning, there was darkness.....from this came a being, a being whose power was immeasurable, this was Black Dragon. It marked a boy, the chosen one. ... was his name, soon he saw his power.... and then there was.....

Forces of life are affected by his existence, for he is in control....

Before the dawn of time as we know it, before the big bang, or theories of evolution that man is still decoding, even before the eras of prehistory, there was a mistake made. A mistake that is too late to change or take back, and if fate was to take its course, oblivious to consequence or morality, this mistake, would bring about what all cultures commonly fear...the end of the world, a cease to all living existence on the planet, the apocalypse.

A transgression can be washed away, but not forgotten. At least not easily, not at some cost, some unavoidable remuneration, and this was life. The Collective knew this. They had been well aware of what their actions would lead to, but with limitless power, and the naiveté of a child, they made the mistake that any mortal would make, toying with life. But The Collective weren't in any way mortal, so their faults weighed greater on the continuance of existence. As the webs of the universe dangled in their hands, they knotted and sew together the galaxy they were to inhabit for all eternity. In this galaxy they made planets, each different from the next. They did have a favorite planet though. They spent extra time creating this planet. The Collective soon found their planet to be barren with no life or intelligence, so they pondered and decided what primitive inhabitants to put on the planet. They chose beasts which they would enjoy watching, dragons. These beasts were entertaining to watch, due to their native destructive nature.

The Collective then saw the difficulty in monitoring the dragons from a distance, and decided to stake a post on their planet. This post was in the form of a castle. They called this castle by no name, for it was the capital of the world, and it was inhabited by the creators of this world. Anything extraneous to The Collective was not allowed anywhere near this capital, and it was virtually impossible to penetrate the walls of the castle. Many dragons attempted this defiance, over-stepping their boundaries, and ironically just as many dragons had failed.

<u>Chapter 2:</u> From sweat, to tears and blood…then life

Control the water, control the fire, and control the earth and the sub-heavens…
These were the jobs of the ancient dragons, and soon this was found to be too much, for these ancient dragons could not even control themselves, and great power was at waste. It took mortals great efforts to check these beasts of pure strength, and ignorance.

Much time has passed, and The Collective has now added more intelligent life. Animals, by land and sea, including humans, were created. The Collective has also stopped closely monitoring their prime creation, the foremost species of dragon known as "the guardians". Dragons roamed free throughout the land, uncompassionate to all other existing life. They were now the guardians of the planet, due to the negligence of The Collective. They were capable of swimming, breathed fire, roamed the land, and soared in the skies, like majestic birds. Since The Collective was out of the picture, and dragons ruled the earth and above, who was left to control the dragons? This factor remained not thought of, but soon it was recognized, for one day, somehow, the dragons gained a taste for blood.

Countless numbers of humans and animals were wiped from the earth, chaos erupted. Humans had developed many irrelevant means of defense against the dragons. Human life was rapidly diminishing, when finally The Collective re-emerged to intervene.

Chapter 3: The One and Only

It was just too much for the mortals, so The Collective saw great need in creating a dragon more powerful than the rest, a dragon that could hold the secrets of life and death which they contained. So it was done. Darkness swept the universe. This dragon soon saw its power and abilities over the rest of the dragons. It was amazed that it could not be stopped, not even by The Collective, the force which created it.

The Collective was sure of what had to be done in order to preserve life. They wanted to make a dragon more intelligent or stronger than the rest, one that possessed the bloodline of The Collective, but was to be of the dragon. They had not, couldn't have predicted the mistake that they had made, but it was done.

~~~~~~

The grass blew, and with the breeze, came the aroma of roasting pheasant. All was calm. For days there had been no sightings of the dragons. Rumors hovered in the town that there was a slayer about. Some said that he possessed the dark magic or witchcraft and killed dragons with single gestures. Others remained curious, yet cautious enough not to wander past the sacred grounds.

A family picnicked in the grasslands serenely, when a young one looked into the sky, pointed, and called,

"Ma..." She and the father responded, by approaching him and asking,

"What Melchah, could it be a bird?" He shook his head and his expression changed, and with this sudden change, they both looked up, and cursed the heavens, for in a matter of seconds they, as well as the landscape, were about to be smothered. Two dragons tumbled to the earth. A split second later, another landed on its hind legs and let out a majestic roar that shook the land. Perplexed as to what they had just witnessed, the family that had just made it to safety, stood cold, as if they were part of the earth. The father slowly approached the rear of the dragon. Sensing movement, the dragon whipped around in a motion that would indicate attacking, and immediately stopped. It was not in this dragon's nature to kill innocent beings, only those who have wronged, deserve to be wronged. The little boy broke free of his mother's vice, and ran to his father's side and tightly clung to his leg, as tears streaked down his face.

"It's alright Melchah; this fellow means us no harm." The boy wiped his eyes and looked into his father's eyes, as if asking what to do next, and said,

"Can I touch it father?" His father approved, and as he reached out to stroke the beast, it parted from the earth as it flapped its huge wings, and departed.

The family rushed back to the town to tell the others of their adventure. They approached the town head, and explained what they had just experienced. He responded by saying,

"Contact our neighboring towns. We must celebrate, for maybe there is hope for us all!"

~~~~~~

The dragon returned to its home after a very busy patrol. Upon entering the castle, the dragon, which was still learning many new things about its abilities, searched for its teacher and mentor. This was the sole female member of The Collective. It located her in her quarters on the roof. She was admiring the view. From here, she observed a world she helped create, a world far from our time, and a world without faith. As it crossed the threshold, she congratulated it on a good patrol. Then for many hours they interacted. They had telepathically communicated, on a cooperative basis; they could interact, only when they had both agreed. They would never breach each others minds without permission.

Late in the day, the woman had duties of her own to attend, and she left the dragon alone to develop its own comprehension of what they had just discussed. Somewhat disappointed, still having questions that were unanswered, it tried to locate an unoccupied member of The Collective. The beast was trained and taught continuously. It was always curious for more knowledge and eager to learn from any teacher. It searched vigorously, trying to locate one of the other members of The Collective. It failed to do so, but what it did find angered it. All of The Collective was gathered in one of the castle's many corridors. The dragon found it very odd that its presence was not requested, for in the past it was welcome to, and aware of all social gatherings The Collective held. It had no great impact on any of the subjects discussed so its views often went unheard. It just wished to be recognized as the member of The Collective that it was. This time though, circumstances were different, for its mentor hadn't even alerted it of the meeting. Outside of the room the dragon waited and waited, continuously making excuses for their crime against it, and it continuously contradicted each one. Then suddenly it actually listened to what they were saying. They were discussing the diminishing need for the dragon, due to "the guardians" dispersion. It realized that it was just a tool, a puppet that they had controlled very well. It had done all of their dirty work like a pawn in the game of life, casting death to all that oppose them. The scaly beast was angered and it wanted revenge. They had ultimately wronged and deceived it. Its anger now turned to hatred, and it was fueled even more by the voice yielding the final decision, which was none other than that of its mentor, the only one it had originally trusted, the only one that seemed to show compassion for it. Now it had nothing, limitless power yes, but it was seriously misdirected. Someone was going to pay, no The Collective was going to pay, and pay dearly.

<u>Chapter 4:</u> Quitters Stay Alive

*Since the dragon was indeed part of The Collective, it was given all of the privileges of The Collective. So it was written, the last surviving member of The Collective would be given all the strengths of the entire Collective. So the dragon became greedy its heart became **"black"**, as it was sent into a rampage taking on its creators, The Collective.*

The dragon exploded into the room, and all became silent; it was as if time had frozen.

"*I think it heard us discussing its non-existing future*", said a member known as Deridus.

"*Quiet*", snapped a member known as Coryphaeus.

"*We must eliminate this problem now!*" A member known as Celerus, whom was known for his split second decisions, leaped into the air at the dragon. It responded by incinerating him mid-flight. Panic filled the room, as the eight members scrambled to different corners of the castle. It dealt with them one by one, starting with Recreanon. Recreanon had put up no fight what so ever. He was hidden in the boundless boughs of his corridors. The dragon let out a burst of flames, igniting the entire room, and disposing of Recreanon. Next to suffer was Euphor. Euphor was almost impossible to defeat, he healed every blow the dragon landed, until he lost concentration and missed his last chance to heal. The dragon clamped on to his neck and cracked it while jerking its body laterally. Next the dragon battled Strife. Strife knew many forms of combat, and had each one at his disposal. This seemed to aid him in battle, until the dragon took flight, and the battle was immediately ended. When it exited Strife's corridors, Deridus was waiting. He and the dragon looked into each others eyes; no fear was present in either. The dragon's lips started to curl back revealing menacing teeth. Suddenly the dragon was attacked from behind by Disorium, they had tricked it. The two of them frequently worked together to train it. The dragon was so surprised it didn't recognize their trick. After the surprise blow and with the two on one situation, the dragon had no time to plan and think. It would be too risky, and with all that was at risk, it really wasn't worth it. The dragon swiped at Disorium with its winged claws, and slapped Deridus with its tail. Both were fatally wounded, so it left them there to suffer. Acumenus was in the process of casting a spell when he was slaughtered. The dragon was curious as to what the spell consisted of or did, but it didn't let it hinder its mission. The dragon flew into the stone spiral staircase at the end of the corridor. This staircase would lead it to the other levels of the castle, more specifically, the roof. As it proceeded to the roof it moved cautiously, for it knew two members remained; Coryphaeus the leader, and **her**! It had almost made its way to the roof when Coryphaeus dropped on its back and stripped its wings from its body. Pain streamed through the dragon, and anger almost entirely consumed its mind. Coryphaeus leaped off of its back as it crashed into the stairs.

"*How say I the pain I felt when my creations began to kill each other? How say I the pain I felt when my brothers were slain? Now say I no pain when I kill you, for you are a beast of no morals, no sense of loyalty or devotion. I am your creator beast; you dare to spurn my word, my command? Reply beast!"* He opened his mind.

"Where are your morals? How could you allow one of your creations to be disposed of? I do as I feel that which will aid me. I show no compassion for you, for you created me. I owe you nothing except to be. How could you assume otherwise? Is my existence so meaningless to you that you can rid the earth of my presence with just as much ease as you bless it with my presence? Or does your consciousness, like mine, revolve around that of your own benefactor. I am in no way defying you, for I am doing what I was created for, to rid this earth of all evil. Nothing will stop me!" Coryphaeus heard enough of it,

"Ignorant beast, you could be annihilated by me with no more than a thought. Since you see me as such an evil being, I will live up to the title. Before I wipe you off this planet, I will let you in on a secret, it was neither my suggestion nor my decision to destroy you, and there was no hesitation in the final word given by your precious Venus!" Coryphaeus was satisfied, and very pleased with himself. He believed that his words struck the dragons heart like a burning dagger; he was wrong, very wrong. The truth had already taken its toll on the mind of the dragon.

"I know of Venus' maltreats against me, and she will pay, just as you will!" With that the dragon locked Coryphaeus in its jaws, and hurled him down the stairwell. The dragon caught sight of Venus and proceeded up the steps. It cornered her on the castle rooftop.

"Don't do this, you have no idea what you are doing", Venus stated.

"Silence..! How dare you? You betrayed me, my trust, and my love. What consequence should I fear, more than that of trust? When broken it can't be mended. I chose to trust you, you pleaded with me to trust Coryphaeus and the others, and now I am plagued by the consequence of those actions. Your deception went deeper though, for you disported with my heart. Your fate is now to be decided by me Venus, and shall I say that it is easy to decide for you, or shall I take time to think about what I am doing...... It could be that a split second decision will do me justice." Tears filled Venus' eyes. In The Collective, she was compassion, but she now felt that she had failed in her mission; her existence was irrelevant. Venus was focused on another problem though; she knew that it was her last chance to save their planet, and the entire universe.

"Listen your actions, if carried out maliciously, will inevitably cause this planet, and all other planets to cease to exist. We hadn't foreseen it when creating you, but your presence on a planet, will bring about its destruction..."

21

"You lie", it said with impatience.

"I am afraid my words are pure. Before the meeting I had spoken with Acumenus to see if there was any possibility of us being wrong, but he augured this, and was sure. In the prophecy as he saw it, with your presence came the end of a world. World after world, even those which we did not create, you would bring about destruction, and it was as if you didn't know it. Indeed you were not conscious of your actions, but there was nothing that could be done. ".

"Is this another form of deception on your part? Before I dealt away with Acumenus, I witnessed him casting a spell, probably to mar me, but I do not believe he was able to finish, because my presence has showed consistency. "

"I know nothing of this spell you speak of, but if you are right, he probably found a way to save the universe."

"Is that what you call it?" With that, the dragon crept closer to Venus, and she backed away. As it went for the kill, she cursed it never to...

With the last member of The Collective besides itself out of the picture, it was beginning to feel all of their energies streaming through the air and into its body. It felt power, true power, and ultimate power. During the battle, its heart turned black. Its actions were carried out through anger and hate. So it was then recognized as The Black Dragon. It had not healed as Euphor had taught it to, and it was hastily weakening. With all the power surging through its body it was neither able to heal nor control it. Suddenly the earth began to tremble, fire lit the skies. Then asteroids, and meteors, struck the earth around the castle with devastating force. Ashes rose to the heavens, the core of the planet bubbled, ready to burst. All the while, the Black Dragon laid there agonizing, and figuring what to do next, for the end of the world was coming, and there was nothing that it could do.

Chapter 5: Soar with the Dragon

Its veins ran with the venom of the deadly scorpion, its mind contained the wisdom of the wise, since the beginning of time. Fire burned in its stomach and in its eyes, shown the sign of dragon rage. The transformation was complete, but "Black Dragon" was weakened from its battle with The Collective, and its body was too weak to serve as a vessel for this new strength it had acquired.

The wind was ripped back and forth, at Rysqo's command. His hand
speed and power was indefinite, he seemed to get stronger and faster
by each movement he did, and he owed this to his devotion and practice of
all the arts he had learned since he was a younger child. He was very
skilled in many arts, and was a tournament champion. He chose not to
openly associate with many, only a chosen few, and even in that handful of
people, they still had known nothing of his private life, or his deep dark
secrets. He only openly confided those topics with his lifetime friend and
practice mate Xavier. While he paused for a refreshing bottle of water,
Xavier had made his music with the wind. Rysqo was undefeated, and
knew if anyone could match his skill, it would be Xavier. He watched as
Xavier went through the motions and practiced, undaunted by any of his
surroundings.

"Yo X", Rysqo called. Xavier finished his movements, and then
joined Rysqo for a bottle of water. He devoured a bottle quickly and
replied,

"Yeah", with an accent that may have taken others by surprise.

"You want to spar really quick, just light, not even to break a
sweat?" Xavier took another bottle of water to the head while eyeing
Rysqo, he still hadn't responded. Rysqo felt sure that he would say yes,
also eager to test his skills, so he proceeded to the center of the yard area
and commenced stretching, his back to Xavier. Then he heard incoming
footsteps, he turned around to divert Xavier's first attack, the fight was on.

The battle went smoothly, the two landed just as many blows, and
they had also increased their mutual respect for each other. As the battle
winded down, they had both stopped paying attention to the area around
them. They stopped while sharing some laughs, and heard clapping. They
turned to see Tanya, the only female to have ever tamed Rysqo. She was
beautiful in every man's eyes, and she had no enemies, male or female.
She was also committed to Rysqo, and their love burned as an eternal
flame. The only disagreements they ever had were the ones that arose
when Rysqo tried to protect her. She was so delicate and precious to him.
He wanted nothing to harm her. He had no concern in losing her to
someone else, because they were "soul mates". When they walked the
streets together, they had complements piled on; they just looked like they
belonged together. With her beautiful personality and an untouchable
body to match, and his confidence and fit body, they were perfect together.
Girls wanted him, and guys wanted her.

"Uh oh", teased Xavier. Rysqo's face lit up, as he laid his eyes
upon his goddess. They embraced each other tightly, as she congratulated
him on a well fought battle. The three of them entered the house for more
water, as Tanya told them of an upcoming party. Rysqo hated social

gatherings, but he complied with Tanya's wishes. Xavier said that he had other things to attend to, so Tanya understood.

The three of them went back outside, and Tanya challenged Rysqo to a fight. He always found her amusing when they sparred, because she only did it to be cute, but Rysqo and Xavier found it to be amusing. She tried to pick up on the movements the two of them did, but she insisted she didn't want to learn the arts. The three of them had more laughs as Tanya gave up when she couldn't land a blow on Rysqo. The city teens always hung out together, and had fun, Tanya was their inspiration, she had always managed to put a smile on both their faces and they all cared for each other. Never had one turned their back on the other, never had they an argument in the bunch. Xavier was the oldest, out of school and on his own. Rysqo and Tanya had attended the same high school and were currently seniors. They had plans for when they got out of school, and were always trying to make them better and better. The group was always together, and they were happy with that arrangement. They didn't see things getting any better......or worse.

The party seemed crowded to Rysqo, they all did. He was in a daze as Tanya dragged him through crowds of people all dancing and having fun. They finally found an area which seemed to have a little room. Then Tanya saw some of her friends,

"Rysqo, I'll be right back I am just going to say hello to Michelle, and Monica", and she ran over to them. Rysqo was standing all alone, but not for long because as soon as Tanya was out of sight, Rysqo was approached by a girl.

"Hey wassup", she asked.

"Nothing", Rysqo said as he looked past her.

"You trying to let me get a dance", she said, trying to be noticed.

"No, not really", Rysqo said getting a little frustrated. He had lost sight of Tanya, and he only attended the party because of her.

"C'mon why not, you tired or something?"

"Yeah that's it, excuse me can you move", Rysqo said as he walked past her and began his search for Tanya. The girl just looked on and watched the short Rysqo walk right out of her sight. All she could say was,

"Um um umn."

"Why don't all of you so-called ballers go back to the party and go dance or something?"
The gang of boys ignored Monica's suggestion, and continued their courting of Tanya.

"So what is a fine looking girl like you doing at a party all alone", one of the boys asked.

"I am not alone, I have a boyfriend, and he is inside at the party",
Tanya sharply responded. The two girls had only come outside for a
second to get some refreshments, and already somebody had tried to talk to
Tanya.

"You know he obviously ain't thinkin' about you 'cause he's
probably in that party with chicks all over him, so how about you let me
know your name, and get a dance." Tanya lost her patience,

"C'mon Monica let's go back inside, Rysqo is waiting", Monica
agreed.

"Now I know you heard me, why you gonna go and try to play me
like that", the boy asked.

"Now I know you heard her say she had a boyfriend", snapped
Monica taking up for her friend.

"Why don't you shut up and mind your business, hater", the boy
said, his frustration growing.

"Naw man, why don't you leave her alone", said Monica angrily.

"Yes...why don't you leave her alone", a male voice said in a very
grave tone. Everyone turned to where the voice came from. Rysqo was
leaning against a wall near the sliding door leading to the party, looking
down with his arms folded.

"What, who the hell is he, or who does he think he is", the boy
said. Tanya and Monica stayed silent but looked at each other, then Tanya
spoke up,

"Rysqo, its okay, Monica and I, we're okay, let's just go. I don't
want any trouble." They started walking towards Rysqo.

"Oh no, don't tell me that's the boyfriend, he looks more like your
little brother", the boy taunted, the rest of them laughed. Tanya walked up
to Rysqo and squeezed his arm,

"Let's go inside". He looked into her eyes, then looked at the
boys one more time, and complied. Then one of the boys said,

"Yeah hero, you better listen to your girl". Rysqo stopped cold.
He turned around, and gave the three a cold look.

"You got an eye problem buddy", the main instigator asked.
Rysqo turned around. Tanya and Monica were almost back inside, and
Michelle had just come to the door. The boys had an audience now.
Rysqo paid them no mind and sped up to catch up with Tanya. Tanya
turned around to see what was keeping him. "Man forget this", the boy
said as he walked up to Rysqo and shoved him in his back. Rysqo spun
around and looked him dead in the eye. "I know you heard me you little
punk", the boy said. Tanya ran up to her man.

"What's going on", she asked.

"Yo I'm tired of you and homeboy here disrespecting me and my
boys!"

"Oh really", Rysqo said with an attitude.

"Rysqo let's go", Tanya said sternly.

"Naw baby girl ", the boy said as he pushed Tanya aside. Somebody in the background yelled

"Fight..!" Rysqo turned around, as he turned back he was greeted by a swift jab, but with his quick reflexes, he dipped back and countered, his blow landed, and down went the boy. His friends came over to be served the same punishment.

The fight didn't last long, one strike each. Rysqo was already annoyed that he was even at the party. He used his skills to quickly end the battle. As he looked around he noticed that the party was ruined, and as he continued to scan the perimeter he saw Tanya. She stood there with her arms folded, and she didn't seem too pleased that he was fighting again. No words were exchanged by the two; they only joined Monica at the front exit. Rysqo apologized on the way home. Tanya forgave him and asked him never to get into any more fights that involved her in some way. Rysqo agreed to this, because he knew that his girlfriend had not wanted him to get hurt, but Rysqo also knew that he wouldn't be hurt fighting, at least not by mortal hands.

Chapter 6: Unleash the Black Dragon

It had to find a vessel worthy enough to receive the power it contained. This vessel in whatever shape or form it took to would be referred to as "the chosen one". The Black Dragon chose to mark the body of a young mortal boy as its vessel. It did so, and the mark took place on the boy's right arm in the form of a stone dragon tattoo. It was a very clever disguise. This time though, a seal was placed so that history would not repeat itself. The boy would control the power at will, but an opportunity like this would call for a reason for the dragon to be "unleashed". This reason would have to warrant releasing such a creature and such dark power into a world.

What was there left to do, could Venus be right, was this apocalypse dealt by it? As the Black Dragon lay there on the castle roof bleeding, agonizing, dying, it tried to concentrate and figure out what it could do. It had repeatedly thought of one contingency. The Black Dragon decided what it would do. Using the remaining strength that it now had, the Black Dragon traveled through time and space, searching for a being to inhabit. It searched and searched until it came across a new world, a new time. This world was known as "the planet Earth". The Black Dragon felt a pure energy being emitted, and it would head towards it to start the second phase of its plans.

Rysqo narrowed his eyebrows as he was about to pass a crowd of jocks with his girlfriend, Tanya. He could already hear their catcalls in his head. He hated it when females were disrespected, especially when this female was as special to him as Tanya, or his mother. He moved to the side slightly while holding Tanya's hand, as if to try to direct her out of their line of sight, but it was too late.

"Damn, look at that...woouuooo." The others laughed and patted him on the back as if in congratulation. Rysqo stopped cold, then looked at Tanya, he saw that she hadn't wanted to be involved in any confrontation, so he resumed walking. The jocks' catcalls seemed to be getting louder, and they were. They were following Rysqo and Tanya to their next class. As a teacher passed by they stopped, and disappeared into the crowd. Rysqo sighed; it was a sigh of relief, yet anger. He wished Tanya would have allowed him to defend her honor.

Rysqo walked Tanya to class. Rysqo put his stuff down at his desk. They had a substitute in his class, and he needed to be excused to the bathroom.

"Excuse me; may I have a hall pass?"

Upon entering the bathroom, he saw some familiar faces. A smile lit his face. As he walked over to the urinal, the smile stayed on his face. One jock said,

"That young boy must have really had to go, he is happy." The rest of them laughed. Another one of the boys recognized Rysqo.

"Hey, that's the dude with that nice looking chick!" Rysqo's eyebrow rose,

"Chick..?" A third jock questioned,

"Yo, what's her name?" Rysqo's fists clenched, then he remembered Tanya. He calmed down, and started to exit the bathroom. One of them blocked the door,

"Yo man, he asked you a question!" Rysqo smiled, and proceeded to the sink to wash his hands. "You think something is funny, do I look like a comedian?" Rysqo looked him in his eyes, and said,

"You don't want to know what you look like." The other jocks laughed and instigated after Rysqo's remark. Rysqo proceeded to exit the bathroom again when he was surrounded, and the one blocking the door made his move. After Rysqo hurt his pride he wanted to redeem himself in front of his friends. That was one of the biggest mistakes that those boys ever made.

Rysqo looked at the two who were closest to him then with maximum speed and power he delivered a back-fist to the face of the jock blocking the door. His face seemed to explode, as blood oozed out. Rysqo then grabbed the back of his head, swung around his back while delivering a paralyzing elbow to his spine, and kicked the door of a stall into the face of another jock. His first two victims dropped. The jock that was behind him was now in front of him, and he was rushing at Rysqo. Rysqo diverted his path, using his own weight and momentum against him, and slammed him into the wall. He held him there by his throat while supporting his arm. Then Rysqo was rushed by a fourth jock. While still holding on Rysqo kicked him in his solar plexus, and spun to land a kick to his throat. He dropped; Rysqo turned his attention back to the boy on the wall, and tightened his choke hold.

"Why can't you people just leave me alone", Rysqo asked. School security entered the bathroom. Things didn't look good for Rysqo, but apparently the security guards witnessed the entire confrontation on a surveillance camera. They rushed to the bathroom as soon as they saw trouble. They thought Rysqo was the one who would be in need of their services, but they were very wrong.

⁓⁓⁓⁓⁓⁓⁓⁓⁓⁓⁓⁓⁓⁓⁓⁓⁓⁓⁓⁓⁓⁓⁓⁓⁓⁓⁓⁓⁓⁓⁓⁓

"Rysqo Dauragon. Why is it that the name sounds so familiar? Oh now I remember you like to test yourself physically against the other students. One Drake Donaldson, varsity football team, busted lip, missing teeth, broken nose, bruised philtrim, and a slipped disc in his spine. One Donovan Treatwood, varsity football team, mild concussion, broken nose. One Brent Jones, water boy, crushed trachea, broken neck. Finally, one Deuce Williamson, varsity football star, fainted, deprivation of oxygen. Rysqo, how do you do it? You deal out all those injuries, yet still remaining the victim acting in self-defense huh?"

"Is there some reason why you are restraining me from going back to class?"

"No", said the principal, "You may leave, but please, try to stay out of trouble. I'll write you a note". He looked at his watch while shaking his head, "you can proceed to your next class". Rysqo took the note, and exited the principal's office. He exited as the bell sounded. He had to return to his previous class to get his things that he hoped Tanya was watching.

As he walked the hallways, he felt prying eyes, and a lot of them. To his dismay word of his bathroom adventure traveled very quickly. Many people were staring as if he was on fire, or naked, or even naked on fire. Rysqo could care less about them, he just hoped that word had not yet reached the ears of Tanya. A few moments later, Rysqo found himself walking slower. He was thinking of what excuse to give Tanya. He was worried that he had messed up, this time really badly. He felt a hand on his shoulder and turned around, expecting some daring teenager looking for a thrill with a stupid question or comment. It was actually his friend Allen.

"Here man, here's your stuff", Allen said.

"Thanks man, I was hoping that Tanya would bring it though", said Rysqo as he put his book bag on.

"Uh, I really do not think that she, or that you want to talk to her right now."

"So I guess that means she heard what happened", Rysqo said in a disappointed tone. He saw this as bad news, he hated bad news.

Chapter 7: Fits of Fury

The boy took heed to all the terms of assuming the position in The Collective, for the world had changed, and all the dragons had been wiped out, for the mortals had lost their tolerance of the beasts. The boy's world was years in advance of the world The Collective had once created. His world had seen the likes of the dragons, and for whatever reason, they had no longer existed in this place and time. Maybe it was because the boy's world possessed many faiths. Dragons and other reptilian creatures were seen as evil creatures in some of these faiths.
The boy, Rysqo was the last trace of the Dragon and Collective dynasties. Rysqo, the Black Dragon soon found it hard to fit himself into normal society, and lost all compassion for that of the mortal world, except for that of his four mortal wonders of the world.

"That's it Rysqo, it's over!"

"Tanya", Rysqo pleaded.

"Don't try to sweet talk me, I asked you to stop getting into fights for me!"

"I know, I'm sorry, but this had nothing to do with you, I was..."

"No Rysqo, it's over, good-bye!" Tanya then walked away. As he watched her strut away his friend came over to pat him on the back.

"You okay man", Allen asked.

"I'll live", he responded.

"Man when I heard what you did to those muscle heads, I was sure Tanya was going to kick you to the curb."

"I guess she finally had enough", Rysqo said. Rysqo was taking the episode with Tanya much better than some would have thought. Dating the most desired girl in school for as long as anyone could remember, he was expected to be devastated when dumped publicly. As they walked the halls, it seemed that the news of this breakup traveled very fast, as fast as that of the bathroom. She was on the market again, and he was an eligible bachelor as well. He felt more and more stares walking down the hallway, but paid them no mind.

They exited the school.

"Man hold on, matter of fact, I'll catch up with you later", Allen rushed back into the school, he had forgotten his coat. Rysqo proceeded walking home. He decided to take the scenic route around the back of the school, and through the football field, he needed to think.

Football season in the public league had not yet begun, and practice was usually tight around that time, but due to some mysterious injuries to some of the star players and the water boy, practice was dismissed. By the time Rysqo exited the school, mostly everyone had filed out. Only those who instigated and discussed the two events surrounding Rysqo took their time getting home on this Friday night.

As he made his way around the back of the football field, he was followed by two masked figures. He paid their presence no mind, thinking that they were just more of his newly acquired fans.

"So happy man,...what now?" With that comment, Rysqo recognized the voice and whipped around. He immediately knew there was going to be trouble. One of the boys had a build like Deuce Williamson, but with them both wearing masks, it would be impossible to tell. Rysqo released a sigh of fatigue and disgust, and just as he prepared for a fight, the sky turned very dark, as if the clouds were made out of lead. The sky then opened up, and the battled body of the Black Dragon collided with the ground. The two masked figures looked at each other, one of them fainted. The other said,

"Man c'mon Deuce, get up". He tugged at the limp body for a few seconds, then dropped the arm and ran. There only remained a shocked Rysqo, whom throughout this whole ordeal, did not flinch or even breathe. His limbs were immobilized, he was rendered paralyzed. Just when he thought things could get no worse, in his day, and life, a voice shook his body. Rysqo could not tell the voice's origin, he looked around to see if someone was playing games with him, he even looked at the body of the Black Dragon, it didn't move. He expected to see the mouth moving, or something, but a dragon laying on a football field, and a talking dragon at that, the thought got more ridiculous by the second. The voice came back, stronger this time. Satisfied that he wouldn't find its owner, he decided to just listen. The voice became even louder, and now Rysqo was able to understand, and make out sounds, but it was a language he had never heard before. Then he thought he heard different ones, until finally he picked up on one of the phrases. This time it was in English, or old English.

"**He..lp.. m.ee...**" the voice said. Rysqo started to look around again.

"Hello", he said with question or self-doubt in his voice. "Who is there", he asked.

"**Help.....me**", the voice said with a slight tremble.

"Okay, where are you", Rysqo was confused, but wasn't scared.

"**Come closer**", the voice said. Rysqo's first guess was to check Deuce's body. Deuce just lay there, as a coma victim would in a hospital bed. Rysqo started to feel like he could move again. He stood there to think for a moment. Rysqo started to believe maybe someone could have been crushed by the creature.

"**Help...me**", the voice asked again.

"Okay, where are you?"

"**Over here, come over here...**" Rysqo walked in the direction of the voice, and he ended up with the body of the Black Dragon in his line of sight. "**Closer**", the voice shook. "**Closer**", rang in his head until he was close enough to touch the body.

"How is this possible", Rysqo questioned.

"**I need your help.....I am the guardian... the universe... I came to this place to save my...self my existence... I am dying... a need a body, a mind, yours...pure...please help...me...please.**" At this point, Rysqo was taken aghast by the whole situation. He was supposed to save a talking dragon's life. He figured things couldn't get much worse, and the poor thing did look in pain.

"What do I have to do", Rysqo questioned.

"**Release your mind ... let me take control**". With those words, Rysqo complied.

Chapter 8: Man of Many Faces

*The Black Dragon was forced to live a cursed life, and was never able to
love again, so his mind was twisted to the point which he could not decide
whose love or acceptance he wanted. His mind was forced to think only
thoughts of promoting the protection and preservation of The Collective.
He was disappointed at first discovery of this curse, but not devastated.
He just wished that one day he could have the heart of his gem, the wonder
of his world.*

...
I wander in the dark, alone...
The voices in the dark tell me I can not leave them,
And that I must be alone...
I listen, but I wonder...
I wonder if one day the light will return,
Then at least I can wander alone,
And see where I am going...
*Maybe I can even see the face behind the voices I heard when I was in the
dark, alone...*

Rysqo was now in a state of unconsciousness. His mind was completely overtaken by the Black Dragon. His body still stood on the football field as it was, for they were in his mind.

"**Rysqo, is that your name..? I am known to some as the Black Dragon. My existence erupted from a need for justice and hope, in a world of anarchy and misery. I was given the tenth and final position, in an order known as The Collective. The Collective created me to watch over a planet in the universe they created far from here and this time. When they believed my duties were up, they felt that it would be in their best interest to destroy me. I once trusted, I once loved, and I know never to make that mistake again. One by one I eliminated my eight brothers and my sister in The Collective, Celerus, Recreanon, Euphor, Strife, Deridus, Disorium, Acumenus, Coryphaeus, and Venus. The battle wounded me severely, and I used my remaining energy to come here.**" Rysqo was still in shock, he had no questions at the time, and he was still trying to figure out if he was awake. Rysqo's mind was very weary, as if he was in a dream. All he could do was listen to the strange voice. He had no idea what had taken place, how long it had been, or who he was listening to, still he listened. "**I will not immobilize your body like this forever. In fact, I will only exist in your mind and subconscious, as thoughts or dreams would. When I was being trained and disciplined, each member of The Collective taught me something different. I now contain their energies, and can't use or harness them. They exist inside of me, and now you, but can only be used by those who are pure of heart, and I am not, not anymore. You shall live life as you normally would, and try to stay healthy. As I get stronger, I will be able to do and share more with you. Remember my words, for you are now Rysqo, the Black Dragon, and each decision you make, each action you take will weigh greatly on your planet, and your universe. You must uphold the same duties as I held though, and you must not abuse your abilities. Your abilities are not apparent and will not emerge, unless it is absolutely necessary, and you seem to be able to handle yourself, so this will not be often. You are in no way invincible; in fact you will stay the same unless I am called upon. Your duties are to protect this planet from this position, with your presence should come justice, and benevolence. These are the duties I give to you Rysqo. Now is the time to decide what you will do with them.**" Rysqo regained control of his mind and body. He looked around, it was late and Deuce was gone. He felt different even though the dragon had assured him no changes would come. He tried to think that it was all a dream or a hallucination. Rysqo saw a glimmering light in the corner of his right eye. He pulled up his sleeve. Then he looked at his arm where he had a tattoo. It was a stone dragon, he had got when he had ended his freshman year...it was glowing, he wasn't dreaming. Rysqo pulled his sleeve back down, and started walking home.

<u>Chapter 9:</u> The Final Chapter

*Greed, hate, and envy; they caused the dragon dynasty to fall. They are the **beginning**...and the **end** , but there can be only one, and he is "Rysqo, the Black Dragon", last surviving member of The Collective, holder of the secrets of the universe, master of the combats, secret to making and breaking destiny, he is...*

The next morning Rysqo sat up in bed. He wiped his eyes and then pressed his face into his hands. He was trying to remember all the words of the Black Dragon. It was far too much to remember, and he was very tired after getting in very late. His mother had already departed to run errands, and he had no plans for Saturday. He decided that a good training might be in order. He was actually anxious to see if the role he had taken up had any impact on his talents.

Xavier made his way up to the counter. He stopped in the middle of the aisle because he thought he heard a disagreement at the register area. He peeked over the row of canned dog food. He saw a couple of young men agitating the cashier, a foreign elderly gentleman. When he had entered the store, he was the only one there besides the cashier, whom was a very peaceful person. He and Rysqo had frequently visited the neighborhood store, and he could not ever remember an instance when there was trouble.

"How much?" one of the young men asked. The cashier responded by pointing to the price on the food item, and tapping it. "This crap", the boy sent the food item hurling into a shelf. The cashier backed up and reached under the counter. The boy saw his movement and reached across the counter to grab his collar with both of his hands and pull him in. "Uh uhn pal, you chill", he looked at one of his associates, and gave him a head signal, "go see what my man was reaching for." His partner went around the back of the counter and searched the area where the man was reaching, to find a slightly concealed baseball bat. He rose it up over his head like a trophy and smiled. The other boy glanced at it, and then returned his gaze back to the terrified face of the cashier. He rolled his eyes. "You know what; I hate it when you foreign assholes come over here starting shit. What did I do to you? You are charging me all this money for all this crap..." He pulled down a rack of candy, "and now you try to hit me with a baseball bat because I disapprove of your services. I'll teach you that the customer always comes first! Man, yo hand me that." He took the baseball bat. "Yo, hold this punk still. I'm going to hit a homerun with his head". His friend pushed his head over the counter, and held his arms. The man began to mumble and cry. "Let's do this ", the boy said as he reeled back in a batting stance. Just as he was about to swing, the bat was snatched from his hands, and his right leg gave out. Xavier threw the bat to the floor,

"That's enough." The other boy released his hold, and jumped over the counter. As Xavier stared him down, he raised his hands in a manner that would indicate submission. He side stepped past Xavier and picked up his friend. They gave Xavier one last look, then they fled. The cashier brushed himself off, and then regained his composure. As he tried to say thank you, a bullet dove into his chest. Xavier ducked behind an aisle, and stayed out of sight.

~~~~~~

Rysqo was low in his water bottle supply, so he headed to the neighborhood store. He greeted the neighborhood youngsters as he walked, and they returned the courtesy. As he made his way to Tanya's house, he took a quick glance, hoping to catch sight of her. She wasn't home, so he proceeded quicker. He felt very bad about their disagreement, but not as bad as yesterday. He didn't want to call her, and he hadn't received a call from her. So he left the situation alone.

~~~~~~

Tanya and Monica walked around the corner, both aching for a snack.

"So, did you make up with Rysqo yet"? Tanya smiled, then forced an artificial frown,

"No, and I am not going to either. I am serious, and Rysqo has got to understand that." Monica laughed at her statement,

"Sure you are girl, you know you love that boy, you may as well stop the drama." Tanya was silent, she knew Monica was right, and she knew that it hadn't been twenty four hours yet and she had already missed Rysqo.

~~~~~~

He looked around the bag of chips as two figures exited the automobile. The two whom he recognized were standing on the street. Those two boys were not alone, and it seemed that they had anticipated trouble. Or at least they anticipated making trouble. Xavier saw them armed with one handgun, equipped with a silencer. With their resources they obviously meant business. Xavier crept to the back of the store; he knew that this task although not impossible, would be extremely difficult. Xavier frequently worked as a security guard. He had just recently quit his security job because he was sick of the stress. Xavier now did cleaning and renovations.

Two of them stood at the front counter, and the other two spread out searching aisles. Xavier knew that he could be spotted soon. Then his heart skipped a beat, his worst fear came true as he heard the voices of two young ladies entering the store, and laughing. The criminals concealed the weapon quickly, and one of them took the counter as a post. He dropped the body of the cashier on the floor. The two searching the aisles stopped to turn around. Tanya and Monica had approached the counter. The armed criminal said, "We're closing up now". The two in the back aisles made their way to the front. Xavier exhaled, he recognized the voices, and he began to get nervous. He did not want anyone else to get involved. He did not want anyone else to get hurt.

"What; Mr. Long always closes at eight thirty on Saturdays! Where is he anyway?"

"He is sick, and we are closing up early today", the criminal cashier said. Tanya looked at him, he was fidgeting,

"Well just let me get this gum then." She reached for a rack that was no longer there. She then looked down and noticed there was blood on the counter. Tanya's expression changed and it made the criminal cashier look down and notice the blood as well. He looked at her. There was silence for a few seconds. "Okay then we'll just go..." Tanya said while heading to the door. "Come on Monica let's leave!" she said as she walked past Monica. One of the two from the back blocked the exit. The armed criminal grabbed Monica, covered her mouth, drew his weapon, and placed the barrel of it on her temple,

"No one is going anywhere."

~~~~~~

His mouth was so dry, he was so thirsty, and the day was nice. Rysqo had tried to re-think a day of grueling practice. He thought it might be better if he ventured to the basketball court for today. He walked slowly, and then stopped while looking into the store window. He saw the situation that unfolded inside, and he saw Tanya. He ducked behind the side of the store. He counted four against one, odds with which he had no problem, for the day before he had the same count. This time though, there was a deadly weapon and civilians involved, and most importantly Tanya was one of those civilians. He had no intentions to go out first thing in the morning and play hero. Calling the proper authorities might take too long, or lead to a hostage situation. He had to think and act fast. The Black Dragon told him that he would have to protect the world, and would have its help, but would this qualify.

~~~~~~

"You really picked the wrong time to come here baby girl." the gunman said. Tanya just agreed with a nod and was quiet. She knew these types of situations from the movies. Her best bet was to keep quiet. Monica was still in shock from the whole thing, so it was easy to keep still.

They all stood there, trying to think what next. It was obvious the assailants had no prior experience with armed robbery. Or could it have been they had never encountered such resistance. Then they heard a knock on the glass. Everyone turned in that direction. No one stood there. Nothing was there at all. Luckily for the criminals, the streets were empty, and traffic passing by the store was less than minimal.

Just as Rysqo had planned, they had approached the window to inspect it. The gunman remained stationary, as did the scab cashier. The other two went to check it out.

Rysqo ran to the back and opened the door. He had worked a summer job at the store so he was let in on a spare set of keys to Mr. Long's store. He and Tanya frequently came to the store, and spoke with Mr. Long. He had enjoyed their company, and they helped him out. He did them a favor by allowing them to fulfill community service hours there. Rysqo felt that it was time that he pays the favor back. Rysqo's first guess was armed robbery, but he didn't remember seeing Mr. Long. Rysqo tripped over something and fell to the ground in a pushup position. It was a mop and a bucket, and the noise startled those up front.

"Go check it out", the gunman commanded. He seemed to be the leader. One of the two lookouts went to the back and opened the only rear access door. He looked in and saw nothing, so he stepped in. The door closed behind him. Rysqo was now on the floor, he could see every movement the young man had made. He got closer and closer. He walked to the back door and opened it to look out. Rysqo leaped up then pushed him outside. Rysqo turned him around and delivered a stunning kick to his solar plexus. He stumbled back to hit the wall. All the air had left his body, and he was hunched over. His back then against the wall, he looked up, to be greeted with a kick to the face. An instant knock out for Rysqo. He dragged the body before the door. He looked at the young man, not too much older than himself.

"What is taking him so long? Yo, go check it out", barked the gunman. As the other watchman left, Xavier, Tanya, and Monica all wondered what was taking him so long.

He went through to the back of the store. All that was in his head was that his associate had stepped outside to smoke or something. He saw that the door was slightly open to the back, and he was then sure of it. He walked through the door leading outside past the mop and bucket. Then he saw his partner's body,

"What the..." Rysqo spun from behind the door, and kicked it closed. The watchman turned around and before he had a chance to speak or react, Rysqo delivered a blow to his throat. He tried to speak, but all that came out was a squeak. Rysqo delivered a kick combo to his right leg. His leg buckled up and he went down. He put his hands up to protect himself. Rysqo stepped on his chest with his left leg,

"Where is Mr. Long?" The boy responded in a gesture stating he had no idea. Rysqo then knocked him out as well with a kick across his face jerking his neck. He left his body as it lay on the ground in the alley.

Xavier was very curious as to what was going on in that back room. From his position he could see the door. He saw the two boys walk in, but saw no one walk out. The door cracked, he saw Rysqo. Seconds later Rysqo saw him. Both were relieved, but it still was not over. Rysqo leaned against the threshold thinking, what could he do, he didn't want to injure Monica or Tanya. He was glad to see he had some help though. Especially help like Xavier's.

"**Rysqo...**" Rysqo looked around then he remembered the Black Dragon, he opened his mind. "**Rysqo...you must concentrate, focus Rysqo. The path to take will always become clear when you concentrate Rysqo. You must listen to my words. You will find a way.**" Rysqo took heed to the Black Dragon's words. He looked around, when he spotted something, and then he got an idea.

~~~~~~

The gunman and the scab cashier became very nervous.

"Man they should've been back by now, something just isn't right", the scab cashier said.

"Stop girlin', they are probably having some smokes", the gunman said. Tanya was getting tired of standing, and she feared for her friend's life. They were at the mercy of these criminals. Anything they wanted, they would have no choice but to comply if they wanted to walk out of the store alive.

The door to the back swung violently open. Rysqo emerged from the back room and all turned to look. Xavier was puzzled at Rysqo's daring action until Rysqo began to walk towards the front. He saw Rysqo walking with a baseball bat concealed behind him.

Mr. Long organized youth sports in the neighborhood. He kept much of the equipment in the back of his store so that youngsters would visit him to borrow some of it. This also made it convenient for him to sell them candy and other snacks to them when they came in; just another excuse really.

The gunman eyed Rysqo steadily. Then he removed the barrel of the gun from Monica's head and pointed it at Rysqo. Rysqo dove into the center aisle, as three rounds were fired at him. He crawled to the back and was greeted by Xavier.

"Yo X, how many shots did he shoot". Xavier took a moment to think, and then he responded,

"One"

"Okay that makes four then. With that basic handgun, he has either four or two shots left. You ready to gamble." Xavier nodded he knew what he had to do. Xavier crawled around to one end of the store, Rysqo to the other. The gunman had now started to walk down the center aisle. He heard some noise to his right, he fired two shots. Then directly opposite to his right, he heard more noise, he fired, one, two, his weapon withdrew, he was out of ammo.

"Shoot, how many of them are there", he asked.

"Just two man." replied the scab cashier. Tanya and Monica looked at each other, for they were both side by side now. They lipped "two". Suddenly they had not been the victims anymore.

"Yo man, throw me a clip." The cashier reached in his pocket and tossed him one. The gunman turned around to catch an ammunition clip. He loaded it, and then turned back around to be face to face with Rysqo. Silence, then they both reacted. Rysqo kicked the weapon from his grip, it landed then went off. The girls were worried and scared. They grabbed each other and turned away. Rysqo delivered a punch combo to his opponent's chest, then a back-fist. The gunman stumbled back, and shook his head to gain his balance, and re-align his equilibrium. He swung, and Rysqo blocked and countered with, two elbows to his head, front then back. He hooked his arm around his neck then delivered a hooking donkey kick, after which his victim fell to the ground buttocks first. At this point his friend went rushing down the center aisle. Rysqo saw him coming. Xavier then appeared. He reached down and spun around to gain momentum and angle, and released his fury. The bat went sailing for the boy's forehead. It struck him dead on, and he left his feet, and lay sprawled out on the floor. Xavier walked to the front now, and he secured the girls' safety. Tanya ran around the counter to call the proper authorities, when she almost fell. She looked down, her eyes opened very wide, and her heart jumped. Laying there was the body of Mr. Long. It was stuffed up under the counter. She covered her mouth, and began to cry. She tried to get herself together a little, and she picked up the phone. Everyone stood up front now, and they all remained quiet.

The authorities arrived some ten minutes later, and the episode was explained to them. They looked at Rysqo.

"Is all of this true young man", one of the officers said. Rysqo nodded. "I'm going to need one of you to come down to the station with us to file a report, and make a statement", another officer said, as he pushed the two cuffed young men towards the front.

"Okay, the other two are in the back", Rysqo said.

"So hold up, you mean to tell me that you were in the back of the store the whole time and didn't say or do anything", Tanya screamed in Xavier's face. Xavier rolled his eyes,

"What, was I supposed to take a bullet for you to save your life? Those heroics are for your boyfriend here." Tanya backed off. She looked at Rysqo, who was in his trademark pose, leaning against a wall with his head down and arms folded. She walked over to him, and stood there. He looked up,

"Thank you", she said. "You know, I have been thinking. Maybe it's good that you fight for me, I am starting to see how things are for you a little."

"I doubt it", Rysqo said, as he looked back down. With that sudden cold remark, Tanya took a step back.

"All I am saying is that, we shouldn't be broken up the same way we met". Rysqo put thought into her words. They had met with him fighting over her. They were in pre-school, and Rysqo got into a battle with another toddler. He looked up and forced a smile, but he hadn't meant it. She saw this as a chance to embrace him, so she smiled back and squeezed him. Rysqo had not hugged back. He did not feel the same way when Tanya was around him now. He knew this, but paid it no mind. He knew that he had just undergone a serious incident. He hadn't known what to blame it on, but he knew one thing, he was still thirsty.

Rysqo and Xavier walked towards the basketball courts.

"So Xavier, why didn't you try to save Tanya and Monica?"

"What; why do I always have to be the hero?" Xavier questioned.

"Just asking man, I was just asking." They looked up as a figure approached them.

"Yo wassup, you two trying to run some ball", Allen asked. Rysqo looked at Xavier,

"I don't care man, what about you". Xavier looked at his watch.

"I have got to get to work, I will see you later", Xavier waved good-bye. They watched him walk off.

Xavier was in janitorial work for this huge cleaning company. His company was currently cleaning some skyscrapers, and he would be quite busy.

Rysqo grabbed the basketball from Allen's grip, dribbled it then shot it. He almost ripped the net from the rim, as was the outcome of mostly all of his shots. He was supplicated by many neighborhood and public league teams. He chose not to pursue a basketball filled life though. He knew it would lead him away from Tanya. He also only saw the sport as a means for conditioning himself.

He played with Allen and some other neighborhood kids until it got boring to him.

"Alright I'll see you all later", Rysqo said.

"Where are you going man", Allen asked. As he interrogated Rysqo, the rest continued to shoot around.

"I got to go somewhere. I'll catch up with you later." He waved to his fellow basketball players, and then shook Allen's hand.

When he returned home from the police station Rysqo went straight to his room. He had lain in his bed and began to review his day. *"*Not bad for a Saturday*"*, he thought. He closed his eyes.

"**Rysqo**", the voice stopped him from dozing off. "**I must tell you something. I am afraid that you are deeply emotionally attached to that female being named Tanya. It is sad to say that you should try to break off any feelings you two have for each other.**"

"Why", Rysqo asked.

"**It is better that I tell you now, before things between you two go too far. Though I should have told you before, when I had first entered your mind and saw your compassion for her. Rysqo, with my presence inside of you, you take up many of my characteristics. One in particular will hinder your romanticism with Tanya. As I murdered the final member of The Collective, the member known as Venus...she cursed me never to love. As I am damned to live a life of solemnity you are as well.**" Rysqo was speechless. He knew that he felt different when Tanya hugged him, now he knew why.

"No, no, there must be a way to break or reverse the curse. I already am in love with Tanya."

"**I am afraid that if there is a way to break the curse, you will have to find it inside of yourself.**" Rysqo was very angry, but he knew that he couldn't let this anger control him, for he couldn't let his emotions affect his thinking. He had to find a way to break the curse; he had to find a way to be with Tanya.

<u>Chapter 10:</u> Darkness has returned....

The ground shook, the sky opened, and the heavens separated. Flames rolled across the land. Life was forced underground, and they turned to their warrior, Rysqo, the Black Dragon. He rose from underground, coming out of hiding, and searched the land for seven days, and was shocked to find, that the sky was returning back to its original dark pigment. The sky opened, and expanded in a circle of flames, and out of this came thousands of dragons...they had returned...

For Rysqo ,months had passed like days. It was summer now. Rysqo and Tanya had graduated and were both headed to college. All was once again quiet, until it happened.

~~~~~~

Rysqo was shook by his mother and woke with hesitation. He slowly arose while in bed, when he saw her go for the blinds to his window. He prepared to close his eyes to avoid the ultraviolet rays, but there were none. It was about ten or eleven thirty in the morning, on a summer day, and the sun was no where to be seen.

"It looks like a storm is coming. Put on the news!" Rysqo's mother said as she sat on the edge of his bed. He reached for his remote. Upon turning it on he saw news coverage on the storm. He went through the channels, in every language, on every channel they all talked about a storm that was approaching their region. It was slowing down, and it seemed like it was going to stop as soon as it reached them. The weird thing was that the storm was happening all over the world, but the clouds seemed to be clearing out of everywhere else and heading towards the city, circling and hovering around.

Usually in this type of procedure, for precaution and safety measures everyone in the city was to head to the closest shelter. For Rysqo, this was the high school gym.

When they arrived, there were designated areas for each family, and people were boarding up windows. They went to their area and got situated. Rysqo then told his mother that he would be back. He went to the spot designated for Tanya and her family, it was empty. He then proceeded to look around for her. He had no luck for about ten minutes, then he proceeded back to his area, and he stopped to notice that Tanya and her mom were having a conversation with his mom. Tanya turned to see him,

"Rysqo" she shouted ecstatically as she rushed to hug him. "You were out looking for me?" she questioned with joy in her voice.

"Yes, I was worried" he responded.

"Ohhh, that is sweet. Rysqo we need to talk." With those words, there was a crackling sound like thunder ripping through the sky. Everyone stopped and looked outside through a window that was not barricaded. The sky turned solid black. Rysqo knew something was wrong. He proceeded to walk outside. His mother called for him, and he assured her that everything would be alright.

He knew she always worried about him. He caused her a lot of stress growing up. Ever since his father was murdered Rysqo was so distant to his mother. She was the one who sent his father to the bank that day. He didn't blame her; he was just in shock that she had cared so much about his father that day. When Rysqo was brought home, the authorities were explaining how his father tried to be a hero to her. She didn't even try to console Rysqo. She just wept and wept.

Rysqo didn't understand how she could be so upset. She didn't lose everything, just a loved one. Rysqo didn't understand love at the time. He grew up with Tanya since pre-school and everyone always said that, as a couple he and Tanya resembled his mother and father when they were younger. He never really knew what they meant.

Rysqo still took offense to his mother's neglecting him. He felt worthless to her; worthless to everyone. He grew up training, and regretting not being able to help his father that day, even though he was young. Through his training he became a fierce martial artist. He did have a temper however, but he always found an excuse to check it. Usually it was Tanya at his side, watching his back, and in his corner.

Rysqo tended to feel like Tanya cared more for him than his mother. He was mistaken though. His mother didn't understand him. She felt like he didn't want or need her consoling. No one truly understood Rysqo. They couldn't figure out how a boy so young could grow up to be so strong without his father. He also hadn't shed a tear since that day. He came off as cold or heartless to those who did not know him. Everyone respected him though. The story of the bank robbery was national news. Rysqo's name was never forgotten. He was pitied all across the country. He didn't need their pity though. Rysqo Dauragon didn't need anyone.

He scanned the landscape. Then he thought he saw something. He stepped outside, and looked ahead of him. He saw something rushing for them in the distance, as far as the eye could see. Then he gasp, he could finally make out what it was. Walls upon walls of fire streamed straight for them. None of its path seemed to be touched, but it was heading for them at an increasing speed. He rushed inside and told everyone to get down. They all began to panic but did as they were told. Rysqo ducked as well. They sat there for about ten minutes. With the speed that the flames were moving, he expected something to have happened. Everyone began to wonder why they were ducking.

"Rysqo, what is going on", Tanya asked. He looked her in her eyes and responded,

"I don't know". He stood up and walked for the door. Everyone watched him, no one objected to his actions. He went outside once again searching for some clue as to what was happening. Then suddenly he noticed that the flames that once rushed towards him were now forming a passageway leading straight for miles. He reached out to touch the wall of fire and he felt no heat from the vibrant flames. Tanya stood up and rushed to him to see what he saw. As she got closer to him, she was forced back by the heat of the flames. She wondered how Rysqo could withstand the intense heat from the flames. He turned to look at her, and without saying a word, he turned and began to follow the path. All Tanya could do was look on.

As he walked through areas he thought he recognized, he realized that the only things the flames had touched were those that got in its path. The flames did not spread beyond the path or burn him. Rysqo was very curious as to what was going on. He knew something was seriously wrong, but he had to continue and see it through to the end. He turned around to see that path behind him diminished with each step, so now he couldn't go back. Every step he took, the scenery regenerated itself behind him.

Rysqo walked and walked. He had altogether walked for seven hours, which seemed like seven days. He had no sense of the time. He had no sense of what was going on.

Back at the shelter, they all wished him luck and hoped he was safe, for none of them had volunteered to go on his journey, and none of them could. That path was chosen for Rysqo, it was his fate, his destiny. He left something very important to him behind though. Tanya needed to speak with Rysqo, and she prayed that he would make it back to her so she could tell him something; something that would change their worlds forever and something that would change the fate of the universe, and possibly bring some hope to mankind.

Rysqo soon saw that his path ended up ahead of where he was, not too far. He still moved with caution though, because it was far from over. He reached the end of the path, his legs aching. Suddenly the flames broke from their current formation to circle above his head. They swirled up higher and higher. The sky opened up above his head, in a ring of fire. What Rysqo saw next was something that did what nothing else could. It sent fear through his mind. He dreadfully feared for the fate of the world, for the planet. He began to step backwards while looking up. Hundreds, which seemed like thousands of dragons, came crashing down to the earth. Rysqo felt the ground moving beneath his feet. He maintained his balance but could do nothing else.

Some of the dragons died upon impact, but those few hadn't even placed a dent in the number that came down altogether.

"What is going on, this is just too much", Rysqo was overwhelmed he needed help, guidance. His heart and spirit were not going to be enough in this battle.

"**Rysqo you must eliminate these dragons, they are a strain on your world. They are not supposed to be here.**" Rysqo then felt slightly relieved,

"Okay, am I to understand that I am to destroy these dragons with my bare hands? What do I look like? How did they get here, what is going on...?"

"**Rysqo, you must calm down and concentrate. I can not tell you the origin of these beasts, but you can defeat them, I will make it possible. Go for their hearts, and be very careful, you are the only chance this planet has. I know it seems unreal, but you must believe in yourself, believe in me...**" With that Rysqo regained his composure. He began to have confidence in all the Black Dragon's words. Energy streamed through his mind and body, he felt power, the ancient power of The Collective, and the Black Dragon. It all had existed inside of him. He was now the Black Dragon, Rysqo, the Black Dragon. He was about to battle for the fate of the world, for they had returned.

Chapter 11: One Man Matrix

Out of the sky they came, and they fought until ten remained...
The rain came first, each drop, a strain on time...
Those who carried with them the burden of faith foresaw this Day of Judgment...
The winged demons plagued a planet that was not theirs to inhabit...
The guardians had lost a few due to the reality that they did not belong...
Each life that was cast away was taken to compensate for this sin...
The planet fought back to aid its creator, but it was not enough...
The only hope was the one that watched from below.
He stood on the battlefield alone...
He was one, but many...

Thousands of dragons seemed to come out of a hole in the heavens. Rysqo soon found himself surrounded by dragons and the bodies of dragons.

He remembered what he was told, and he approached the rear of one of the dragons, for they were not aware of his presence yet. Rysqo hesitated for a second though. Where was a dragon's heart? This question now plagued him, and before he could decide the answer, the dragon whirled around to meet him face to face. The rest did as well. It focused on him, and he focused on it. It sucked up his scent with its huge nostrils, and then it exhaled. The force sent air surging at Rysqo, but he did not move. It rose its neck up and let out a roar that shook the land. Rysqo saw more dragons flood the area. It seemed as if the dragons had recognized him, but were not making any sort of move. Rysqo looked around, he was puzzled. He then decided that he would just have to be the one to make the first move. He looked at the dragon, then rushed over to it, and drove his fist into its torso. The dragon let out another roar then it began to fall. It crashed to the ground and disintegrated into the air. Rysqo was now utterly amazed. It was as if with the dragon went all the traces of its existence. He turned around to see the rest dispersing. He knew that he could let none escape, so he began to go after each one. Rysqo started running through a field of dragons, swinging and missing each one. The dragons ignored him as they scattered.

What amazed Rysqo was that panic had taken over the dragons. They began to turn on each other and fight. They had resumed their native violent practices. Rysqo navigated through the battle field occasionally striking a dragon, while trying not to be crushed. Dragons began to die at an increasing rate. Then some dragons took to the air. Ten of them had taken flight. The dragons on the ground had not even battled for five minutes after the ones in the air had begun to scorch them one by one. Rysqo took cover, and shielded his face from the heat of the flames. Rysqo had noticed that the amount of dragons on the ground had reduced to none. It seemed to be ending, or so he thought.

Rysqo was drained. He rested on one knee and pushed himself up. He looked around, it was eerily quiet. Then he was surrounded by ten dragons, as they landed simultaneously.

"Rysqo be very careful, I sense trouble."

"You think?" Rysqo questioned sarcastically. The dragons began to move closer to him. One of them snapped at him from behind, and then another did from the side. Rysqo turned around; he knew that this was not going to be as easy.

"Dragon, give yourself up", a voice said. Rysqo was confused, the voice came from his head, but it was not the voice of the Black Dragon. Another voice came,

"Dragon you will now die, your actions against us have sentenced you to your own death". Rysqo was confused, he was not a dragon, he did not look like a dragon, but the voices were surely addressing him. Suddenly the Black Dragon responded.

"Could it be my brothers and sister? How did you...never mind how, you will still be destroyed as you were in the other time."

"No...My brother, we have changed, as you will see." Rysqo was very confused at this point, he thought that The Collective had been dealt away with for all eternity, he was wrong, as was the Black Dragon.

"Rysqo you must defeat them all, I don't know how they have returned but you must send them back, for the fate of the world". Rysqo agreed they had to be vanquished as well, but then he stopped. He counted ten dragons, something was not right. He did not bother to think about it any more, because he was being attacked. He struck the first member as he did the dragons, expecting the same results. Instead they had disintegrated, but into a stream of energy, and it blew past Rysqo and headed for the direction of the shelter. The same result came each time, until he was the only one remaining.

The Black Dragon got a strange feeling, but hesitated to say anything. Rysqo was completely worn out; he could not catch his breath for about five minutes. When he got a hold of himself, he began to walk back to the shelter. It seemed that he had won the battle. It seemed that The Collective had once again been defeated...but it also seemed that history was repeating itself, and with all the efforts of the Black Dragon, it could not be stopped. Still things seemed too easy to Rysqo, and he became very wary.

As Rysqo walked the streets, he heard the sounds of animals in the alleyways. All else was silent though, it was as if the city was dead. He thought he heard footsteps behind him so he turned around. Nothing was there. Rysqo was displeased with his paranoia. So he continued walking. He was very tired now and he wanted to just go back to the shelter to rest. Then suddenly, he heard clatter behind him, it sounded as if a trash can had been knocked over. He turned around, and indeed, there was a trash can rolling into the street. Rysqo was fully awake now. With the day he was having, it seemed like anything was possible. He had started to believe everything was possible.

He started to walk, but he switched up his path, and entered an alleyway. He pressed his back against the wall. He waited for the right moment, and he sprung out from behind the wall. He had timed his surprise attack perfectly. He had spun around the corner of the building to grab the stalker, and was now holding him by his lapel against the wall.

"Why are you following me?" Rysqo questioned. The victim was a delivery boy who had apparently been sent out by a superior to keep business going.

"Geez buddy, I wasn't following you, I got a job to do", the delivery boy said as he broke away from Rysqo's grip. Rysqo eyed him, he hadn't looked like he posed a threat, but he could not be too sure. Rysqo also wondered who could be ordering a pizza at a time like this.

"You should not be out here, it is too dangerous", Rysqo said as he was walking away.

"Yeah, you don't know the half of it", and with that the delivery boy kicked Rysqo in the back. Rysqo flew about three feet and landed on the ground. He turned around, and the delivery boy was now standing over him.

"You poor, poor, beast; you are still so naive, so ignorant of the many secrets of The Collective. What a shame that you have gotten innocent mortals involved in your vocation. No matter, I will enjoy destroying you and delivering the justice for The Collective". Rysqo sat there writhing in pain. He was being addressed as the Black Dragon again and was unsure of what to do.

"Is it Recreanon?" Rysqo knew of the member of The Collective known as Recreanon, but he hadn't expected to see him, especially not in mortal form.

"I pity your wretched soul, for your eyes can not discern the victim whose death was dealt by your hands. Tell me brother, what is it like to murder your own blood. Tell me how you can go about living in another time knowing your inescapable past."

"What, you dare to judge me after you were to take part in my execution. My past was not my will, and it makes me who I am. I can not make it my burden. You try to impress guilt into my mind, and restrain me with the chains of my past, but you are no better."

"Ha, ha, ha; you still have not figured it out, never mind; you will, in time figure it out; as it was seen by Acumenus. But it is already too late, for you, and this planet."

As Rysqo stood up he found the conversation between the two very interesting, and he felt like some clues were missing, he felt like some secrets were yet to be uncovered.

The Black Dragon was indeed hiding things from Rysqo, but it was information it felt Rysqo had not needed to know, at least not now.

"You and the rest should give it up and realize your destiny is to die."

"Fool, you are our destiny..." Recreanon swung at Rysqo. Rysqo dodged it only to be struck with another blow. He staggered back, holding his ribs. Recreanon leaped into the air and tried to land a kick to Rysqo's face. As Rysqo saw him coming he too jumped into the air and blocked and countered his kick with his legs. Recreanon fell to the ground. He was angered, and his mortal vessel did not seem to adhere to damage very well. He charged at Rysqo with a rage of punches and kicks. Rysqo blocked each one while moving backwards until he was forced against a wall. Recreanon took advantage of this. He tried to sweep Rysqo with his right leg. Rysqo leaped into the air, and spun his body one hundred and eighty degrees. He elevated himself some more with his left leg by kicking the wall and spinning another one hundred and eighty degrees while still in the air. As he had almost fully spun around, he delivered a kick to the jaw of Recreanon. Recreanon was spun around and stumbled backwards and to the ground. He looked up at Rysqo who was closing in on his position. He stood up and ran into the shadows of a dimly lit alleyway. Rysqo chased him into the dark area. Rysqo ran down the alleyway to reach a dead end. The light above him surged then completely blew out. Rysqo was now in complete darkness. He was blinded now, and he felt his way back to the street. He was close to the exit when he walked right past the well hidden Recreanon.

"**Look out Rysqo!**" Rysqo turned around and was kicked in the chest by Recreanon. He flew backwards, this time into a car across the street. He had dented the vehicle, and the impact left him unstable. He looked up to see the blurry image of Recreanon soaring through the air directly at him. He stepped out of harms way just in time. Recreanon's attack connected with the driver's side window. Before he could pull his leg out of the wreckage, Rysqo delivered a few quick kicks to his leg to disable it. Recreanon fell to the ground. Rysqo stood over him.

"Why did you attack me" he questioned.

"**Finish him off, stop playing games.**" Rysqo was surprised at the Black Dragon's eagerness of killing Recreanon, but he did not argue, for he had no wish to prolong the battle any further. Recreanon smiled at him and began to laugh.

"Ha, ha, ha; you are foolish mortal. You aid in your own planet's destruction". Rysqo had no idea what he was talking about, and he did not have time to ask. Recreanon laughed and laughed, until Rysqo put him to peace. He saw Recreanon as a raving madman and he was assured by the Black Dragon that he was such.

He leaned against a wall for a rest; for the shelter was now well in his sight. He felt somewhat relieved. He knew that as soon as he entered the shelter he would be able to rest. Rysqo was thinking of how he would be welcomed by his mother and Tanya with open arms.

He was about thirty feet away, when he saw the door to the shelter open. Tanya stepped out and she made immediate eye contact with him. They both stood there not saying a word. He began to walk towards her, when all of the sudden, a figure vaulted into his path. He and the middle aged man made eye contact, and it was on. The man attacked Rysqo without warning. No words were exchanged at all before this battle. He tried to kick low, and Rysqo blocked, and then as he blocked, countered. The hit didn't even stun the attacker. He kept coming at Rysqo like a runaway freight train. Rysqo diverted attack after attack and he began to tire. Then he caught Rysqo with a fake, and landed a menacing blow to Rysqo's face. Rysqo backed into a wall, and wiped his mouth, blood. He spotted the school bus lot in the corner of his eye. He looked at his attacker, who was slowly walking towards him. Rysqo ran for it. The gate was locked. He was still being pursued. He hurdled himself over the gate by using his legs to kick his way up the wall in a zigzag motion using the gate and building. He reached the top and swung his legs over. He landed on his feet then ran to the cover of the school buses.

He leaned on the side of a bus, as he waited between two school buses that were parked. He was out of breath. His mind and body were so tired from his last battle that he was overwhelmed with fatigue. He felt it was his fault though, for he should have ended the battle quicker and never let his guard down. Suddenly, the bus he was leaning on began to lean back on him, and then it began to shadow him. He had to act fast so he dove forward, and rolled under the other bus. The school bus crashed to the ground.

He was relieved, and then he got a hold of himself. For a second he had forgotten about his pursuer. He knew to stay on guard from here on out. He continued to roll to get from up under the bus, then he stood up. He now was between two more school buses. Euphor looked down on him then crouched down.   "You have any guesses", Rysqo questioned.

"Yes, I believe it is Euphor. The way he had withstood each of your blows seemed odd to me, then I thought. When you fled he hadn't pursued you immediately. He had probably stopped to heal." Rysqo smiled,

"So he did feel my hits. Good, I was beginning to doubt myself." Euphor jumped across the gap between the buses. He had timed his jump so that he would be slightly below the edge of the bus opposite to him. He had used his right leg to spin around just before he reached the other side. Rysqo saw his movement, and he knew that a kick was coming. Rysqo stepped to the side and turned towards him while he was in flight.

Euphor's kick had connected with one of the school bus' windows. His leg was cut and he eyed it as he landed. He and Rysqo now stood between the school buses. He stared at Rysqo with no emotion. Rysqo slowly started to back away. Euphor smiled, he saw his chance, so he quickly healed his leg wound. He looked down, no wound; there was only blood on the clothes that the human body was wearing before he took control. Rysqo stopped, and saw that his leg had healed. He knew that he had made a mistake. Euphor jumped diagonally from bus to bus without landing, and then as he got closer to Rysqo he spun fully and kicked. Rysqo dipped back. Euphor had missed Rysqo, but he dented a bus. Rysqo now thought he was in a movie, for the things he had just seen were like those in a martial arts action flick. Euphor landed and began to throw hand techniques at Rysqo at a dizzying speed. Rysqo did his best to divert and avoid the attacks, but it was no use. Euphor landed half of his attacks to some part of Rysqo's torso. Rysqo saw that using defense only, would not prove very helpful in this battle. He would have to send a flood of devastating attacks at Euphor so that he could not heal. Rysqo blocked a final attack by Euphor when he countered. Euphor was hit by surprise after leaving his guard down. Then another one of Rysqo's hits landed. This one had dazed Euphor. His vision was blurry. He shook his head to see if it would help, but it hadn't. The mortal body he had inhabited was much worn. It had taken all the punishment it could receive. He had enhanced the human's strength, but that obviously was not enough. Euphor needed to heal, but he saw no opening; Rysqo was relentless. Euphor now stood on his feet, unable to keep his balance. Rysqo looked at the pathetic warrior. He once served as the healer in The Collective, and now he stood before him, dying. Rysqo saw no need to feel compassion though, because to him he was already dead. He delivered a spinning kick, locked his leg around the rear of the neck of the powerless Euphor, and he snapped it.

His limbs were very sore, and his lip now bled more than before. He wiped his mouth with his sleeve, and then he stood up.

"Rysqo you have taken care of two of my brothers, only seven remain."

"Eight, eight remain, I counted eight."

"What...that can't be. It must be some form of Acumenus' treachery. Be careful. I must warn you though. I believe that my brothers extended their existence like I did. They are occupying mortal bodies and carrying out their will from them. I have inhabited your mind only, but them...they take full control, mind and body. It seems harder to destroy them. "

"It isn't that much harder, I mean all you have to do is destroy the vessel right", Rysqo seemed sure it was this simple.

"I ...I am afraid it seems that simple but it is not. The mortals...their subconscious minds are tossed into limbo. When you kill their body they do not inhabit them, so it is like killing innocents."

"So when I kill them, it is like The Collective has removed their soul to make room? Why can't the Collective members perform this transference repeatedly? I mean, it would make sense if every time I defeat one of their puppets they can hop to another body."

"It can only be done twice from two different vessels. You can not interchange between bodies or vessels as you use them. It involves three specimens, the starting form, the new form, and the ending form."

"I suppose those forms are The Collective, the dragons, and the innocent. Wait a minute, does this mean you have a second form to take to."

"...No this is my second form..." Rysqo said nothing, he was confused. "When The Collective, my brothers created me, I was created like any of the rest. Each member of the Collective was created by the preceding. Coryphaeus was first. He created Acumenus, whom created Strife, whom created Euphor, whom created Deridus, whom created Disorium, whom created Celerus, whom created Recreanon, whom created Venus. Each one had their own position in The Collective, each their own unique ability. When they stood together they would stand as an unstoppable force. Venus was created last. She was the last one to have the right to create. Together though, The Collective spawned many things. Venus saw a need to create someone when one of their planets was in peril. So Venus created me.

I was one of them, I looked like them, and I fit in. The ability she gave me was the ability to learn. She wanted me to learn to do many things, like to feel, and have compassion. That is what she taught me. Coryphaeus had powers that controlled the unimaginable, he taught me to control myself, or you could say my mind. Acumenus was a genius. He taught me about the world, and its wonders. Strife, a master of the combats and war, he taught me to defend myself. Euphor, the healer, he taught me to feel no pain in battle. Deridus, the one whom derides, he taught me to spot an enemy's weakness and exploit it. Disorium, slave of chaos, he taught me to survive in any situation. Celerus, the speed demon, he helped me to enhance my reflexes. Recreanon, the sly chameleon, he taught me to stay hidden, sneak attack, and use camouflage in my surroundings. I picked up each lesson quickly, and there is no limit to my knowledge, and I have no capability of forgetting.

One day we met to discuss an end to my full time training. They were ready to send me out against the dragons, but they did not see me as effective against them in my original form. They created a vessel, another dragon, a different dragon. They asked me if I would be its caretaker. I had agreed, but I knew that the rest could have volunteered or been suggested just as I was. They then killed me and I exchanged bodies. I quickly got use to the change, and I began to hunt. So my ability was to learn, and I used it against them, for I did

not make the same mistake twice. They expected me to die for them twice. So Rysqo, now you can see why I have a grudge against The Collective. With all of their deception, all of their deceit...you see. ...Venus, my creator... now you see Rysqo...now you see." The Black Dragon's speech hit Rysqo hard, and answered quite a few questions, but he still felt that there were things that he needed to know, things that would help him, things that were being kept from him, and he was unable to lose the thought.

Chapter 12: The Jade Crane

Love is as painful as Betrayal...

Long ago, in a small village, there lived a man...
This man was trusting of no one, except for one...
A woman...
The woman told the man she loved him,
He believed her...
She asked him if he loved her...
He didn't answer...
She asked why he did not answer...
He said because he couldn't...
She asked why...
He said because he was not sure...
She asked how he could not be sure, for she had said she loved him...
He said yes she did, and he said that he believed her...
She started to cry...and she asked why he did not love her...
He said he was not sure, and said that he did not want to lie to her...
He said there is one way I can be sure I love you though...
She asked how...
The man walked away...
No one in the village knew where the man went
For fourteen days he was gone...
He came back the fourteenth night...
The woman was sitting there weeping...
She asked him where he had gone...
He held out his arms and in them was a Jade Crane...
This is for you he said...
The woman looked at him...and said I can't take this...
He asked why...
She said she was not sure...
He asked how she could not be sure...
She said she was sorry.., but on the third night she had betrayed him...
He said okay...
She asked what he meant...
He said okay means he knows if he loves her...
She asked if he did...
He said no.., and he walked away never to be seen again...

Rysqo returned to the shelter; battled and bruised. He was stared at by everyone as he entered. He knew to them, he must have looked horrible, because that was sure how he felt. He returned to his area, his mother ran over to him and squeezed him tightly.

"Ouch", he whined.

"What happened to you", she asked.

"I'll tell you later. Hey where is Tanya." His mother ignored his question as she wet a cloth and began to nurture his injuries. "Hey did you hear me mom, where is Tanya?"

"Rysqo, she was supposedly out looking for you", his mother finally replied. Rysqo's heart jumped. He had seen her when he was first attacked by Euphor. Where had she gone? He jumped up from a cot and started to run for the door. His mother saw the look in his eyes, and she hadn't tried to stop him. He ran the opposite direction of the school bus yard.

"Rysqo you must slow down, you haven't fully recovered from your other battles, and you have no idea what you could be getting into." Rysqo ignored the Black Dragon's words and continued running. The fortitude he now displayed showed that he had cared deeply for Tanya, but many would question if he loved her.

~~~~~~

Some three to six hundred feet from the shelter he saw her standing. She was just standing there looking up at the sky. Rysqo stopped running when he was about three feet away.

"Tanya." She hadn't moved. "Tanya", he shouted. Suddenly she turned around while executing a spinning back-fist. It hit Rysqo hard. He had just taken it and his neck turned back. "...Venus then huh?" She charged at him, but he stood his ground. She repeatedly tried to hit Rysqo, but she repeatedly failed. Then she swept backwards, and his legs were taken out. He fell on his back, though he tried to brace himself. She then brought her leg high above his chest, and dropped it down like an ax. Her hit landed, and he spit up blood.

"Rysqo, you must fight her back, I know that she is in Tanya, but you must. If you ever cared about Tanya then you will rid her body of Venus." Rysqo knew he was in a position he had no intention of staying in.

"If I destroy her, will Tanya's mind return to her body, will she still be dead?"

"There is no way to tell, but you must destroy her." Rysqo thought about it. He was scared for once in his life. His emotions took hold of him. He locked up her leg and took her down. He then crawled over to her and locked up her neck. They both stood up, he let her go.

Venus looked at him, and then she looked around while turning away from Rysqo.

"It's beautiful isn't it?" she asked as she looked at him. Rysqo readied himself, as she walked forward, and again turned her back to him.

"It looks to me like the end of the world!" Rysqo replied.

"No Rysqo, it's not the end, but a whole new beginning, a second chance, a chance to start over and not make any more **mistakes**!"

"But...Tanya...Venus...we learn from our mistakes, our past, it is how we prepare for the future. If we erase them, then where will we start?" Rysqo walked up to her side.

"Rysqo, you are different from the Black Dragon. Like Tanya, you shouldn't have been caught up in this. I can see that you do indeed love Tanya, but can't show it with my curse on the Black Dragon. It may be too late, but I strip my curse from you Rysqo, the Black Dragon, may you find love. Now Rysqo, do what you must, she...it...it is in control now, hurry before it is too late....and remember, trust your mistakes, follow your heart." With those final words from the lips of Tanya, Rysqo walked up to her body and released Tanya from the hold of The Collective.

Rysqo did not know with whom he had just spoken, it seemed like they both were talking to him.

Rysqo was very upset; the Black Dragon saw it inside of him. He had not spoken. Rysqo picked Tanya up by her head, then her legs, and he began to walk towards the shelter, carrying her body. It was almost morning now, but outside there was no way to tell. The sun was blocked out by the dark clouds, and it was as if they were in an eternal night.

He kicked the door to the shelter three times. A young man opened it and looked at Rysqo. Rysqo looked deranged, he showed no emotion and he did not blink. He walked past the boy without saying a word. He sat Tanya down at their area.

"Don't let anything happen to her body" he said. Then he walked out. No one knew what had happened and no one asked.

Rysqo walked to the center of the football field to the place where he and the Black Dragon had first met and bound together.

"I need you to teach me all the abilities that you received when you defeated The Collective the first time." The Black Dragon was shocked at this request, but it knew that it would eventually come.

"**Okay**."

One by one they reviewed each one of Rysqo's new capabilities, and how to control them. Rysqo repeatedly asked the Black Dragon if there was anything else that he needed to know about it, and, or The Collective. The Black Dragon said there was not a detail left. Rysqo healed his injuries by using Euphor's generous gift. He felt so weird though, it was as if he was in a dream or another reality like a video game.

The Black Dragon assured him this was all real, its abilities were with him to stay. Rysqo sat down on one of the bleachers. He saw that his clothes were pretty much done for, so he decided to go home, to his real home and pick up some more clothes.

He walked past the store where the incident of the attempted robbery had taken place, and he walked past all his neighbors' homes.

Rysqo went through his front door, looking around, he was tired of surprises. Everything looked normal; in fact it was just how he had left it. He climbed the staircase leading upstairs, and he walked down the hallway and into his room. He entered his room and began to extract clothing from his drawers. He was comparing different combinations, based on flexibility and weight. He had almost decided what he wanted to wear when he looked on the top of his dresser. He walked over to it, and picked up the picture of him and Tanya. He had remembered where it was taken.

"Black Dragon, where can I find the rest of the members at?"

"Rysqo you do not have to concern yourself with finding them, chances are they will find you." Rysqo did not expect that answer, and he did not take it very lightly. He sat down on his bed and looked at the picture once more and then he lay down.

Chapter 13: The Sunrise of Doom

The warrior has found his way mangled and twisted.
The warrior has found his way alone and true.
The warrior has found his way foreign to all others.
The warrior has found his way and he fights for you.

R ysqo sat up in bed and he looked at his clock; then he looked outside. It was supposedly dawn, though it looked more like midnight. Dawn had light, some light. He got up and wiped his face, and took a deep breath. The picture was still in his hands, and he left it on the bed as he stood up. He proceeded to the bathroom and he entered the shower.

He felt so calm and relaxed under the warm water of the shower head. It was almost enough relaxation to allow him to fall asleep again while standing up. He had almost finished his long soothing shower when he heard a very loud crashing sound. The origin of the sound seemed to come from downstairs. He rushed the remainder of his shower and ran to his bedroom.

He quickly slid on all of his clothes. He poked his head out into the hallway. He began to walk slowly down the hallway towards the steps while using stealth. His back rested against the corner of the wall. He looked around the corner, and down the stairs. He saw that the front door was missing from the threshold, it lay on the floor. It was as if it had been knocked off the hinges. He was still peeking around the corner and scanning the area for any sign of trouble. Then he turned back around to be face to face with another young man around his age or older.

"Hi", Rysqo said in a friendly tone. He kicked Rysqo down the steps. "Now that was not nice", Rysqo said in a less friendly tone. The boy ran down the wall while on his side using the banister to keep his balance. Rysqo saw him coming so he kicked the banister, and the wood split open. The boy fell down the remaining steps. "Now that was not very smart now was it? Do you want to try again?" Rysqo stood up while looking down on the young man. The boy sprung up and tried to hit Rysqo. Another miss, but it was barely a miss, because the hand speed of the boy matched that of Rysqo's evasion. Rysqo paused for a second, "Hold on, Celerus right, should've known it." Celerus was so quick. All his attacks were based on reflex and split second decisions or improvising. Rysqo saw this and he also saw that it would not be difficult to outsmart him. Rysqo backed up into the kitchen; he grabbed a broomstick, and detached the bottom. He spun it behind his back. He signaled Celerus with his hand to come on. Celerus ran at him full speed. Rysqo spun the stick forward. He struck Celerus' leg then his hip and kidneys. He then inverted the stick and drove it into his opponent's solar plexus, then his sternum. Celerus backed up while holding his chest. He charged at Rysqo again, and this time he kicked the stick. It snapped in half in Rysqo's hands. Rysqo smiled because he now had a two handed set of weapons; the disabling Escrima. He repeatedly went after the legs and rib cage area of Celerus' body. Celerus kicked one of the sticks from Rysqo's hand. Rysqo threw the other at Celerus then he exited the back door. Celerus ran after him, but when he made it to outside, he saw no sign of Rysqo.

Rysqo had the advantage now, for they were in his training area. As Celerus looked around he noticed Rysqo's weapon set. He walked over to it. He noticed that some things were missing. A knife struck the corner of a wooden chest inches from Celerus' head. He turned around, and just in time to catch another knife. He threw it down. He looked around, trying to detect some movement of any type. A knife went through the left shin of Celerus. He reached down to pull it out, and then he stopped. He saw Rysqo walking towards him. Rysqo stood over Celerus in his crippled state. Celerus leaned back and pulled the knife from his leg. He then quickly threw it back at Rysqo. It was aimed directly at the throat of Rysqo. Time seemed to slow down, as Rysqo dipped back and to the side while throwing a knife at the forehead of Celerus. Time sped up when Rysqo was in no danger. The knife whizzed past Rysqo. His knife landed in the center of the forehead of Celerus.

Rysqo walked into his house and got some water from the kitchen. He sat down in the dining room area, and he put his head down. He thought about something and he quickly looked up and around. He smiled; his eyes had made contact with what he was looking for.

Rysqo slowed to a complete stop at a red light.

"What am I thinking", he asked himself as he drove through it. The streets were his, no law enforcement, no rules, no order, chaos. He turned a corner suddenly, a figure landed on his windshield. It cracked the front almost completely. The figure then rolled off. Rysqo skid the car to a stop. He was very upset and he didn't know who or what to check first, the human victim, or the auto mobile victim. He walked to the front of the car to see the body of who looked to be a dead homeless person. He looked closer, and bent down. The eyes opened,

"Boo". Rysqo jolted back, he saw that this was no homeless person. There was a loud boom behind him. He turned around to see that he was surrounded by two middle aged men. One stood on the sun roof of his car, the other in front of him on the street. The one in front of him grabbed Rysqo and threw him about twenty feet in front of the car. Rysqo was slow to get up, and he was a bit shaken up. The car accelerated to a very dangerous speed and was heading for Rysqo. Rysqo jumped into the air, doing a spin flip. He had cleared the car, but it had kept going, then it did a one eighty. The car had picked up speed once more. Rysqo readied himself for the jump. The car swerved and tried to pancake Rysqo into the glass store front of a building. Rysqo tried to make this jump but he failed. The car tunneled through the glass with the force of a herd of elephants. It jolted to a stop once it was inside, and Rysqo was sent flying. His body slid through the debris of the glass to an abrupt stop. He was laying face down on some glass, when the driver exited the car's interior by standing up through the sunroof. He observed the path of destruction. The other one came running to enter the new entrance to the store.

"Disorium, check the body!" Deridus ordered. Disorium walked over to Rysqo's body, it had not moved. He looked at Rysqo's face; it was filled with cuts and glass. He was a bloody mess. Disorium looked at Deridus,

"Dead..." Disorium looked back at Rysqo's face. He saw no cuts or bruises anymore. "Uh oh..." he said. Rysqo's eyes opened and he jumped up and grabbed Disorium. He ran forward while pushing him backward until he sent him crashing through one of the remaining glass doors. Deridus looked at Rysqo, "Nice car", he yelled. Rysqo spun around and walked hastily over to his car. Deridus was trying to exit at this point. Rysqo kicked the car door back closed and hit Deridus' leg. Disorium re-emerged on the scene. He jumped through the window and headed in the direction of the other two. Rysqo heard the sound of crunching glass so he turned around, and rolled backwards across the hood. Deridus looked at him standing on the hood. Rysqo eyed him, and threw a kick through the windshield. Deridus ducked down and rolled out of the car door. Rysqo jumped off the hood.

Only the car had separated the three now, inside of the dark store. They stood there looking at each other. Rysqo knew that this two on one with the members of The Collective would prove as a difficult handicap. Rysqo looked in the corner of his right eye, and spotted some elevators, past a store of clothes. He was in the mall. He knew that there was another way past the elevators. He would have the advantage if he could separate the two inside of the mall. He waited about thirty seconds more and ran for it, almost slipping on broken glass and debris. He ran and ran and he did not look back.

The mall had three floors, they were all sub floors though, and the street stores were all on the ground level. Rysqo made it through the store and he reached the mall. Rysqo looked over the railing; the fountain was still going. The lights were suddenly switched on. In an empty mall, in the dark he felt more confident, but that was no longer the case.

Disorium cornered Rysqo with his back to the railing. Rysqo saw he was by himself, so that meant that Deridus must have turned on the lights. He knew they would not let him get away, so he made his move. Rysqo leaned his back over the side of the railing and flipped over it while extending his arms to grab hold of the sub level one railing. Disorium peeked over it, and Rysqo peeked up, and waved. Disorium backed up, and then he ran and flipped over the railing, twisting his body while in the air. Rysqo saw his body drop to the center of the mall, and he landed on his feet.

"This guy is crazy!" Rysqo exclaimed. He turned around to see what store he was in front of. Rysqo was in front of a cooking store. Rysqo suddenly got an idea. He ran to the store front, it was locked. Rysqo slammed his hand against the gate in anger.

All the stores in the mall closed at the same time, so they were controlled by the same electronic gate operation system. He had to find gate control though.

~~~~~~

Deridus was riding a glass elevator to the bottom level, when he saw Disorium running up a stationary escalator to the first sub level. Rysqo peeked over the railing once more to see one of them running up an escalator, and the other riding an elevator. Rysqo ran around the outside brim until he was at the elevator door. Deridus had exited the elevator and it headed back up. Disorium had made it to his destination finally. He looked to the left then the right, and then he looked down at Deridus,

"I don't see him." Deridus got angry, and then he saw the elevator doors open up behind him. He looked inside, and no one was there. Disorium had watched from the railing as Deridus inspected the elevator. Deridus entered the elevator, and looked around, the doors closed. The panel had been smashed in after all the buttons were pushed several times. Deridus was stuck on the elevator. Rysqo crept behind the unsuspecting Disorium, whom was leaning over the railing still.

"Boo!" he said. Disorium spun around. Rysqo kicked him in his chest, and his body went over the railing. He landed on his back, but was not dead, he was severely injured though. Rysqo dropped down next to him. Disorium struggled to get up on his feet. Rysqo kicked him again, this time he had stumbled back to the fountain. Rysqo grabbed him by his collar and prepared to hit him, raising his right hand and clenching his fist.

Deridus saw the scuffle through the glass elevator. He could not open the doors though. He hurled his body through the glass and to the ground. Rysqo heard the crash, and let go of Disorium. He fled the area and then he spotted the customer service area. He ran to the booth, and saw the security panel. He found the gate operation unit, and he opened the gates. The stores' front gates all started to open. Rysqo now had to use this to his advantage; he had known the mall well.

~~~~~~

"Get up! We must get rid of him, and find the others!" Deridus was very ashamed of being defeated by a mortal. It was not over yet though. Disorium dusted himself off, when he noticed the arms store about ten feet ahead of them. They had never seen arms. In their time, they were exposed to many things, for the humans were very intelligent. These weapons of destruction, meant to inflict damage to the frail human body, were something The Collective had never seen. The Collective were no fools though, for they were very intelligent and very resourceful.

Rysqo equipped himself in the various stores, and then he was ready to set out against his enemies.

Rysqo was sure he had the advantage now, so he had no hesitation going out into the open anymore. He went back to the fountain. His enemies were gone, and it was eerily quiet. It was way to quiet for Rysqo. He circled the fountain and from that confined area, looked all about the mall.

He walked slowly around it again, as his footsteps echoed throughout the floor. He was about to leave the area, when he saw a red light come from somewhere. He looked all around then he looked at the fountain. In its clear water, he saw his reflection. He then saw that he had a red dot on his head and a red dot on his chest. He immediately dove forward onto his stomach. Bullets ripped through the water, and ricocheted off the stone. Rysqo crawled forward until he was no longer under the cover of the fountain. He got up and started to run for a pillar he saw straight ahead. Bullets whizzed through the air around him, and some collided with the stone structures. Rysqo deduced that they had visited the arms and ammunition store, and borrowed some weapons. He was now on the short end of the stick. He decided that he would have to use an ability to find them, and reach their position. He decided that Recreanon's would suit him best.

"Ha, ha, ha, you think we got him?" Disorium asked. Deridus shook his head,

"I doubt it; he is a very slippery one." They emerged from their hiding place to look for Rysqo. Rysqo saw them moving on the floor above him. He rushed to the emergency stairwell directly in his line of sight. He opened the door and forgot to catch it as it slammed shut. Deridus heard a noise behind the door to the emergency stairwell. He signaled for Disorium to go check it out. Rysqo pressed his back against the wall.

"**Concentrate**." Rysqo heeded the words of the Black Dragon. He let his mind take control. Disorium opened the door and walked through. He stood side by side with Rysqo his target, but he was unaware. Using Recreanon's camouflage trick, Rysqo went unseen to the human eye, and since the bodies Deridus and Disorium occupied were human, this helped him to regain the advantage. As Disorium turned around to exit the emergency stairwell, Rysqo left the safety of the wall. He grabbed Disorium's weapon, and he pointed it upward at his throat. Disorium now saw Rysqo, but only for a second though as his eyes froze up. Disorium had pulled the trigger while panicking.

Deridus had heard the commotion. He walked slowly to the emergency exit, his gun facing that way. He grabbed the handle to the door and pulled it open. Rysqo waited readily on the other side. In his hands, Rysqo held a kitchen lighter, and a spray can of pan greaser. Deridus was greeted with a stream of fire to the face. He dropped his weapon and grabbed his face with both hands. His upper body was now covered in flames and he started to scream.

Rysqo emerged from the emergency exit stairwell. He dropped his utensils to the ground. He stood there as Deridus suffered. Then Rysqo got a running start and leaped into the air to deliver a kick to the chest of Deridus. Deridus' flaming body fell over the railing to the floor. Rysqo looked over the railing. Deridus was sprawled out on the floor of the bottom level, he was surely dead.

Rysqo went back up to the ground level, and exited through the same store he entered. He walked past the debris and he noticed his car. It was beyond total recognition, at least in his eyes. Rysqo then decided he would pay his friend a visit. He could use some help.

The building Xavier's company was working on had a shelter inside of it, he was sure Xavier would be there. He also knew that Xavier's boss would probably still have him working there.

Rysqo headed out of the mall. Rysqo was tired of walking the streets; he knew he badly needed a set of wheels. His destination was all the way across town. He had to speak with his friend Xavier though.

"Rysqo four members remain." Rysqo stopped walking, "You told me that there were nine other members"

"Yes I did, but you assured me that there were ten members on the scene when they first came to this planet." Rysqo tried to catch up the Black Dragon in its own words, he had failed. Suddenly Rysqo felt a slight tremor. Then he felt a more intense tremor.

"What was that?" Rysqo lost his balance. The tremors stopped a few minutes later. "This city does not usually have earthquakes. Can you please tell me what is going on?"

"It is the end of your world Rysqo."

"What...I thought it was my duty to protect the world. I mean...I am destroying The Collective, what else is there to do?" Rysqo stood up.

"That's just it, there is something else. Acumenus had tried to cast a curse at his death. I am not sure what it did, but it has to be in some way linked to your planets destruction." Rysqo was very angry now,

"I thought we agreed not to keep anymore secrets!"

"It was not a secret; it just had not come up before. Anyway, when you find Acumenus, I am sure you will find out what his curse does." Rysqo continued to walk. He was annoyed with the Black Dragon. He felt that he was not being told everything once again, but maybe when he found Acumenus he would get some answers, more answers than the

71

Black Dragon was expecting. For the moment though, he was going after his friend.

Chapter 14: The Eternal Chain is Broken

Friendship seldom lasts forever, but evil has maintained its existence through the beginning of time and will always thrive.

When a life is lost, a soul floats freely into oblivion...
The souls of the pure hearted find their way to sanctuary...while the souls of the black hearted roll together into a deep void...
Each soul is then chained down, preventing it from haunting the living world, and resting in the world of the dead...
For all eternity, these souls are subjected to suffering for some crime they committed while inhabiting a body...
These eternal chains have been cast off by those who would dare to rewrite the laws of life and death as they had been etched, and disturb the flow of existence...

Some three hours later Rysqo had made it to the building. He stood out front and looked up to marvel at the height of the sky scraper. It was the mere height of the building that caught Rysqo's eye.

The building, Divine Heights, was a relatively new building in the city. It was undergoing some minor construction, and structural changes before its grand opening, the next month. The building had to be spotless for this occasion, due to the expectations of the city. A great deal of money was expended for this project. Xavier's crew was one of the top services in the city, so they were called upon.

Rysqo knew the history of this building since they first started on it three years ago. He entered the front door. The building supposedly was equipped with a shelter of its own. He had no idea where to start looking. Could Xavier be in the shelter, or was he still working? He decided to just search each floor for some sign of his friend. He had no idea which floor Xavier was working on, so he decided to search each floor one by one.

Almost another hour had passed, and he still had no sign of Xavier or his position. He had searched over thirty floors, and he had come across much of the other crew, but still there was no sign of Xavier. He exited the elevator and proceeded down the long dark hallway. Finally he had reached the floor Xavier was on, but he had not figured it out yet.

~~~~~~

Xavier was in the back of the room still tending to his duties. He heard the elevator doors opening. He was not aware that anyone was coming to the area. He had no help on any of the other floors, and he had not requested any help on this floor. He took this cleaning job because it was more peaceful than the security work he used to do. He had asked to be left alone, and he knew that usually his fellow workers respected his wishes.

He listened closely, and then he crept up to a wall as he heard footsteps. They were definitely getting closer. Xavier now had his back against the wall. He was armed with a mop. As the foot steps seemed to enter the room, he jumped out from behind the wall, mop in hand.

"Whoa, slow down man, it's me."

"Rysqo what are you doing here? I almost had to hurt you. You should know not to sneak up on people!" Xavier stopped though, he heard another sound.

Rysqo had also heard a sound. He ran down the hallway trying to reach where it came from.

"So Rysqo, why aren't you in a shelter, like the rest of those prisoners?"

"I did not feel like waiting around in a shelter." He walked over to Xavier, whom was at the window, opening it to let the floor dry. Xavier turned around with a smile on his face, and looked at his friend. He looked at him, but in the distance, in the corner of his eye and behind the one that stood before him, he saw Rysqo. Xavier's smile faded away, the impostor turned around. Rysqo was out of breath, he looked at the face of the mirror image of himself. Suddenly the face distorted, and formed a face Rysqo had never seen before. Xavier stood on one side of the impostor, Rysqo on the other. The impostor signaled them both to come on with his hands. They attacked him with full force. He dodged and countered every move that they tried to pull off. Then he stopped their assault by knocking them each to the ground.

"You know all of my moves! Who or what are you?" Rysqo demanded to know what he was up against.

"I am the tenth member of The Collective, known as Compeerus." Rysqo had not recognized him from any portion of the Black Dragon's stories. Could he be another secret or a lie? Xavier was standing there listening to their brief exchange of words. He had no idea, no clue, what either of them was talking about. "It's time to die", Compeerus said in an informing tone to Rysqo. Xavier ran up to his back to attack. "You stay out of this", warned Compeerus. He knocked Xavier backwards. Xavier sprung up to his feet to try again. Rysqo saw him ready himself,

"Xavier, no, wait!" It was too late; Xavier had already started his next attack.

"You fool", said Compeerus as he leaped into the air, and kicked Xavier back. Xavier fell backwards and into his mop bucket. The water washed across the floor. Rysqo saw his chance. He rushed the mirror man Compeerus. Compeerus was caught off guard, and was struck in the face. His neck twisted with the direction of the blow. Compeerus felt the pain, and he felt anger. He twisted his neck back very quickly and looked at Rysqo. Their eyes locked, and the fight was on. Rysqo threw many different combinations of attacks at him, but each one had not landed. Compeerus was impossible to defeat in a straight forward one on one fight to the finish. Rysqo knew that he was really in over his head this time.

Xavier had stood up. He saw Rysqo struggling against the opponent, and he knew he had to help. He walked over to his mop, and grabbed it. He detached the head by snapping the stick at the bottom with his foot. He ran over to help out. Rysqo saw his help coming, and so did Compeerus. Xavier attacked with his stick, a weapon of choice. Rysqo also attacked Compeerus. Compeerus still managed to divert their attacks though. Rysqo went low, and Xavier went high, and vice versa, and still, neither had landed a significant blow to the body of Compeerus. They all paused. They were out of breath, and worn out. Compeerus then made his move. He kicked Rysqo and sent him flying through the door and out into the hallway. Rysqo was dazed from the blow and it took him a while to get up. It was now one on one with Xavier and Compeerus. Xavier saw this and he threw down his weapon. They now engaged in battle. Xavier put up a good fight against Compeerus, but he did not have a chance. Rysqo re-entered the room, holding his ribs. He saw his friend battling Compeerus; he knew there was no match.

Xavier turned to see Rysqo. Compeerus struck him with a few sharp sneak attack blows. Xavier went down to the ground hard. Rysqo knew that he was done for if he had not helped him. Xavier stood up, to lean on some of the furniture in the room. He spit up some blood. Compeerus was about to finish him off when Rysqo blocked his attack for Xavier. Compeerus eyed Rysqo.

"Your courage is impressive", he smiled at Rysqo. His smile turned to a frown, as he started to attack Rysqo. Rysqo was now on the defensive. He was backed up to the window. Compeerus attacked with all his force. Rysqo grabbed him, and used his power against him to force him through the glass.

Rysqo held on to him as they fell dozens of floors. Rysqo saw the ground getting closer and closer. He used Compeerus' body as a shock absorber, as they crashed into the roof of a car. Rysqo rolled off the body of Compeerus. He was glad to finally have his feet on the ground again. Suddenly Rysqo felt some of those tremors he had felt earlier, but these were way more intense. He knew he had to hurry up and find Acumenus.

Chapter 15: The Book of Truth is opened

A hero who tries to make sense of a senseless world is deceived by his only
answer to the questions that now plague his planet.
His only hope is lost in the trust he chose to let go...
As time runs out, answers to all his questions now come to him, but are
they the answers that he wanted......or needed...

Rysqo returned to the side of his friend. He saw that Xavier was dying. As he listened to his Xavier's last words, Rysqo informed him of everything that happened, even with Tanya and Venus. Xavier looked at his friend like he was crazy, but he had not doubted a word he had said. The fighter he had just gone up against was unlike any he had ever laid eyes on. He seriously doubted they were capable of those types of fighting skills.

Rysqo sat there with his friend, until he stopped responding to his words. Rysqo used his fingertips to close the eyes of his friend. He exited the Divine Heights building, and he swore to avenge the death of his friend, his love, and his planet.

Heroes that go undiscovered and whom are under-appreciated usually have the greatest impact on society. Rysqo walked the streets of his city, once again in a wretched manner. He knew he was fighting for the human race. He was responsible for defending them for the unspeakable evils which The Collective would undoubtedly bring. He took some time to think. When he did away with the evil of The Collective, mankind still would have to deal with the evils of humanity. Was it worth his risking his own life? Yes, he was the chosen one. Yes, he accepted the responsibilities of the Black Dragon. But had the Black Dragon known the evil it was defending? Had the Black Dragon seen the world it had protected. Maybe the evil was the world itself, not the earth, but its inhabitants. Would mankind appreciate his efforts in years to come? Rysqo had no intentions of being recognized as the man who saved the world. He just wondered if he was doing the right thing. He was sure that The Collective was evil and that they were doing the wrong thing, but was he doing the right thing. He absolutely had to rid the planet of The Collective, but would the evil still remain?

Rysqo thought and thought. He reviewed all of his memories, good and bad, with the help of the Black Dragon. He remembered his good memories, and tried to forget his bad ones. He revisited a memory he had repeatedly tried to forget. The murder of his father, as it was witnessed by him as a young child. That was an act of human cruelty being portrayed. This was a very bad side to humanity, greed. An armed robbery took the life of his father. He chose to be a hero and protect his fellow man, and he found himself in a grave because of it.

Rysqo at this point had no fear of death, for he didn't have much to live for left in the world. The world was also being destroyed. He knew that everything was riding on him; fate was in his hands. He did not like being in this position though.

Rysqo then remembered Tanya. He remembered all the good times he had shared with her. His love for her is what finally convinced him. This world he lived in was a great place, and it was worth him fighting for it. At least if he ever doubted his actions, the world would always be worth fighting for. So he now had no reason to look back and regret his actions.

Rysqo proceeded down the street, a little faster now though. He had healed while he was thinking about what he would do, and he became anxious to end the war with The Collective. Minutes later there was a very powerful tremor. The street cracked around him, flames rose up, and stretched forward for miles. Was this another path? It was as if the planet was leading him somewhere, somewhere else. He started walking down the path, to see where he was being led.

Strife prepared for Rysqo's visit. He and Acumenus were determined to halt his quest.

Each of the previous members had failed at capturing Rysqo. The Collective indeed had some tricks up their sleeve. None of the members Rysqo had battled had intended to kill him, just injure or disable him so that he could be apprehended. They wanted to keep Rysqo alive for some reason. Strife had other plans though. He had not appreciated being murdered by the Black Dragon in his last lifetime. He was going to do his best to return the favor to him.

Strife was a rebel of sorts, and he only saw things being done his way. Who else in The Collective could stop him though? Only Coryphaeus was powerful enough, but he was preoccupied with other matters.

Rysqo entered the structure. He looked around as he walked through the stone threshold of what looked like a castle, ruined by it's years. Rysqo walked through the courtyard as he passed trees, and crumbling stone structures. He was not alone though. In the shadows moved a warrior.

"What is this place? This is not part of the city! I mean at least I do not remember this part but..."

"Rysqo be careful, you are in the castle The Collective once dwelled in. I don't know how they made it possible, but somehow they brought the castle to your time and planet." Rysqo observed the castle from the courtyard. He thought he heard a noise in some bushes to his left. He turned to see what it was. He saw the bushes rustle. He approached the bushes very cautiously. He leaned forward to see what was in the brush. Strife launched himself forward at Rysqo. He had tackled Rysqo to the ground. Rysqo flipped him off with his leg. They both jumped up, and began to fight.

Rysqo landed the first two blows quickly. Strife backed up after being hit and moved in again. He swung at Rysqo; Rysqo had leaned to the side, and grabbed his arm. Rysqo then proceeded to throw Strife. He sent Strife about seven feet. Strife kneeled on his right knee before standing up, and pulled out a weapon. Rysqo ran directly at him. When he saw Strife's weapon he slowed to a stop, some five feet away. Strife had pulled out a lightweight sword. Rysqo had never seen that type of sword before. Strife was in a sword stance waiting for Rysqo to make a move. Rysqo backed up into a statue. Strife tried to trap him there. He slashed at Rysqo twice. Rysqo evaded his attacks and moved away from him. The sword struck the statue. The end had turned blunt, and it was useless. Strife spun and launched the sword at Rysqo. Rysqo almost got hit with the deadly projectile, but it penetrated another statue right next to Rysqo.

Strife pulled out a chain. Rysqo saw he had many weapons concealed in this thin black over coat he was wearing. He also had a vest which held projectiles. Strife swung the chain around and around, as he crept closer to Rysqo. He attacked, swinging the chain through the air as a whip. Rysqo shortened the space between them, and then he grabbed Strife's arms. He got the chain out of his hand. Strife pushed him back and reached into his coat. He quickly threw a series of small knives at Rysqo. Rysqo caught two, and he dodged all the rest. While Rysqo was preoccupied with the projectiles, Strife slipped on a set of claws.

Rysqo tossed the knives back. They both landed in Strife's left arm. One was lodged in his forearm, the other in his shoulder. Strife pulled the two knives out of his arm. He stripped the left claw from his hand and let it drop. His left arm was now disabled; Rysqo must have hit some nerves. Rysqo approached him slowly; stalking his wounded prey. Strife swung at Rysqo with one hand, the other dangling at his side. Rysqo dodged his attacks. He finally grabbed his arm and locked it up, while removing his claws. He knocked Strife to the ground. Strife continued to fight back. Rysqo knew that he should end the battle. He prepared for a chance to land a deathblow to the body of Strife. Strife charged at Rysqo. Rysqo moved in to get behind him, and lock up his neck. He snapped it with ease, and let the body drop. Only two members remained.

The scenery around him faded, and Rysqo increased his guard.

"What is going on", Rysqo asked.

"The castle was just an illusion", said a voice. Rysqo turned around to be face to face with a relatively old man.

"Who..."

"I am Acumenus". Rysqo put his hands up ready to battle. Acumenus looked at him. "I do not wish to fight you boy." Acumenus circled Rysqo, whom slowly put his hands down.

Rysqo never took his eyes off of the old man though. He was curious as to why Acumenus chose this elderly body over a fresh new one. Rysqo figured the sorcerer probably just wanted to remain as actualized as possible.

"You and the dragon have come very far. What a shame though." Rysqo looked puzzled.

"What do you mean", he asked.

"Rysqo you must not fall for the trickery of Acumenus, do away with him."

"What are you hiding Black Dragon? I have questions he might be able to answer!" Rysqo turned his attention back to Acumenus. He ignored the words of the Black Dragon.

Suddenly, a dart whizzed through the air and hit Acumenus in the temple. Acumenus died instantly. "No!" Rysqo shouted. He caught Acumenus as he was falling. He saw Acumenus as the last hope to save his world. A dart whizzed at his head. Rysqo caught it just in time. He looked at the tip; it had a substance on it. It was not poison though, it was a substance that would put him to sleep. He stood up and looked around. He saw no one anywhere around. There were just empty streets around him. He needed to think again, so he decided to revisit the shelter.

Chapter 16: Judgment

Judgment is but a bridge to the stars of a shining galaxy of wrong doing in this universe.
At any given time it can be made..; but when the trip is made across it, the path usually can not be reversed...

Rysqo sat on his cot in their area at the shelter. His mother talked with Tanya's mother about her daughter. Tanya's body was laid out on a cot near Rysqo. Her mother had not yet decided what to do with her daughter's body, but for the moment she had decided that she would listen to Rysqo, trust Rysqo.

Rysqo looked at the body of his girlfriend. He was stripped of the curse Venus had placed on the Black Dragon, and was able to love, but he had not wanted to love again. After a love like Tanya, he had no desire to be with anyone else. They had fully committed their lives to each other. They shared the same dreams, each containing the other. Rysqo had lost that part of him, but he was not yet ready to let go. He just sat there, looking so pathetic. The two women saw in his eyes that he was seriously upset, so they did not say a word to him.

A young man stood over Rysqo, looking down. Rysqo saw the shadow, and he looked up slowly.

"Rysqo, there is someone outside asking for you." Rysqo looked confused, who could have come to see him at the shelter. With the city quarantined, who would risk coming out to request Rysqo's presence personally? Rysqo thought about it, and he jumped to his feet. He was sure of who was outside. He went over to his mother and hugged her, and then he grabbed her hands.

"Mom there is something I have to do. I don't know if or when I will be back, but I must go. Do not try to stop me, just trust me...believe in me." She looked into his eyes, and knew that he was up to something. She saw no reason to hold him there though, so she nodded in approval. He kissed her cheek, "I love you mom." Rysqo turned to the young man and followed him.

"I love you too Rysqo…"

~~~~~~

They proceeded to the back door of the gym, which led out to the football field. He pointed out in front of them. Rysqo looked in the direction he was pointing, but he saw nothing. He turned back to the boy,

"Where..." He had disappeared. Rysqo shook his head. He walked in the direction he had pointed. Rysqo walked for a very long time. He had even crossed the whole football field.

Rysqo continued to walk. He was now off school grounds. Rysqo stopped to look back. There was no sign of his high school. He turned back around; then the tremors started again. They were more violent than ever. The earth split behind him, and around him. He looked into the holes, and they were deep, they seemed bottomless. Rysqo backed away from the edge.

"Rysqo Dauragon", a voice said. Rysqo turned around to look at the face of his last opponent. He was suited for battle definitely. Though his vessel towered over Rysqo, he was the least bit intimidated.

"...Coryphaeus?" Rysqo said in an interrogative voice.

"Ah, I see you have studied your opponents." Coryphaeus circled the area. They were now on a platform; it was basically a small island of earth, surrounded by deep crevices in the ground. Rysqo watched Coryphaeus as he walked around. "Poor boy... I pity you Rysqo. You should not be involved in this war. The Black Dragon is a delusive beast. Why do you fight for him Rysqo? What has he told you? What lies has he told you?" Rysqo had not expected to engage in deep conversation with Coryphaeus.

"What are you talking about? You are up to something." Coryphaeus mocked him with laughter.

"Foolish boy, you chose to join the wrong side. I am up to nothing Rysqo, but you will see the truth before the night is over." Coryphaeus put his hands up. Rysqo did the same. Coryphaeus and Rysqo met halfway at the center of the platform. They gave each other very cold stares.

Rysqo had no idea what to expect from Coryphaeus. He knew that since they had lost most of their abilities after their first death, he was facing all new opponents. He had no guidance in this fight, and the Black Dragon was silent. Coryphaeus was tired of waiting it out. Rysqo saw this in his eyes. They started the battle by executing the same technique. From then on it was a fight like no other. He and Coryphaeus battled, but Rysqo was somewhat disappointed. Rysqo expected the almighty leader of The Collective to put up more of a fight. Coryphaeus had seriously given Rysqo difficulty though; just not what he was capable of.

Coryphaeus stopped the fight. He knocked Rysqo back, and to the ground. Rysqo almost went off the edge as he held on and pulled himself up. Coryphaeus stood over Rysqo, and smiled. He turned his back, and started to walk away. Rysqo held his ribs, which were very tender. He now knew the true power of Coryphaeus. One hit ended the fight for him. Rysqo was very confused with his actions though.

"Why do you walk away, and turn your back to me." Coryphaeus flagged him off,

"You can do me no harm." Rysqo was confused, but then the Black Dragon spoke to him.

"Rysqo, you must destroy Coryphaeus. Do not be fooled by his trickery. Kill him now." Rysqo saw the words of the Black Dragon as strange, and uncalled for. He was fully aware of what he had to do. Rysqo stood up and looked at the back of Coryphaeus. Coryphaeus faced darkness. He looked back as far as he could in the corner of his eye. He knew Rysqo would attack. He smiled as he heard incoming footsteps.

Rysqo struck Coryphaeus in the center of his back. Coryphaeus went down hard. Rysqo had fatally wounded him, but he was not dead yet. Rysqo walked over to him and looked down at the body of the once powerful leader of The Collective.

"Why did you let me kill you?" Coryphaeus smiled, and spit up some blood.

"...You still ...don't...get it do you..?"

"Get what? Stop with your riddles..." Suddenly, the sky opened up again. Dragons entered the atmosphere, and soared through the skies. Rysqo and Coryphaeus looked up. Coryphaeus laughed,

"Ha, ha, it has begun". Rysqo looked at him, and he crouched down,

"Why do your dragons still invade my planet? How can I save this world?"

The ground shook.

"...There is nothing you can do. You can not stop that which has been willed by The Collective..." Rysqo got angry,

"What do you mean, that which has been willed by The Collective? Tell me what I must do." Coryphaeus laughed, he had truly been humored by the boy's ignorance. He spit up more blood.

"...There...is nothing...you...or the dragon...can do. If he lives your planet dies. What boy, did he not tell you of the prophecy of Acumenus."

Rysqo was even more angered.

"What is this prophecy that he speaks of...answer me!"

"It is just a lie Acumenus told Venus. Do not believe what Coryphaeus tells you." Coryphaeus laughed, he had heard their whole conversation.

"Why did you not tell me this? You and your secrets...I am tired of it all...I will no longer do your bidding. How I am to know who is telling the truth?"

"Look boy...yes it was a lie told to Venus, but the rest of us had known the truth. We knew she would have interfered." Rysqo was even more confused,

"Interfered with what"

"Yes Acumenus showed her a prophecy, but only half. He read to her that every planet which was occupied by the dragon whose heart was black was destroyed. This was true, it was very true. Fate, ha, ha, we will fate. It is at our command. Our power is truly far beyond the imagination, the comprehension of the Black Dragon, or you for that matter. Do you know why every planet the Black Dragon occupies is destroyed? ...It is because, every planet the Black Dragon inhabits, is inhabited by The Collective. We were not as foolish as you may have thought. I know the

Black Dragon told you stories. Why would we be so inept to create a beast that could destroy us? Yes he told you of the transference system, but we do not follow that. We watch over the Black Dragon our prime creation, no matter what he does, or where he goes. He can defeat or destroy us limitless times, but never rid himself of us. Thanks to the spell performed by Acumenus, this is all possible. He could not figure out the riddle we made of his life. All this time we played him and Venus for fools. That brings us to why your planet is being destroyed. When the Black Dragon kills a member of The Collective, a part of the planet dies. With virtually all the members dead, this planet is dying. Think of it as security, a precaution. We knew that someday the Black Dragon would realize his power, and we made it so that all life would be wiped of a planet when this happens. When each member dies, it is as if life resets on the planet. We are given another chance to create the planet from scratch. We never did anticipate the Black Dragon's violent actions toward us, but we were prepared. So you see Rysqo, as long as the Black Dragon lives, we live, and there is nothing that can be done. The Black Dragon is immortal, since he took all of our powers and combined them. So with my death, my brothers will be reborn to help me restart this world."

Rysqo was shocked at each of Coryphaeus' words. The Black Dragon remained silent. There was nothing that the Black Dragon could have possibly done, but he should have told Rysqo. Rysqo believed he now knew who murdered Acumenus.

Coryphaeus died and then it began.

Dragons soared around through the air, igniting everything in sight. Only one person could correct the mistake made...there was darkness. He was Rysqo, the Black Dragon...the ground separated more, molten lava spewed through the cracks...last surviving member of The Collective. Flaming hail entered the atmosphere and struck the earth with force that split it instantly, it landed on every continent, and the destruction was massive...he was the holder of the secrets to the universe, and its future. Pain and suffering was carried by the wind...he is...the only hope...the right to the ultimate wrong...he is Rysqo, the Black Dragon. Every natural disaster known to man occurred in different parts of the world simultaneously. The core of the earth bubbled, as the earth above was annihilated.

Rysqo had to think fast, before everything he loved, everything he fought for, was destroyed. Rysqo then knew what he had to do. To make it all right. Rysqo started to run with all his speed, all of his heart. He leaped into the crack. **"Noooooooo..."**

Light returned to the sky. The dragon warriors were destroyed, and The Collective was through, forever. Tanya and Xavier were brought back, and all things of negativity to the planet Earth were reversed and or destroyed. The Universe was saved... The Black Dragon was no more... The Black Dragon was immortal but its mortal vessel was not. Rysqo destroyed the evil of The Collective for good, but he had given up his own life in the process. He gave up his life, so that the planet could live, so that life could go on. He did what he thought was right, what his heart told him to do...just like Venus had told him.

EPILOGUE

"Here, go give this to your mother." The man handed the pan of barbecued meat to the little boy.

He was just a little thing, but he was very strong and obedient to his father. He loved his mother and his father very much. He walked slowly with the pan of meat in his hands. He entered the kitchen, and looked for a place to put the pan. He saw no where that he could reach.

"Mom", the little boy screamed. His mother walked through the threshold laughing with a smile on her face. She was in the next room having a conversation with some other adults.

"Yes sweetie?" The little boy outstretched his arms, so she could grab the pan.

"Here mommy", the little boy said.

"Hey, tell the cook to come on in, we have got enough food", another voice said from the other room. The woman smiled.

"Okay", she yelled back.

"Hey baby, go tell daddy to come on inside now." The little boy shook his head and he went outside to get his father like he was told.

"Daddy, daddy, mommy wants you to come in." The man agreed. He carried his daughter inside, while holding his son's hand. When he got inside, he put his daughter down and she walked away, and his son ran to the other room after her.

"Yes Tanya, what is it." She wrapped her arms around him.

"You have got all your guests waiting and me too."

"I am sorry", he said as he kissed her.

"Go ahead, Xavier is getting bored, and he is about to drive your mother crazy." Rysqo hugged his wife tightly, and then smiled as they walked hand in hand into the other room.

Rysqo,

the

Black Dragon
Part 2

The Dark Heart

INTRODUCTION

Throughout life, we are faced with many obstacles, many challenges and decisions that we have to make. Some decisions that we have to make or that we are responsible for, we would rather relinquish to others. Some people neglect these difficult decisions, avoiding their problems or responsibilities.

Taking responsibility for your actions should be just as simple as committing them. People whom run away from their problems have many different reasons for doing this. It could be any number of reasons, from fear to just a lack of responsibility. It could also be the severity of the decision.

When heavy pressure is applied to something, chances are that it will snap. Then there is always the other way of looking at it. How did they get in this position? If you are not capable of taking up a responsibility, do not get into the situation, for you will have to live with the decision for the rest of your life. Sometimes though, the decision may seem to be virtuous, then, you realize the true severity in the decision, and realize that you have made a very big mistake, a mistake that only you can change. So then you are faced with more and more decisions to make, until you find yourself under the stress and expectations of others, and quite possibly even yourself. It gets worse though, because you can't decide that you want to walk away, or abandon your responsibilities. All you can do is make right what you have done wrong, and hope that you have done the right thing. The only way to be sure though, is to follow your heart. If you follow your heart, you have no one to blame but yourself. This is a little bit difficult though, when you heart is black...

PROLOGUE

With arms folded Acumenus finally complied,
        "Then it shall be done, but I see not the reason for the
heavy security. What is it that you fear so?" Coryphaeus smiled,
        "You could not imagine. It is still good to be sure. I am sure we
will not regret it." Acumenus shook his head and looked at the ground.
        "How will the others see clearly what you see? They might
protest, and Venus, I know Venus would be the first to protest this."
Coryphaeus began to get annoyed with the impudence of Acumenus,
        "They would not dare to countermand my orders, and
Venus...Venus is no problem."
        "So be it my lord, so be it. What shall we name him, and what
shall be his virtue?" Coryphaeus walked to the window that over looked
the fields where wild animals were born and matured. He watched as
young birds learned to fly, from imitating their parents. He watched as
young animals became young predators. A baby bird fell from a tree, and
its mother landed on the ground next to it. Suddenly a lioness pounced on
the mother. The squeaks of the baby were silenced when the cub pounced
on it. Coryphaeus turned back to Acumenus. He walked away from the
window, and up to Acumenus.
        "We shall name him, Compeerus. His virtue shall be to mimic."
With that Acumenus and Coryphaeus joined their energies to form the
mirror warrior Compeerus.

        Venus walked down the corridor swiftly until she saw that
Coryphaeus was already talking to Acumenus. Her pace slowed down as
she had moved closer to them. Coryphaeus turned to see her as she
enclosed on their position.
        "Venus, what brings you to seek Acumenus' wisdom?" Venus
hesitated to answer at first, wondering why she was being questioned.
"What was Coryphaeus doing here", she thought.
        "I was summoned here by Acumenus. What brings you here my
lord?" Coryphaeus looked into Venus' eyes and he saw a spark of defiance,
so he quickly submerged it,
        "Do not question me! My matters here are of no concern to you."
Venus felt that she had pinched just the right nerve with Coryphaeus, so
she turned her attention to Acumenus.

Acumenus had seen Venus coming, in one of his premonitions. He had to quickly assign the mission to Compeerus, and destroy him. He had covered up the situation very well. He now stood nervously in front of Venus. He felt her eyes turn on him, and he looked up. "Ye...yes Venus. Oh, Venus has come here to discuss our problem my lord. Remember what I had told you before she came in, about the prophecy that I wrote, as I saw it?" Venus looked at him hard.

"Ah, yes I see. She has come to protect her precious beast. It is for the best anyway, Negroblatus is becoming more and more of a pest." Venus was shocked at the coldness of Coryphaeus, but she knew that he always had it in him.

"Please Acumenus, just show it to me. I must see if there is anything that we can do to avoid ... You are aware this is already hard for me, you are making things more difficult." Coryphaeus sighed,

"Stop your pathetic act; it's for his own good." Venus stared at Coryphaeus, as he turned and walked away. Acumenus readied the prophecy. Venus then gave him her undivided attention.

Tears streaked down Venus' face.

"Are you sure that there is no other way. Please look again before our meeting." Acumenus saw the pain in her face,

"You know that it is very likely that I will auger the same prophecy Venus." Venus wiped her eyes, then her cheeks.

"Yes..., I know...but...why...why my creation, my most loved creation." Acumenus did not answer. "I know that Coryphaeus is happy. He is happy because I am not happy. Promise me Acumenus, if there is anything that you can do or anything that I can do...please I swear on my own head, then I will do it."

Venus wept and wept. She was forced to make the final decision at the meeting, because, she was the final member of The Collective before Negroblatus. She was to cast the final decision, in the execution of her own creation. He was her prized possession, and she loved him, as any mother would her child. A mother was what she felt like, but she could do nothing to protect her child.

As Venus left the room crying, Coryphaeus waited in the shadows. He left the cover of the shadows when she was out of sight. He walked through the threshold of Acumenus' quarters. Acumenus looked up to see Coryphaeus walk over to him.

"What a piteous waste. Venus is holding us back. She is becoming a little bit of a problem too." Acumenus did not answer; he just looked lost in thought. "Acumenus, I know you do not sympathize with Venus. Ah, she plays games with the head of the genius. Never mind any of that, you gave Compeerus his mission correct?" Acumenus looked into Coryphaeus' eyes. He saw the same coldness that Venus had seen. Without answering, Acumenus stood up and walked away from Coryphaeus, and prepared a spell his lord requested earlier.

~~~~~~

     Venus had regained composure, and was now in her own quarters on the roof of the castle. She looked outside into the forbidden lands, and she saw the dragon. It was headed back to the castle, and it would arrive any minute now. Venus felt her pain eating away at her again. She almost wanted to yell, "No don't come back, they are going to kill you", but she knew that Acumenus had told her that it was the only way to save all life in the universe. The dragon landed on top of the roof, and it proceeded to cross the stone threshold. Venus left her quarters, and met it halfway.

     "Hello... you did well patrolling today. I doubt that there were any deaths on this day."

     Just saying the word death was hard. How could she hide its fate from it, but what could she do? She deduced that nothing could be done. She could not allow her selfishness to destroy the universe. Maybe that is why Coryphaeus snapped at her. Maybe he was surprised at her selfish thinking. Maybe Coryphaeus was only concerned for the well being of the universe. She was unable to stop thinking of the dragon, when she had realized that it was getting late, and she would have to go to the meeting soon. All she could do was wait…as her last few moments with her beloved creation, slipped through her hands. Then she looked at her hands, she saw that it was the dragon's blood that would soon be all over them.

Chapter 1: Two Sides, Two a Story

Light is shed on a dark past as secrets are revealed. Hearts do not always turn black due to hatred. It could be greed, hate, or envy. One warrior's quest for unmatched power leads his heart to turn black. His greed and ambition twist his mind so that he can not see the truth, so that he could not see the answer to the question... What would you risk to gain absolute power? What would you give up to have your wishes come true? What would you give to live your dreams?

The elevator came to a stop at the basement floor. Xavier stepped out with all of his cleaning equipment in hand. The Divine Heights building was already very clean, but Xavier's supervisor wanted it to be immaculate on opening day.

Xavier knew that this was a very big job, and a great deal of money was riding on the success of this job. Their whole company was scattered throughout the building. Each person worked from top to bottom cleaning the floors of Divine Heights over and over. The people cleaning throughout the building were stationed inside of the building until the end of the city quarantine. With the scenery outside, one might argue why they would even try to leave.

Xavier looked left and right, he was trying to decide where he would start. Suddenly the ground began to rumble. Then another tremor came seconds later, and it was powerful enough to knock him off his feet. He did not try to get up until he was sure that they had stopped. It was the safe thing to do he thought.

Xavier rose to his feet, and he walked over to a window. As he peered out the window at the empty streets of the city, he almost got lost in thought. A few days earlier, those streets were packed. Now it was as if a nuclear holocaust had taken place. He looked at his watch; there was no sign of the sun, no sign of life. He remembered the theory of how the dinosaurs were wiped from Earth. He wondered what was going on. He had been inside this building for quite some time now. Xavier began to think of his friends, he wondered if Rysqo and Tanya were okay. He wondered if they were in some place safe like him.

Xavier found the window to be a great distraction, so he turned away from it. As he walked away, he got a cold eerie feeling, as though he was being watched or followed. He decided that he was just experiencing childish paranoia, and should get back to work. Xavier dipped the tip of his mop into the water. Xavier watched as the water was absorbed into the strands of the mop head. Xavier felt a cool breeze pass through the room. He looked around, trying to detect some open door or window. He scanned the room a few times before resuming his duties. Another breeze hugged his body. This time though Xavier paid it no mind. All of the sudden, Xavier heard a sound. It sounded to him like a giant coin that was flipped, settling its way to the ground. Xavier knew there was another presence in the room with him now. He became a bit annoyed. He was starting to think that one of his co-workers was playing a trick on him. In the corner of his eye, he saw something glistening. He turned to his right, and walked over to the object. He stood over it and looked down. It was a silver medallion. He bent down to pick it up. His body and all of his limbs froze up. He stared deep into the emblem on the medallion. It was a yin and yang based design. He heard a voice in his head.

"Who are you? Where am I? Why ..." Xavier had not known what to say or do. Was he possessed? Xavier decided that he would answer the questions in his head. The voice he heard was frantic, and panicky.

"My name is Xavier. I am not sure where you are, but you seem to be in my head, no my mind. I do not know why." There was a pause for a moment.

"My name is Compeerus. I was...sent here...to...help...must save galaxy..." Xavier could not really make out what the voice was saying. It was as if the voice was trying to remember a speech, or was nervously reciting a verse. **"The...Collective...mirror...two men...may... bad...fate...must help me."** Xavier was confused, but he understood "help". **"I am Compeerus. I am the mirror man of The Collective. I need two people to help me. I must split into two vessels. There will be absolute power for the two vessels. ".** Xavier had no clue what was going on. He had heard all of the last speech. He decided that he would do what he thought he was asked. From what he took from the last statement, he would be the one to gain absolute power, something he craved.

~~~~~~

Xavier crept up behind a fellow employee. He waited to do what he was instructed to do next, but he knew what had to be done. He cupped his hand over his mouth, and dragged the man back to a wall. He struck him hard so he would be knocked out.

The voice gave Xavier one final order. The voice told Xavier to release his mind. Xavier complied. He felt the energy stream through his body and run through his veins. He felt it's pulsating in his limbs. He felt completely rejuvenated from all of his work, and he felt stronger. He saw the body of the man stand up and face him. He was surprised that this was actually happening. He was so overwhelmed that he almost forgot what he had agreed to do. Xavier did not care about anything or anyone else at the moment. It was as if his life had certainly changed for the best.

He felt this strange power. He was promised more as time went on. Xavier became taken over with selfishness and greed. He felt a rush of energy and power, and no longer cared. He was willing to do whatever it would take to get more. He was willing to go through any obstacle. He felt invincible, and he was almost correct. His gift from this group of people known as The Collective did come at a high price though, he would have to sell out his friend, and he would have to sell out his world.

~~~~~~

Rysqo walked away from his dying friend, fists clenched. He vowed to take revenge, he vowed to get justice. Xavier lay there waiting, waiting for his friend to leave the Divine Heights building.

Xavier stood up slowly. He brushed himself off. Rysqo had just watched his friend die at the hands of Compeerus. Xavier was in no way dead though. When he bound with Compeerus, he was given a sort of clause immortality, in which both parties have to die simultaneously. Xavier felt like some sort of god. This power had gone to his head, and he had already committed his first act of deception against his friend. Xavier had not even really cared about Rysqo anymore though. He had his own problems to deal with. Xavier made a deal, and he intended on keeping his word.

Though Rysqo had told Xavier of the story of everything that he had seen, and how the Black Dragon chose him, and how he was now fighting off The Collective, to save the world, Xavier thought nothing of Rysqo's words. Xavier's logic was that The Collective was not evil, because they did nothing to him. Xavier had no idea of his ignorance. His heart was completely black now. Compeerus made his way back up to the floor which Xavier was on.

"You okay". Xavier smiled,

"Great". Compeerus smiled as well.

So far The Collective's plan was working, but his mission was not over, it had not even begun. He knew that he had tricked the young man. He had formed a false sense of security around the boy. As long as one of them lived they both lived. Compeerus was safe, and The Collective was insured, no matter what happened.

Compeerus pointed to Xavier,

"You must always keep this medallion safe, do not let anything happen to it. This is very important. Do you understand?" Xavier shook his head accordingly, while he looked at the medallion in his hands. "Ha, ha…very good."

I must give you a new name to represent your existence. I know one that is suiting, "The Black Tiger". The tiger represents balance and skill. I think it suits you. The yin and yang medallion is also a symbol of balance. Yes I think things will work out just fine."

Compeerus and Xavier then discussed the future, and what they would have to do. All the while Rysqo was out defeating the rest of the members of The Collective. He had no idea of his friend's treachery; though it would not take him long to find out, one way…or another.

97

Chapter 2: Crystal Clear

The Black Tiger finds his secrets being revealed, and is forced to speed up the plan, as everything begins to fall in place for The Collective...

There is a misconception that crystal clear means actual appearance when it comes to perception...
A crystal though, like a prism, bends the light...
So what you see while peering into a crystal will not be clear...but instead a distortion of the truth by a shiny rock...
Just as all that glitters is not gold, all that you see is not the truth...

Rysqo grabbed his keys and headed for the door. He heard thumping noises coming from upstairs. As he crept closer to the bottom of the stairs, he saw his son Damian running through the hallway half dressed.

"Wait, wait I want to go. Wait for me Daddy!"

Rysqo sat on the steps,

"Okay"

Damian ran down the steps and jumped when he almost reached the bottom. Rysqo eyed him; he had obviously rushed to put his things on. "You ready?" Damian shook his head. Rysqo reached for the knob. He paused, "Did you tell your mother where we are going?" Damian shook his head again. Rysqo shook his head as well, as in congratulation. Rysqo opened his front door. Standing there as soon as he opened it was Xavier. They all looked at each other for a while. Xavier put his hand up to give Damian a high five. Damian slapped his hand hard. Xavier mocked him by faking pain.

"Where you guys headed?" Rysqo looked at his watch.

"...Nowhere if we don't hurry up."

They all exited the car and entered the bank. Xavier walked behind Damian, whom walked next to Rysqo. Rysqo approached a teller.

"Hello I would like to make a..."

Bullets hummed through the air. Rysqo and all turned to see a gunman firing rounds into the air.

"Everybody get down, now!" Rysqo complied, as he pulled his son close to him. He saw that Damian was scared. There was no use trying anything and putting their lives in danger. Playing hero would prove to do just that. Rysqo looked up at Xavier. While Rysqo and the others in the bank were down on the ground, he defied the gunman, and remained standing, facing the teller's station.

The gunman fired more rounds into the air, and barked more orders. The gunman then noticed Xavier was still standing. "Hey I said get the fuck down. Don't play games with me asshole, get down." Xavier made no response, with neither actions, nor words. The gunman felt that he had lost control and became enraged. He cursed to himself, and he walked over to Xavier. He pointed the gun to his back. "La...La...look don't make me say it again. I ain't afraid to kill you dude!" Sweat streaked down the gunman's face.

Rysqo looked up and saw that this was bad news for Xavier. What was he trying to prove? He was going to get himself killed. Xavier spun around very quickly, and looked into the eyes of the gunman. He began to walk closer,

"You can't kill me. Once you lose your cool, you lose the battle".

The gunman backed up,

"...I...I said get down!" The gunman was not expecting this sort of defiance. He wanted an in and out deal, no trouble. The gunman back up into a red velvet rope. Xavier saw this and made his move. The gunman's finger squeezed the trigger, and bullets streaked from the barrel of the gun. Xavier was all over him though. He freed the gun from his hands, and knocked him to the ground with one hit. Rysqo had covered Damian's eyes and ears when the whole ordeal had started. People in the bank began to cheer and suddenly the bank was in an uproar. Xavier took it to his head. He displayed no modesty as he raised his hands into the air.

Outside of the bank Rysqo waited for his friend to exit. As the door opened Rysqo could hear the cheers.

"Uncle Xavier", Damian screamed as he rushed over to hug him. Rysqo was in his trademark position.

"Damian, get in the car!" Damian heard the sternness in his father's voice, so he quickly followed his orders.

They loaded into the car, and went home. As soon as Rysqo was parked, Damian was out of his seat belt and into the house to tell his mother of his first adventure.

Rysqo and Xavier went to the back. Rysqo grabbed some bottled water. Soon after, Xavier did as well. Rysqo twisted the cap off and began drinking his water not saying a word. Rysqo removed the tip of the bottle from his lips.

"Xavier, what were you trying to do back there? What was that all about?" Xavier smiled, and walked on an angle a little further from his friend.

"Trying to do…It seemed to me, and all those people, like I saved all of your butts." Rysqo did not expect such a remark from the lips of Xavier. He knew Xavier had quit his security job because he tired of confrontations; always having to be he hero.

"Xavier you put everyone in more danger. That man was obviously not going to do anything to harm anyone if his orders were followed. The bank tellers knew the procedure. Chances are no one would have been hurt. Why did you go and make things more difficult? Those types of people disregard all other human life, just for a couple grand. He had a mission while he was walking into that bank." Xavier smiled,

"Tell me then Rysqo, oh mighty Black Dragon, why is it that you did nothing to save them? Were you planning on letting the criminal escape? Were you planning on letting him get away with the crime he had committed? I believe that I did your job for you. Do not become cross with me because it was too much for you to handle..."

Rysqo was not angry, he was just shocked. Xavier did not use to act like this, but he was starting to notice a change in his behavioral habits.

"Xavier, all I am saying is that you have no idea what could have happened. He was armed and he was scared. All of those people..." Xavier interrupted him,

"All of those people could have died if it was not for me." Rysqo lost his toleration for reasoning with Xavier.

"No Xavier, all of those people could have died because of you. What is wrong with you, can't you see the mistake that you made." Xavier rolled his eyes,

"All I can see is that you are jealous". Rysqo's mouth dropped, and he smiled sarcastically.

"Jealousy...is that what you think it is. Oh I see, you want to play hero. Well go ahead Xavier, but see that you don't get yourself killed in the process. By the way, what happened to your clothes?" Xavier turned to look at Rysqo. Then he looked down at his torso, it was plagued with bullet holes. Xavier looked up again. He thought that he had hidden it from Rysqo but, his friend's eyes were way too quick. Xavier smiled to himself. "So what happened Xavier...bullet holes, but no blood?" Xavier did not like to be interrogated.

"He missed me." Xavier knew that what he said had sounded stupid, and unbelievable. Rysqo mocked him by looking closer.

"Oh really, all those times? Wow, you have got some kind of luck. I mean something is watching over you big time." Rysqo watched Xavier turn his back again. Rysqo had no idea what Xavier was hiding, but he knew that it would be best to leave him alone. Eventually he would come around.

Xavier bent down to tie his shoes. The medallion slipped out of the chest pocket of his shirt. It clanked to the ground, and spun until it settled. Rysqo reached down to pick it up. Xavier intercepted it and slipped it quickly back into his pocket. Rysqo became more curious to his secrecy. "That is one mean looking medallion you have got there Xavier. When did you get that?" Xavier stood up,

"It was a gift..." Rysqo nodded his head. Xavier looked down at his watch. Rysqo threw his capped water bottle into the air at him. Xavier caught it without looking up.

"Don't go getting yourself killed doing anymore stupid stuff like that." Xavier looked at his watch and said,

"I have got to go" and he tossed the water bottle back at Rysqo. Rysqo saw Xavier to the door. As he turned around Tanya was coming down the stairs. He turned back to Rysqo, "Don't worry, I don't do funerals". He smiled and started to walk out. Rysqo grabbed his arm,

"Hey, and don't me call the Black Dragon. Rysqo, the Black Dragon died a long time ago." Xavier smiled and exited.

"That's strange, Xavier did not even say hello to me." Rysqo stood with his hands on his hips, and looked down.

"That is not the only thing strange about Xavier." Tanya did not know what he had meant but she did not ask. They walked into the living room area of the house.

"I heard what happened at the bank Rysqo. You okay?" Rysqo smiled at his wife's concern.

"I am fine, but you know, I just can't seem to catch a break." Tanya smiled, and hugged him tight.

"You put too much pressure on yourself. I love you to death, and your children love you to death. We expect nothing of you, but you. I think you should take a vacation. We could go somewhere to just relax, somewhere far from banks and stores. I am already off for the rest of the year. Michelle or Monica could watch the kids." Rysqo thought about it,

"I don't know Tanya." She kissed him softly,

"Well then Rysqo, you should think about it."

Chapter 3: Balance is broken

The forces of the universe all quiver, as an old evil is reborn into the world different...
It is now once again a tragedy for the planet, as old habits are also brought back...
This evil's inherited forbidden power has given it the ability to once again throw the universe into limbo...
Semi-god ignorance leads this evil to cross boundaries that mortals dare not cross...
Once again the Earth and the universe, is thrown into the hands of those who find the will to fight...
Those who can follow destiny...
Those who are of the dragon...

Xavier drove around the corner of the warehouse and parked. He set the car alarm and entered the building. He walked past all the workers that he saw and he made his way to a heavily guarded back room. They acknowledged his identity and allowed him to proceed through. Xavier turned when he had entered the room and opened a door which revealed a long dark stairwell. He began walking down the steps.

Warriors waited behind both sides of the door as the footsteps got closer. Then they timed their attack. They sprung out from their respective sides, and attacked the man. Xavier blocked and countered both of their attacks, sending them to the ground. They held their stomachs and rose to their feet slowly.

"Sorry sir. Just precaution..." Xavier smiled a little, and proceeded to walk. He made it to the back. Compeerus turned to see him.

"Ah, you made it Black Tiger, and you are right on schedule. The sun will be setting soon."

Xavier looked past Compeerus at this engraved stone structure. He looked at the symbols. It was about a six or seven foot stone wall. It stood in the middle of a circular platform, with ten holes around it. Steps led to the top of the platform where the structure stood. The structure had eleven circles. Ten were in a ring, each with their own symbol, and one was in the middle.

Xavier walked up to Compeerus.

"You have the medallion", Compeerus asked. Xavier quickly grabbed it from his pocket, and showed it to Compeerus. Compeerus smiled. "Good, good. This is no ordinary medallion, as I already told you. This medallion was given to me with instructions, by a man known as Acumenus." Xavier looked at the structure again.

"Man? Rysqo told me that The Collective was like an order of semi-gods. They had the power to create life." Compeerus held the medallion up to a candle.

"Huh, Rysqo has no idea what he is talking about. Yes, The Collective was a very powerful force. Almost unstoppable, but they were far from gods, or even semi-gods. The Collective was in actuality one person, a human. This man was named the head of a cult order. They believed that they could achieve godlike powers from following out a series of tests written in a prophecy they had discovered. They were tests based on human temptation, sins, virtues, things of that nature. There were ten tests in all. The first test was the test of leadership, which he had already attained. He and his cult order had shown their devotion to the task, and he was their leader. The next test was the test of genius. A man would have to make decisions based on gut, and logic. They had to navigate through a certain area, an area of certain peril. The next test was the test of war. When the man reached the center of the area, he was forced to battle a series of warriors, until only he remained. The warriors were actually spirits of the fallen, who had previously attempted and failed the same trials. So each time a man failed in the quest it would be harder for the next man to follow in his footsteps. The next test was the test of healing. A man was cut across the chest with a specially baptized sword and left to bleed for a day. The next test was the test of humility and will. A man was stripped of his clothes and forced to lie in the snow for seven days. Then he was forced to keep everything but his head submerged in a deep vat of water for seven days. Then they were to sit in the sun for seven days. Then the man would have to be buried into the earth with only his head exposed. Finally the man would have to survive seven thunderstorms outside. This test brought one closer to nature. The next test was the test of chaos. A man was placed in a dark pit for seven days with no food or water, or sunlight. The next test was the test of haste. A man was forced to run across flaming rocks, for what was said to be thirty two miles. The next test was the test of cowardice. A man was to stay submerged under water for seven days, using only an air pouch. The next test was the test of love. A man's genitalia, more specifically his testes, were cut off and burned before him. The ancient teachings repeatedly stressed the importance that the chosen had not reproduced. The final test was the test of sacrifice. He was to kill himself. It was said, that if all the tests were done correctly that you would be given the powers of a god.

Indeed it did work. The man made a mistake though, playing god. He realized it when he was cast from the earth with his false powers. He was expelled from this planet and galaxy to a distant place where his body floated aimlessly in nothingness. Somehow he managed to form his own universe with his mind and newly acquired powers. He soon found his punishment too hard to serve, at least alone, so he created members of his own order known as The Collective. He made each one of them name the next according to the tests that he had to pass. His powers were granted to him through forbidden arts and faithless acts. He made their gifts and abilities reflect this. He named himself Coryphaeus after his first test. Coryphaeus means leader. Next he created Acumenus, based off of the word acumen for genius. He created Strife, a man whose name meant war. Euphor was created by Strife, his name meant euphoria. He created Deridus, a jester of sorts, or the one whom derides. Deridus created Disorium, master of chaos; ironic, because no man holds dominion over chaos. He created Celerus, the manipulator of celerity. Celerus created Recreanon, the recreant one. Recreanon created Venus, who was named after a love goddess. She created Negroblatus. His name represented two words; negro and oblation; or the black sacrifice. I am sure Rysqo has told you the rest." Xavier nodded. "Things that I am sure he hasn't told you are how and why I was created. I am Compeerus, the mirror man of

The Collective. Coryphaeus and Acumenus joined together to create me. The rest of them do not know me, but they are sure to know me soon. I was created to come here and prepare this structure. They intended on disposing of the Black Dragon before he posed a serious threat. They knew that the Black Dragon would find a warrior strong enough to defeat them, and they knew that they needed a backup plan. Their first was halted when Rysqo sacrificed himself. They were prepared though. They had me created. I was told to come here, and not to die. So I formed the bond with you. Rysqo would never suspect this, and that is why it will work.

They killed me a long time ago, so that when they were brought here with the Black Dragon, I was as well. My spirit energy does not float around like theirs' though. It is consistent with this medallion. Yours is the same now. As long as the medallion exists, we exist, and as long as we exist, so shall The Collective."

Compeerus found what he was looking for, and he turned the medallion. The yin and yang were now reversed. Xavier watched as Compeerus scaled the steps leading to the top of the platform. "So shall the forces of life be reversed, so shall the death of my brothers." Compeerus placed the medallion in the center circle of the stone structure. Xavier looked around as everything seemed to hum. He felt many breezes flow through the room. The medallion's outline lit up, and the energy streamed through the middle. Suddenly the structure began to sink, and the ten holes lit up. When the structure was level with the ground, it stopped sinking. Energy pushed through the holes streaming out in rays of light. Then one by one, the holes opened, and revealed the members of The Collective. Compeerus turned to Xavier and smiled, "It worked".

Coryphaeus exited his hole first. He stretched his body, and let out a type of growling yawn. Compeerus stood there waiting to be seen by his lord. Compeerus said, "Well". Coryphaeus looked at him. Then he looked at his hands

"I do not feel right, I feel weak, vulnerable. I feel like a mortal again. What did you do?" Compeerus raised his hands,

"Calm down". Xavier looked at Coryphaeus, the real Coryphaeus; he expected much more of a huge man than him. Coryphaeus looked at him, and then he looked at Compeerus again,

"Why do my powers not inhabit me", he asked.

"The spell is not complete yet. You must drink the blood of the child that was given a second chance. I do not know what that part of the spell means. I was hoping that Acumenus could clarify."

Coryphaeus was upset, but his anger was directed toward Acumenus now. He felt that Acumenus should have cleared up any riddles that the spell might have. He did not like the fact that something was standing between him and his powers. He felt vulnerable, susceptible to any man's wrong doing. He decided to calm down and wait for Acumenus to wake. They then ran through the plan once more.

~~~~~~

  All the while Venus waited. She had heard everything they had said. She realized that they had deceived her throughout the whole ordeal just like the Black Dragon. She found herself justifying its actions. She wondered why she was still here. She saw her second death as justice being done. She thought that it was right that she suffer at the hands of her creation. She wondered why she was born into this life of power and suffering. Then she realized that it was Coryphaeus and the rest of The Collective that was behind all of the wrong doing. She was a part of it all. She was killing the planet; she was wiping out the universe. Venus was hurt. She decided that there was only one hope left to save the planet. She had to figure out what the riddle meant, and reach Rysqo before The Collective was brought back.

<u>Chapter 4:</u> Forgiveness

Lies become clear, as an innocent sinner is given a chance to make things right...

Throughout time, one thing remains true...
The past is the past, and the past shall not be if all of time is harbored within at present times...
We can not hope to reach the future if we do not remove the burdens of the past...
The past will never become present if we do not let it pass...
Without a past there can be no future...
There can be no future if we live in the past...

Venus climbed out of her hole slowly and quietly. She looked at the three of them as they waited for Acumenus to awaken. She crept to the side until she was satisfied that they would not see her. She looked back a final time, and then she made a run for it. She ran to the area where the guards stood and she saw them just in time to step to the side. They were headed down the steps. They had left when the ritual had started. Venus waited then she sprung out and attacked them.

Venus dragged their bodies to the side. She made sure that no one else was around, and she ran up the stairs. She opened up the door leading to the back room. She looked back trying to remember the way she came. The two guards were gone, luckily for her.

The factory was closing and security was headed home. The two men had come upstairs to lock up.

Venus opened the front door. It was now dark. She knew that it would be very difficult to locate Rysqo. Venus started walking towards the street. She was almost hit by a car, as it swerved around her, and the driver cussed on his way by. Venus felt the weak feeling that Coryphaeus had talked about. It was her first time experiencing mortal life. She knew that she would have to get use to it.

Venus had no idea where to start looking. She had only been in this world once, and it was in utter destruction the last time.

Venus walked the streets for hours, and she was now very close to Rysqo's home. She had no idea though. When light started to return to the sky, she took some time to rest against a mailbox. She was very fatigued. She felt her eyes beginning to close, when she felt an arm catch her before she fell to the ground. She looked up and saw a blurry figure, and then her eyes shut.

Rysqo applied a cool compress to the woman's forehead, and exited. Tanya stared at her face. She studied its contour. The woman's face was beautiful. She had long dark hair which draped over her face. Tanya extended her finger to her face, and tried to move the hair strands from her face. The woman suddenly awoke and grabbed her hand tightly. Tanya's eyes opened wide,

"Rysqo, she's up". The woman's eyes narrowed at the sound of his name. She watched the doorway, as Rysqo entered. She released her grip on the wrist of Tanya. Tanya grabbed her wrist and rubbed it as Rysqo stepped in front of her. Rysqo crouched down in front of the woman. He looked into her eyes. He now saw her strong facial features, and her beauty. Rysqo looked at her for a moment. He then noticed that he was staring, and she did as well. Rysqo cleared his throat.

"Good morning. I see you are now awake. I also see you have met my wife Tanya. Do you feel okay now? When I found you, you passed out in front of my house. What is your name? Do you have family around here?" Tanya put her hand on Rysqo's shoulder. He realized that he was pummeling the woman with many questions, and giving her no time to respond. She looked at him, then Tanya.

"Are you Rysqo, the Black Dragon?" Rysqo stood up and looked back at Tanya. He looked at the woman's face. He saw that she was serious.

"Yes, my name is Rysqo. Who are you, and what brings you to my home?" The woman's face lit up.

"I am glad to see that you two have rekindled your love for each other. I guess you were meant to be." Rysqo looked at Tanya again. He returned his glare to the woman.

"Who are you? What do you want with me?" The woman swung her legs off of the chair she rested on.

"Rysqo, it is Venus of The Collective." Rysqo was not expecting that answer, and he did not like to be played for a fool. Rysqo stood up.

"What? What type of games are you playing? I am about to escort you from my home."

Venus looked into Rysqo's eyes not blinking and he saw her seriousness.

"Rysqo, it truly is me. I know it seems impossible, but you have to believe me. I have a great deal of information for you. I need you to trust me. Trust your heart." Rysqo heard those words before. He heard them from the lips of Venus. Rysqo decided he would hear what she had to say.

Venus spent hours explaining the situation to Rysqo. She spent hours apologizing for all of her actions. Rysqo and Tanya saw her sincerity. Tanya had wished that she would be able to look into the eyes of the evil person that inhabited her body. She wanted a chance to ask her why she had done what she had done. Tanya now knew why. She knew the whole story, even what Rysqo had not known. Rysqo was shocked at how the story was now developing. Rysqo felt sure that there were things that the Black Dragon had not told him. He now knew those secrets and more.

Rysqo paced back and forth as Tanya sat and talked with Venus. Rysqo had to think. How could he battle The Collective again? He was no match for them. Though they were mortal, he knew that the task would still prove difficult. Rysqo decided that he would need some help on this mission.

"So you are telling me that all we have to do is find this second child, or second chance child; that will prevent them from completing the ritual?" Venus nodded yes. Rysqo was happy with her answer, but not with his mission. "What could Acumenus possibly have meant, *a child with a second chance*? Why does he have to speak in riddles, why can he not say what he means?"

"If you let someone detect your meaning, they will realize your wisdom. Acumenus is smart; he hides his meaning behind his words. This insures that his knowledge will be safe. Only those who are worthy of it will be able to see his meaning." Rysqo listened to what she had said. Rysqo decided that he would go get his friend. If he was going to take on The Collective and get some answers, he knew that his best backup might be his friend.

"I am going to go and get Xavier. Maybe he can help us somehow." Rysqo walked towards the door. Tanya and Venus walked over to him. Venus began to follow when Tanya blocked her path.

"You should rest. Rysqo can do this by himself." Venus understood. Rysqo walked through the front door.

Rysqo was now long gone, and the two women continued to talk; but now Venus was curious about some of the details of Tanya and Rysqo's life. She paid close attention as they discussed their life, and their past. She found mortal life interesting. She decided that she might have to get use to it.

<u>Chapter 5:</u> The light of a dark riddle

As the answer to a wise man's riddle is revealed, our hero finds that it is too late...
Our hero returns to find out what he searched for he would never find, his friend becomes his enemy, and his world is twisted upside down.

Disorium dragged the second body to the feet of his lord. Coryphaeus was very upset. He knew that Venus would find some way to interfere with his plans. She had been a problem for him since she was first created. Coryphaeus knew that he was now in a dangerous position. He had no doubt in his mind that she had turned on him. He suspected that she had gone to seek Rysqo. With no powers he saw difficulty in doing anything to stop her. Her threat was growing in his mind more and more. He decided that it was time to take action.

"Acumenus, you must tell me what the answer to your riddle is. Time is not on our side, I am sure that the dragon's warrior will be here soon."

Acumenus turned to Coryphaeus. He saw the panic and fear in his eyes. He was just awakened after a rest he cared not to take. He remembered that it was Coryphaeus that had killed him in his past life, or so he thought.

"As I wrote it, it was that the child that was given a second chance at life would give us a second chance at life. This is no ordinary child though. Also by second life, I do not mean something like a miracle taking place. I mean a second chance to live the life it had not yet seen, not yet had a chance to live."

Everyone in the room had been awake now, and they were all informed as to what was going on. They all stood even more confused with Acumenus' riddle. Acumenus did not like to just reveal the answer of one of his riddles, but he saw no other way, their ignorance was showing.

"This child though, was given life in a time of death. This child was to be born in the time of the planet's death, and this child was reborn in the planet's life. This child is even more special though. This child is born within the bloodline of the vessel of the Black Dragon."

Xavier realized that they were talking about Rysqo and one of his children. He realized that it was up to him now, as they all turned to look at him.

"Tell me what I have to do!"

Tanya and Venus sat there and talked. There was a warm feeling forming between the two. They felt very comfortable sharing topics with each other. They had almost nothing in common. It did not stop them from forming a bond though. They both had smiles on their faces since Rysqo had left. He had been gone for quite some time now. He was still out searching for his friend. He had no clue where he was though.

The two of them smiled and smiled, as they had found peace in each other's words.

"So you say you and Rysqo have two children." Tanya smiled with pride.

"Yes there is Damian, and Hope. Damian was born four years ago. Hope was born five years ago." Venus smiled,

"Hope is a pretty name." Tanya smiled as well.

"Yes it is isn't it? She gave us hope I guess you could say. It is weird though. When Rysqo and I were in the shelter when all of you came to Earth, I tried to tell Rysqo. I tried to get his attention. I told him we needed to talk. As soon as I said this, all of the commotion started. I never got a chance to tell him that I was pregnant with her." Venus' smile faded.

"You were pregnant with Hope when I inhabited your body." Tanya nodded. "That can't be. You died, I died. That means that the baby should have..." Venus suddenly realized what Acumenus had meant in his riddle. Tanya did not understand the sudden mood swing of Venus, but she wanted to know what was wrong. "Quickly Tanya, where is Hope? You must get Hope! She is not safe." Tanya was curious as to what was going on because she still had not figured it out.

"She is upstairs in her room. What is going on; is something wrong?" Venus jumped up, and ran up the stairs. She began searching for Hope's room. She was almost to her room, when she heard the doorbell ring. Tanya proceeded to answer the door. As Tanya reached for the door knob, Venus made her way to the top of the steps. Tanya looked through a peep hole and opened the door. As the door opened fully, Venus let out a gasp as she saw who stood behind the door. She had recognized him from the warehouse. She began to make her way down the steps. "Hey Xavier, you know Rysqo is out looking for..." Xavier turned to see Venus heading down the steps.

"No, he is the one I saw with ..." Xavier hit Tanya, sending her into the next room and to the floor. Venus ran up to him and tried to attack him. He blocked and countered her attack. He parried others as she tried to stop him from reaching Hope. Venus was ineffective against him.

They fought their way up to Hope's room. Xavier reached it quickly, because he knew where it was. He kicked the door open. The child was sleeping peacefully on her bed. He scooped up her legs. She had not come out of her deep sleep. Venus entered the room as he exited. He fended her off with kicks to her body. She found it impossible to do harm to Xavier in her mortal state. All she could do was watch as he carried Hope off.

Tanya stood up. Xavier's hit had left her a little bit shaken up.

"What are you doing Xavier, where are you taking Hope?" Xavier stared at her and smiled, and then he exited.

Chapter 6: An old evil is reborn

A warrior whom has battled on both sides is now in a position in which he found himself in once before, only this time, will he make the right decisions?
If a lesson is not learned the first time, the same mistakes tend to be made with different circumstances, but the same consequences...
Such redundancies are prevalent in life...
Man tends to never change; only he adjusts to the cycle around him...

They all looked at Coryphaeus. They wondered what would be their next step. If Xavier had failed, what would they do next? Suddenly everyone turned around. They heard commotion behind them. Standing there was a not too familiar face. It was a long time since this face was looked upon, and most of The Collective had not remembered.

Coryphaeus remembered though. He stared the man down. All was silent; it was if time had frozen them in place. Coryphaeus did not know what to expect next. He remembered his past with the man, but did the man remember. He could not decide what to do next, when the man made his move.

He walked slowly up to Coryphaeus, past all of his brothers in The Collective. He stood in front of Coryphaeus staring coldly upon him.

"Are you sure that it will work?" The other men all looked at each other. Coryphaeus had been holding his breath. He had no idea what the man was going to do, but he knew it could be very bad. He was especially nervous in his mortal state. He feared what each minute brought him. He had forgotten what it was like to be mortal, to be human. He had felt a wee bit relieved now though, because with all the man's possible actions, he chose to ask a question. Coryphaeus felt that he had gained the advantage. He knew something that the man wanted to know.

"I have confidence that Acumenus' spell will prove dependable." The man smiled. This was good news to him.

"Where does Venus lie?" Coryphaeus shrugged.

"That is knowledge I have no access to." The man nodded as he started to walk past each of the men. He had remembered them. He had remembered all of their actions, all of their decisions. He remembered everything.

"I must say that I am surprised that you did reach this far. I mean I would have expected none such luck and genius from you in any other lifetime. That just shows that you, all of you, that much has changed, you are different." They all looked at each other, then at Coryphaeus.

"What do you mean?" The man laughed and shook his head.

"Well I guess some things have stayed the same. You should choose to live in a time other than the past. In the past you were spawned under the name The Collective. Why live under that same name now? Has it not caused us all enough pain?" They all agreed with groans and head nods. "Since we are all reborn, we should all be born under a new title. The Collective is no more, it died with our past. We were born into darkness to die in darkness. Now we are reborn into light, and into light we shall live forever, but under a new name." They all cheered at the man's words. They all cheered at the words of Negroblatus. Coryphaeus stared at him while the rest of them praised his suggestion. Negroblatus had achieved his goal, for he had gained their support, which might prove useful if things did go well in the future. Coryphaeus still stared though. He had no way of thinking what Negroblatus was up to, but he surely did not like it.

Chapter 7: Betrayal

Sadness sometimes fuels the flames of vengeance...as each tear plummets into a burning ember...
The more tears that are lost, the more you wish the cause would feel your pain...
Trust is sometimes a gift best not given...

The night was cold. The full moon added an extra shade of eeriness. Rysqo was very exhausted from searching for his friend Xavier. He had not seen his family for hours. When he had left, Tanya and Venus seemed to be getting along very well. His son was at a basketball game, and his daughter was sound asleep in her room. He turned around the corner slowly. As his car had fully made the turn, he was greeted by a serenade of sirens, and a colorful assortment of lights.

Rysqo immediately jumped to the conclusion that a crime had been committed. Rysqo had always thought of his neighborhood as peaceful and safe, regardless of the robberies and typical city violence. With the army of law enforcement vehicles parked on his block, he saw the possibility of otherwise. As Rysqo navigated slowly down his block, he noticed that the police cars seemed very close to his home. In the next few seconds though, everything in Rysqo's life changed.

Tanya's hands were soaked with salty tears. Down her face there were streaks left from tears, and imprints from her hands. Her eyes were red and bloodshot. This appearance did not represent Tanya's beauty very well, and if you had not seen here before, you might argue if she was ever beautiful. Venus patted Tanya on her back, and even then, Tanya was still doleful. Then suddenly Venus stopped patting on Tanya's back and trying to comfort her. This caused Tanya to look up slowly. Her vision was vaguely blurred by tears, but she could make out Rysqo's figure walking towards her. Tanya wiped her eyes, and she saw him clearly now. He was walking very slow, looking directly at her. She ran up to him and squeezed him tightly. An officer approached them. Venus looked up, but Rysqo and Tanya paid him no mind.

"Okay, we are going to do whatever we can. We are going to leave an officer here to stand guard, and watch for anything suspicious. If you need anything at all, he will take care of it. You should get some rest. We will do what we can. With the information that you gave us..." The officer realized that they were not listening to a word he had said. He turned and walked away. Venus watched him leave, and say something through his radio.

Tanya told Rysqo everything she had seen. Rysqo was silent as he sat with his wife and held her. When Rysqo had returned home, she seemed to feel a little better. They sat there silent for a few moments. Rysqo stared off into space. Venus broke the deep silence.

"I see and feel your pain, but Rysqo, I know you know...Rysqo you and I both know that these po...lice are likely to have no luck finding Hope before it is too late. They may not know where to find her at all. We know where she is. We have a better chance at stopping Coryphaeus. You can not let your sadness blind you. You know what we have to do!"

Rysqo looked at Venus. He saw the sincerity of her words in her eyes, though it came out callous. Rysqo then looked at Tanya, whom was staring admiringly at him. He kissed her softly on her forehead and stood up. He did not say a word as he walked for the door. Venus followed him.

Chapter 8: Conquest

The hunt is on for the answer to many questions, but should the warrior stop to ask them..?
What possible excuse is there for betrayal? What believable reason is there for wrong doing?

It was very early in the morning, still dark outside. Rysqo's car darted down each street with breakneck speed. Venus was amazed with the ride. Her first time in a car was going by so fast though. Venus had to watch the road to remember which way she had come. As she pointed, Rysqo drove in that direction. Then they reached an area near the warehouse that was not accessible by cars.

Rysqo looked to see if there was another way to the entrance, but Venus insisted that this was the way she had come. Rysqo and Venus exited the vehicle. They proceeded to the entrance. As Venus saw the guards blocking the door, she stopped and put her back against a wall. Rysqo continued to walk towards the entrance at the same pace. Venus saw that he was not slowing down, so she hurried to his side. Rysqo tried to walk past the guards as they acted like they did not notice him.

As he attempted to walk past they extended their arms to Rysqo's chest, and held him back.

"You are not allowed in here without authorization." Rysqo looked down at their hands on his chest, and then he looked at them.

The workers in the warehouse were working diligently in an almost robotic rhythm. Suddenly a body flew through the front door and to the ground. The workers turned around, everything stopped.

There were many workers in the factory. They all looked at the man's body as it lay on the ground. Then two more figures appeared through the door, then a third. Rysqo held the man by his hair. The man's mouth was bleeding, his neck outstretched. Rysqo looked around, as if to take a quick count. Rysqo struck the man in his neck, and let his body drop. As it struck the floor, the workers looked at it. Then some of the workers left their work and walked over to Rysqo and Venus.

"What the hell do you think you are doing? You come in here beating on our guards. Are you looking for some trouble?" Rysqo looked at the man. He started to walk in his direction, but he walked past him. He walked over to one of the stations and picked up something.

"What's this?" he asked, as he touched their merchandise. No one answered. Rysqo looked around, still no response. Rysqo then dropped it to the ground. The workers began to mumble, until the whole warehouse was in an uproar. Rysqo silenced their commotion with a question. "Where are they?" The workers started laughing.

"Who the hell do you think you are? You should leave before you get yourself in more trouble. We wouldn't want any accidents to happen to you." Rysqo tilted his head.

"Accidents... Really? Wow I didn't know you cared!" Rysqo smiled then he grabbed some of their equipment and pulled it down. "Oops!" Then the fight was on.

They charged at Rysqo. They had forgotten about Venus as she slipped her way to the back room. It was unguarded, because everyone had gone after Rysqo.

Rysqo fought with all of his heart, but he found that there were many workers in the warehouse, too many to fight all at once. He ran through an area filled with boxes. He had split them up. The remaining workers scattered out to find him. They searched through each aisle of boxes. They did not see him. Rysqo found that he was in control now. He stood on top of a stack of wood, and looked down as three men walked through the aisle. He jumped down and he swept one of the men's feet from up under them. As he rose, he kicked off the wood and into the chest of another man. He then stepped on the knee of the third man and jumped past his head, while delivering a kick to the back of his cranium. The hard hat the man wore cushioned Rysqo's blows. The other two men gave chase as the man stumbled forward. Rysqo looked back and saw them coming for him. He ran around the corner of another stack to the next aisle.

"He's over here!" the men shouted.

Rysqo stopped as he heard footsteps moving down the aisle. He pressed his back against a stack and waited for the man to appear. The man ran out and was greeted with a kick to the sternum. He stumbled back, and Rysqo saw that he held a red axe. It read *Use only in case of an emergency*. The other two men ran up behind Rysqo. He turned around, and jumped off the stack delivering kicks to both their faces. Rysqo swept one of the men with his left foot while standing up. He delivered a back fist to the temple of the other. Then Rysqo turned back around, and the man was already swinging the axe. Rysqo used the stack again, and back flipped out of harms way. The axe pierced strait through the wood. The man struggled to pull it out. Rysqo kicked it in deeper, and with the same leg kicked the man back. The man lost his grip and stumbled backwards. Rysqo walked towards him. He swung at Rysqo. Rysqo dodged his punch and locked him up using his elbow and driving it into the man's back, and grabbing the man's chin. While doing this Rysqo continued in the direction the man swung, sending the man face first into the stack of wood. Rysqo released his hold, and gave him two back elbows. The man's body dropped. Then the other man came running through the aisle towards Rysqo. As he had almost made it out of the aisle Rysqo spun, driving his elbow into the chest of the man. He delivered a back fist to the face, and then a fore fist to the groin. The man dropped to the ground. Rysqo saw more men running down the aisle, all the way down at the other end. He ran the other direction.

They chased him. There were three men behind Rysqo as he ran down a long aisle. Rysqo could see the other exit now, when three more men entered at the other end. Rysqo turned around and stopped. For a short moment he had forgotten that he was surrounded. Rysqo kicked from side to side to reach the top of one of the stacks. He was close to the back room now, and he could see where Venus was waiting. She saw him too, and she waved. He smiled and waved back. The men started climbing the stack. Two stood on both sides of Rysqo. A third heavy set gentleman started climbing directly in front of Rysqo. Rysqo kicked him down. He fought the other two as they stood atop the stack of wood. He knocked them down one after the other. More men started to climb. The stack of wood began to lean towards another stack. Rysqo saw that it would not hold their weight too well. He jumped in the direction that the wood was falling. Rysqo jumped from stack to stack as a domino effect was created. Men between the aisles were crushed by heavy wood. Rysqo tried not to look down as he jumped each hole. If he fell it would be all over. Rysqo slipped, and the timing of his jump was off. He grabbed the edge of the wood slab as it was struck by the preceding pile and leaned forward.

Rysqo saw that all he could do was go for the ride. The pile leaned forward not colliding with anything. Lucky for Rysqo, it was the last one. The pile fell to the ground and Rysqo rolled off. He laid there on his back trying to catch his breath. He stood up and looked at the destruction he had left. No workers remained standing.

Venus ran over to Rysqo as he looked down at his hands.

"Aw man, I got a splinter."

Venus led Rysqo to the steps she ran up when she had first escaped. They went down the steps quickly. Rysqo stood still as he reached the bottom of the steps. He looked directly ahead of himself. He saw his daughter's body lying on what looked like a bed. She did not move. Rysqo did not even think he saw her breathing. He walked forward, and then he noticed the members of The Collective all standing behind his daughter in a half circle. They did not move. They just watched Rysqo walk forward. Rysqo walked up to his daughter's body. He looked down at it. She looked so young and innocent to him. As he looked into her eyes and they stared back, he then noticed how much she looked like Tanya. He saw Tanya in his daughter's eyes. Tears left his eyes. They streaked down his face and onto his daughter's. Rysqo scooped up her head, then her legs. He picked up her body, and he turned around. He walked over to Venus. She looked at him. Venus stretched her arms out, and held onto the body of Rysqo's daughter. The child seemed so light to her. They had obviously completed the ritual.

Rysqo wiped his face. He outstretched his fingers, and shut his daughter's eyes with the tips. Rysqo took a moment to get himself together. Then Rysqo turned to face The Collective. Rysqo turned to face his former friend Xavier, a traitor to all humanity. Rysqo knew that it would be a great risk to ever trust anyone and call them your friend. He knew that once again, he found himself regretting past actions.

Rysqo walked to the center of the semi-circle.

"Where is Xavier? I want to fight Xavier first!" They were silent. Xavier stepped out from behind a pillar. Xavier and Rysqo's eyes met. They focused on each other. Rysqo walked up to Xavier and stood about five feet away. Rysqo did not say a word, nor did Xavier.

"Finish him quickly Xavier, we have other things to tend to" Coryphaeus said.

Xavier listened to what he said. Xavier knew that even with his enhanced strength, he might not be able to defeat Rysqo. Xavier then made a very cowardly move that no one was expecting. He pulled out a gun and pointed it at Rysqo. Almost as soon as Xavier's arm was fully extended, Rysqo's left hand was on the barrel. Rysqo's palm covered the tip of the gun and the barrel. Rysqo and Xavier still never took their eyes off one another. Xavier pulled the trigger. The bullet dove through Rysqo's hand and into his chest towards his heart. Rysqo released his grip on the weapon, and he grabbed his chest with his right hand. He let his left hand lay on his side.

Blood oozed out of Rysqo's chest. He fell to the ground, and leaned back into a pillar. His vision started to blur. Rysqo's eyes began to close. His eye lids felt heavier and heavier. He wanted to sleep badly. It was cold. Rysqo wanted to escape the cold and sleep. His eyes closed.

The group of men formally known as The Collective, walked past the bleeding Rysqo. As they walked past Venus, Deridus said,

"We will catch up with you later." Venus did not respond. She just watched as they walked past. She was still vulnerable, and she knew that they were all too much of a match for her. As they disappeared up the steps, Venus began walking to the bed which Hope's body had first lay on. She put the body down slowly, gently. Then Venus ran over to Rysqo. She grabbed his head with both hands. It was slouched to the side.

"Rysqo..." No response. "Rysqo, Rysqo you must open your eyes. Look at me Rysqo!"

Rysqo did what Venus had told him to. Rysqo looked drugged up. His eyelids were heavy and his awareness was dwindling.

"Rysqo, I need you to concentrate. You must concentrate." Rysqo winced with pain.

"What...What...do... you mean...?" Venus rubbed Rysqo's face with her hands.

"Rysqo listen to me. When the Black Dragon entered your body, it left all of its power with you. Though the Black Dragon left your body, its life source and power still exist inside of you. Rysqo you must use this power now, Rysqo you must heal! Concentrate, focus your energy!"

Rysqo closed his eyes as great pain came with his injury. Rysqo began to have flashbacks, flashbacks of the time he had spent with Tanya, and with his children. He was sad, and he felt like he had lost a great part of himself once again. Then Rysqo remembered his wife Tanya. He had flashbacks of all the times they were there for each other. He remembered every moment that they had spent with each other. He remembered their love for each other. He knew that he had to stay alive. He had to do it for Tanya. Rysqo concentrated. He remembered when the Black Dragon taught him to use his abilities.

Rysqo took the next few moments reviewing all of his abilities. He saw the great power that he had not yet used. He knew that this new evil may pose a great threat on his planet, and that he may have to use these new abilities. Rysqo took a deep breath, and he opened his eyes.

Chapter 9: An Unforgivable Act

Trust is rescinded as a chain is once again broken....
This time death is not the breaker of the chain, but it is the chain itself...
Though it takes two hands to break a chain, two sides to hold the chain,
one can do just as much damage...

Rysqo held his hands and his head down low as his daughters body was lowered six feet under. Rysqo kept the funeral private. He had invited only Monica, and Michelle. The only other guests were Tanya, Damian, and Venus. Rysqo looked directly to his left. He watched as Tanya went to her knees and plucked flowers onto the coffin. He expected her to have lost her composure by now, but she seemed to be holding up well. Rysqo suspected that she had enough crying since the day he returned home with the body.

The funeral was arranged two days after the incident at the warehouse. Time was not on Rysqo and Venus' side. They knew that the longer they waited, the greater their enemies' power grew. They would be almost unstoppable if they reached their full strength.

Rysqo was still in a sort of shocked state. With his former friend's actions against him and his family, he new that revenge was in order; though Rysqo deeply knew that revenge should never be a reason to fight. The planet was in danger, and Rysqo had to keep telling himself that he was fighting for the planet. It was hard though, because his mind was filled with rage. Rysqo saw this battle as a determining battle. The last time, he had a choice whether or not to get involved. This time, he was sucked into a chaotic battle.

The Collective's terrible acts against him and his family made it clear that he was the target. They did not care who or what they had to go through to get to him, but they were assured that they would get to him and kill him. Rysqo knew that they had a definite plan this time though, because of the fact that they did not finish him and Venus off. Rysqo had no clue what they were up to, and he did not intend on waiting to find out.

Rysqo sat next to his wife inside of the limo.

"Are you going to be okay? If you'd like I will stay." Tanya looked into her husband's eyes and said,

"I'll be fine. I just need a little time to think." Rysqo shook his head and he grabbed his wife's hand.

"Okay, I gave the driver directions to the house. You should be safe there okay. I have to go take care of this okay. I must put an end to this for good!" Tanya did not respond. Rysqo softly kissed his wife's cheek. "I love you", he said. Tanya smiled and said it back.

Rysqo released his wife's hand and he exited the limo. Tanya now sat in the limo alone. The other guests, other than Rysqo and Venus, were in another limo.

Rysqo walked away from the limo. Tanya watched through the tinted windows. She put her hand on her head then slapped her thigh.

"Okay driver you can go now." The driver looked into the rear view mirror. He then rolled up the separating window. A smirk crossed his face as he put his foot on the accelerator. The limo headed out of the cemetery. Rysqo had bought his own private land for his family to be buried on, so it was difficult to get there. Only if you had directions, could you reach it. It had something to do with Rysqo's ideas of eternal peace, and a serene final resting place.

Tanya sat back in the limo. She had many mixed emotions. She had somewhat expected Rysqo to come home without her child alive, but she was not too sad. She was as sad as you could expect from a mother. Tanya knew that she would not be able to lead a normal life though. She knew that things would never be the same. Tanya also knew that she was deeply in love with Rysqo, and no force in the universe could break the two of them up again.

Suddenly the locks clicked on all sides of the limo doors. Tanya was confused, she already felt safe, was this extra precaution really needed. Tanya looked through the tinted side windows. She saw no familiar landscape. Tanya was very confused now. Then a second layer of tinted windows rose to fully block sight of outside. Tanya now sat in complete darkness. She couldn't even see her hand in front of her face. Tanya also felt very tired. She was running out of oxygen. Suddenly the weight of her eyelids over powered her. Her eyes shut, as her body fell to the seat. The separator to the limo's front and back lowered. So did the rest. Through the rear view mirror, Compeerus looked at her. Then another sinister smirk crossed his face.

<u>Chapter 10:</u> A New Breed of Evil

Nothing worth doing is easy...especially if it is to save the world...

The phone rang once, twice, three times.

"Hello", Monica answered.

"Hey Monica, it's me. Hey where is Tanya?" Monica looked at Michelle.

"What? Rysqo..? Rysqo what are you talking about, isn't Tanya with you and that other woman?" Rysqo's facial expression changed. He turned around and faced Venus. "Hello...Hello...Rysqo!" Monica did not receive an answer. She hung up the phone when she heard the operator come on the line.

Monica walked away from the phone. She had no idea what was going on. She knew one thing though; she did not want to be involved. She grabbed her stuff, and she went to Damian's room. She grabbed some of his clothes hastily. "C'mon" she said to Damian. They went downstairs and they regrouped with Michelle. She did not even have a chance to ask where they were going, because they were all out of the door and headed down the walkway.

~~~~~~

Rysqo and Venus were driving towards his home. Rysqo had broken almost every speed limit in the city. Rysqo's new car was certainly capable of this feat though. He loved this new car, but he loved his wife more. Rysqo would definitely risk his car to save his wife. Rysqo barely made each turn, and skidded down each street when the burnout came. Everything seemed like a blur to Venus. Then Venus caught sight of some scenery. She still did not believe where she was going. The car finally turned around the corner and onto Rysqo's block.

Rysqo jumped out of the car and proceeded to walk behind his house to his training area. Venus had to run to catch up with him.

"Rysqo, why are we here?" Rysqo ignored her momentarily as he scanned the perimeter. He looked quickly until he found it.

"We are here Venus...because I know how Xavier thinks, and he knows this. He was probably here while we were at the funeral." Rysqo walked up to this wooden wall he practiced throwing knives at. He grabbed a knife, and ripped it out of the wall. He grabbed the note as it fell. "He always did hate funerals..." Rysqo thought.

Rysqo began power walking again, this time headed back towards his car. Venus stepped into his path.

"Where are we going now?" Rysqo looked at her, and handed her the piece of paper. Rysqo continued walking as she looked down at the paper. They got into the car, and Rysqo put his seatbelt on. Rysqo looked at her, still trying to figure out what the paper meant. All the paper had on it was two letters, a capital D and H. Venus looked up at Rysqo. "Rysqo I still don't get it. Where are we going? What does this mean?"

Rysqo faced the road ahead of them. He turned the key and started the engine.

"That paper means...put your seatbelt on." Rysqo said as he put his foot on the accelerator.

The car started off.

"Rysqo please just tell me where we are headed." Rysqo sighed.

"We are headed to a memory."

Rysqo and Venus were indeed headed off to a memory, a memory that Rysqo had tried to forget. It was the memory of his past that plagued him. The memory of how he had first joined with the Black Dragon. He felt as if that was the biggest mistake he had ever made in his life. None of this would have ever happened if he had chosen to leave the Black Dragon's offer on the table. He made a deal with the Black Dragon. The Black Dragon was so deceptive, so evil, and Rysqo now felt his conscience eating away at him. He wished he had never become involved with the Black Dragon. He saw that he played a great role in the destruction of his planet. He cared so much for that of which he had no significant involvement with. He saw the mistake of his ways. If he only were responsible for his own life, and did not try to help out the Black Dragon.

Rysqo knew that he could not keep stating all of his ifs. Making the past his burden would only prove to pour stress onto his mind and body. Rysqo also knew that his visiting of his old city would prove to be a task he wished he could walk away from. He did not know what to expect when he reached the city, but he knew that he would have to ready himself.

~~~~~~

Rysqo and Venus got out of the car. They stepped into a horde of people. They were all standing outside of the Divine Heights building. As Rysqo proceeded to the front of the pack, he saw ambulance lights. He realized that something had already taken place here. Rysqo began walking towards the front door, Venus close behind him.

There was news coverage and media everywhere in the front. Police had taped up the area, and declared it was a crime scene, some sort of hostage situation. Rysqo stepped over the tape. A security guard was being lifted into an ambulance, as a police officer watched. The emergency medical technicians worked as if they did not notice the man standing there. The man was screaming, and was obviously in some great deal of pain. The E.M.T. shut the doors to the rear of the ambulance.

Rysqo stood there and watched for a little bit. He knew that the man had a run in with The Collective, and that was the result. He also knew that the same result would occur if anyone or anything else had a run in with them. He had to locate them fast, and put an end to their merciless behavior.

As Rysqo watched, he was approached by a police officer. Rysqo turned to see him walking directly towards him.

"Sir I am going to have to ask you to please step behind the barrier." Rysqo looked at him but did not respond. "Sir, please!" Rysqo started walking forward towards the door. "Freeze!" Rysqo stopped and turned around. The man held his gun steadily aimed for Rysqo. "Put your hands in the air, where I can see them."

Rysqo put his hands in the air. In the corner of his eye he saw Venus about to make her move. She kicked the gun from the officer's hand. The man turned to look at her and backed up. Rysqo and Venus ran through the door. The other police officers were preoccupied with the crowd.

Rysqo and Tanya were running swiftly through the lobby of the Divine Heights building. It was now deserted. The most exquisite and luxurious building in the whole region was now a ghost building. It had been evacuated. It was said to be a hostage situation. Swat teams would be on site soon.

Rysqo and Venus paid no attention to any of the talk going on outside the building, for they were inside now, and whatever happened was just going to happen. Rysqo stopped on the dime. Venus continued running for the four elevators until she turned around and looked back. She saw Rysqo looking down and backing up. He was staring at the floor.

"What now", she asked. Rysqo lipped the words that appeared before him. She did not see the writing on the floor. Rysqo had caught sight of it, when he noticed it was red, like blood, and in high contrast with the color of the floor.

"They are on the top floor. They wrote *your prize lies atop the building.* Be prepared for anything Venus."

Venus agreed that she would be ready for anything, but she was confused, why did it seem so easy to her she wondered.

"Rysqo, this is way too easy, they have to be planning something. This must be a trap." Rysqo smiled,

"Then let's go spring it!"

The elevator doors opened slowly. Rysqo and Venus stepped out cautiously. They scanned the perimeter, looking for anything that seemed abnormal. Rysqo looked straight ahead. He saw a chair with rope tied around it. It looked as if someone was in the chair, but it was facing the other way. Rysqo stretched his arm out to his right. Venus felt Rysqo's arm halt her progression. Venus stood still as Rysqo continued walking. Rysqo walked through a very dark room while looking left and right. He crept slowly closer to the figure in the chair.

"Tanya", he whispered. The figure in the chair squirmed and mumbled stuff. Something was obstructing the speech of the figure in the chair. As Rysqo crept closer to Tanya, he saw that there was one big knot in the back of the chair. Rysqo looked around one final time, and he kneeled down behind the chair and took out the knot. Rysqo then reached around the head of Tanya and pulled off the tape. Rysqo backed up a little. Tanya stood up and turned around slowly to face him. It was then Rysqo saw that he did not just free Tanya; it was a woman whom was probably the hostage.

"Thank you", she said, as Rysqo stood in shock.

The swat teams moved into the Divine Heights building and the crowd was backed up even more. The police were losing their patience.

From inside of the assemblage, Deridus and Disorium came. They were wearing disguises. They waited until Rysqo and Venus had entered the building. They proceeded to Rysqo's car, and dropped a note with the final instructions on it into the driver's seat. They then left the scene and disappeared into the city's night crowd.

The woman ran past Venus and into the elevator. Rysqo was still looking around, hoping that they had brought his wife to the building, but he was losing hope. Venus held the elevator doors open while signaling Rysqo to come. Rysqo ran into the elevator and Venus released the doors. Rysqo pressed the button to go to the ground floor. The woman stood stiff. She had her arms wrapped around her body as if she was cold, her long hair, blocking her face. Rysqo and Venus paid her no mind though.

"There is an elevator headed this way sir." The man thought for a second. "Disable the elevator now!" The man opened the security panel and stopped the elevator in its tracks. He noticed that it was stopped on about the thirtieth floor. The swat team piled into two elevators on the ground floor, and headed up to that floor.

Rysqo turned around to look at the woman.

"What is your name?" She was startled that Rysqo had tried to speak to her. She began to stutter, and she caught herself,

"...Shelly, Shelly Sweets." Rysqo nodded.

"Well Shelly, everything is going to be okay now. We won't let anything happen to you." Shelly smiled and she blushed. She thought Rysqo was flirting with her. She didn't realize he was only trying to be nice. Suddenly their elevator jolted. They were almost thrown to the ground. Rysqo looked at the floor number; eleven. They did not know what was going on. They tried to open the elevator doors but it was not working. The elevator jolted again, and started to ascend. Rysqo saw the numbers climb steadily. They all looked at each other.

~~~~~~

Some of the swat team piled out of the second elevator. Seconds later, the rest of the team piled out of the fourth elevator. They all cocked their guns and aimed for the doors of the elevator. The commanding officer signaled one of them to go open the elevator doors. The man walked up to the third elevator. He put his gun on his back. He reached out slowly to press the button. His finger was fully extended, and was almost to the button when suddenly the doors to the first elevator opened up. The men pointed their guns towards that elevator.

Shelly, Venus and Rysqo exited the elevator.

"Hold your fire!" the leading officer commanded. The men were all at ease. The man began walking away from the elevator, when the doors opened up.

Suddenly many black figures exited the elevator. They all wore black ninja uniforms, and they were all masked. Before the officers had a chance to react, a ninja ran up behind the man who was going to operate the elevator. The men saw blood shoot out from the chest of the man. He looked down to see a sword protruding through his stomach. The men pushed Rysqo, Venus, and Shelly back. They opened fire on the men. The ninja used the man's body as a shield and grabbed his gun. He used it to return fire. The other ninjas ran for cover.

Rysqo grabbed Venus' arm,

"C'mon". He led her behind some pillars near an emergency exit. Bullets were sprayed throughout the room. The swat team was losing the battle. Both sides were armed with bullet proof vests, and automatic firearms.

Shelly ducked for cover behind another pillar. She could not see where Rysqo had gone to. She put her hands over her ears. She looked left and right. Then Shelly caught sight of Rysqo. He was holding the emergency exit open for Venus. As bullets ricocheted off the pillars, Rysqo turned and looked back. He saw Shelly. Rysqo's heart jumped, *she's going to do it*, he thought. Shelly and Rysqo's eyes met. Rysqo shook his head and screamed, "Don't do it". She could not hear him with the noise of live fire, and with her hands cupped over her ears. She stood crouched and she started to run.

Bullets whizzed past her head and into a wall adjacent to the emergency exit fire escape. A bullet grazed her hair, and she screamed. She kept on running as Rysqo watched. Then one of the ninjas turned and pointed the gun at the running Shelly. A swat officer saw his gun focusing on her. The officer started running towards Shelly. Suddenly bullets tore through his left leg. He continued to push forward. He was very close to

Shelly, when she turned around. He tackled her to the ground. Shelly felt the air leave her body. She felt the swat officer's body vibrating, as bullets collided with his vest.

When Shelly stood up she was about five feet from the emergency exit. She immediately ran through the door.

As the battle raged on outside the door, Rysqo, Venus and Shelly ran for the bottom level. Rysqo read the floor levels as they descended. They had reached about the thirteenth floor when Shelly needed to take a break. Rysqo and Venus stopped. Rysqo kept his eye on the steps above them. Suddenly, the fire escape shook. Rysqo grabbed a railing to prevent himself from falling. He grabbed Shelly's arm, as her body went down. He pulled Shelly to her feet. Venus looked down below them. She saw smoke billowing its way up the fire escape.

"That is not good. That smoke means fire, and there should not be a fire in the fire escape." They all looked at each other. Rysqo saw a door below them open up. "Run!" Rysqo shouted as five ninjas piled out of the door. Rysqo ran to the ninjas while Venus and Shelly ran up the fire escape.

Rysqo kicked one of the ninjas as he tried to climb the stairs. He fell into the rest of them. One of them fell down the steps while screaming. Rysqo wondered why he was screaming. The Rysqo thought about it, and he realized that the screaming did not stop. There was a ledge at every corner. The falling should have stopped with the screaming. Rysqo knew that the falling did not stop. That boom that they felt must have been a grenade or a bomb of some sort.

Rysqo saw total blackness behind the ninjas. He knew that they would have to get out. It did not seem like the ninjas showed any care for their fate. They were probably on a kamikaze mission, and told not to come back unless their target was eliminated. Rysqo turned around and he ran up the escape. The four ninjas stood up and gave chase.

Rysqo saw a fire extinguisher at floor fifteen. He grabbed it and waited until the ninjas were in a close enough distance. He saw one of them come around the corner. He sprayed the solution into the man's face and into the air. Then Rysqo continued running. He made it safely to the next floor, when he saw Venus and Shelly standing at the top of the landing above him. He started to run forward. The door next to him started to open up. Rysqo turned and kicked the door into the face of the man on the other side. He ran up to Venus and Shelly. They ran through the door.

They were on the seventeenth floor and needed to get out of the building quickly. Rysqo looked around the room they had entered, he saw nothing of use. He remembered that the ninjas he had just encountered did not carry firearms. They were equipped with grenades, and swords.

Rysqo tried to think how they could have reached him from below. There must have been another fire escape on the other side of the building. Rysqo had to get to the other side of the building, but he knew that he would never make it if he left the room that they were in. It would be a while before the ninjas discovered their position, but he knew that they were swarming all over the building. Rysqo walked over to a window. He looked out onto the city. Seventeen floors up, all of the people outside of the building looked pretty small. Rysqo knew that if he could get to a floor below the ninjas, he might be able to make it. They were under the impression that Rysqo and the others were climbing to the top.

Suddenly the door opened up. Venus pulled Shelly to the side. A ninja came into the room. He turned to his left to see Venus and Shelly. He started towards them. Rysqo ran and jumped into the air kicking him in the back. The man stumbled forward. He reached for his sword. Rysqo kicked the handle of the sword and held it in the scabbard. The ninja knocked Rysqo's leg down. Rysqo spun away from him. A pair of ninjas entered the room. One of them was armed with a gun. The man Rysqo was fighting turned around and ran at Venus. Rysqo kicked the first ninja who entered back. The second ninja pointed his gun at Rysqo. Rysqo grabbed his wrist with his left hand, he then locked it up. Rysqo spun while holding his arm, and delivered an elbow to the back of the man's skull with his right elbow. Rysqo then wrapped his arm around the man's neck in a headlock position. He let go of the man's right arm. Rysqo kicked the man's right knee inward hard with his right leg. The man's leg inverted. Then Rysqo kicked the inside part of the man's left knee with the same leg. The man's leg bent sideways. Rysqo turned as he heard Venus and Shelly screaming.

The ninja pulled out his sword and was about to slash at the women. Then there was a boom. Smoke came from behind the man's head. He fell forward at the women's' feet. The gun shot wound became evident, as they saw a gaping hole in the back of his head. Rysqo threw the gun down. The first ninja turned and went after Venus. This time, Venus pushed Shelly hard to the side. Shelly fell to the ground. Venus hit the man with a quick hand combo and he dropped backwards onto the other ninja's sword.

Rysqo dragged the bodies to the center of the floor. Venus propped the door with a chair. Rysqo began searching the bodies, he was looking for something. Rysqo was just starting to get frustrated, when he found what he was looking for.

Shelly and Venus walked over to him, as he searched the other two bodies in the same place and had the same luck.

"What are those?" Shelly asked. Rysqo smiled,

"They are our ticket out of here. Also they are one of the ninja's most reliable utilities, the grappling hook."

They walked over to the window. Rysqo secured each line. He tested them to make sure that they were tight enough to support everyone's weight. Then he broke the window with a chair. He threw the lines out the window. "Now are you sure you two know what to do?" They shook their heads in unison, and then Shelly hesitated.

"Just one more time..." Rysqo sighed,

"We are going to rappel down about one or two floors, and kick our way through, then run to the fire escape on the other side." Shelly was satisfied that she knew what to do, so she shook her head.

Rysqo led the way. He stood on the ledge, his back to the sky. He told Shelly to get in position next to him. He watched as she got up next to him.

"Okay now go! Use your legs and don't let go!"

Shelly went down as far as her rope would allow. Rysqo looked down, as she dangled. Rysqo spent a few moments to talk to Venus, and then he joined Shelly. Moments later, Venus was on the other side of Rysqo. Venus was on the left side of Rysqo and Shelly on the right.

"Okay one, two, three, now!" At Rysqo's command they bounced off the glass. They all entered the window at the same time. Just as Rysqo had thought the momentum was enough to break the glass. They all stood up and brushed glass off themselves.

Shelly led the way, to the door and Rysqo and Venus followed. Shelly put her hand on the knob, and began to open the door. Rysqo kicked the door closed.

"You know I have been thinking. Why did we all stop on the same floor as those ninjas? Oh and why did the ninjas attack you two? I mean, ninjas, good and bad, follow an honor code. They do not attack the innocent, only their target. They did not initially attack me. It was only when I interfered that they approached me. They were aiming for one of you two. Another coincidence is that you were so close behind Venus when that ninja swung his sword. How did these ninja's know exactly where we were going? Those are too many coincidences, and you know what Shelly, if that is your real name? I also do not think that you are the target. So start talking, this is as far as you go!" Shelly backed up and smiled.

"Ha, ha, ha, ha, ha, ha, you fool. Rysqo you are clever, because indeed, you are not the target. There is someone who wants to deal with you personally. She is the one whom they want." Venus kicked at Shelly. Shelly grabbed her leg, and elevated it; then she swept Venus' other leg. Venus hit the ground hard.

Rysqo stood back; he knew not to interfere with their fight.

Shelly started to kick Venus while she was on the ground. Venus rolled to avoid the barrage of kicks. She grabbed Shelly's leg and took her down. They both jumped to their feet at the same time. Shelly charged at Venus. She pushed her to the window. She pushed Venus' torso out of the window. Venus' back was leaned out, and she looked down. Venus delivered a stunning knee to Shelly's stomach. Shelly screamed and stumbled back. She charged at Venus again, and this time Venus grabbed her, leaned back and used her foot to catapult Shelly through the window. Shelly was sent screaming through the air like a missile. Her screams were silenced when she collided with the pavement before the building.

Rysqo and Venus ran through until they reached the other side. They ran down the emergency exit to emerge on the other side of the building.

They walked around to Rysqo's car.

"What about those police officers?" Rysqo sighed,

"It's a tough job isn't it, but so is mine." Rysqo opened the door. He was just about to sit down when he noticed a note. Venus saw the expression on his face, and then she looked down at the note as well. She and Rysqo both knew who the note came from, and who it was for. Rysqo picked up the envelope, and he prepared to read it. Rysqo then realized that he was looking at a map. Rysqo clenched his fist, and he threw the note into the back of his car. He and Venus looked at each other. They were both ready for what they had to do next. Rysqo started the ignition, and he put his foot on the accelerator. Rysqo's car sped off into the city streets.

He was taking the last trip to find The Collective. He was getting ready for his final battle. He wanted to put an end to The Collective's trail of destruction in the world. He wanted to end it all now, no matter who he had to go through. Rysqo suspected that he probably would have to fight his friend and possibly kill him. He was prepared to do that and much more. Rysqo thought, *is that is whom they think is going to deal with me personally, huh...* Rysqo tried not to think too much of his upcoming battles. He had to concentrate on rescuing Tanya, and avenging Hope. Everything else could wait, nothing else mattered. Rysqo was going to get his justice, and Xavier would be a fool to try to stop him.

Chapter 11: Justice

Injustice requires a response...
Justice, no matter how severe, should go unquestioned...?

Rysqo and Venus reached their destination. Rysqo parked his car. Rysqo and Venus stepped out of his car and began walking towards the entrance to the warehouse.

This warehouse was on the other side of the city. It was abandoned and was a very dangerous place to be. The warehouse was very large and it manufactured many different things, from iron products, to wood products. A fire had left the building dilapidated and unsafe.

Rysqo peeked into the building's front door. He saw nothing as Venus waited behind him. Rysqo decided he would step inside to take a look around.

Venus remained standing outside. There were no buildings in sight, so Venus felt confident that she could see danger coming. She folded her arms and rested her back against the wall. She took a deep breath, and then exhaled with a sigh of boredom. Then in the corner of her eye Venus thought she saw something run up the wall of the structure.

Rysqo saw that the place was dark, but not too dark. It was lit up by the sunrise on the horizon. He looked left to right at the abandoned machinery. Rysqo stepped over debris as it lay in his path. He saw a door that looked like it had been propped open. He started walking for it. Rysqo thought for a moment. He was going pretty deep into the building. Should he go and get Venus? Venus was too weak in her mortal form to engage in a battle to the death with The Collective. She would just be in the way or slow him down he thought.

Rysqo decided that he would proceed without Venus at his side. He grabbed the corner of the door and he slid through it very swiftly. This room was moderately darker. Rysqo felt a breeze of uncertainty, and moisture pass through his body. He wiped his brow. As Rysqo looked down at his hands, he saw sweat. Rysqo then noticed that things were a bit warmer in this room. Rysqo looked back at the door. There was a caution sign, which had a rather lengthy safety label on it. Rysqo deduced that he was in an area of the building which would require extreme heat. Probably a furnace to melt the various metals the workers had worked with. The room had no windows, no insulation. One would think that you would probably suffocate after a short period of time in the room.

Rysqo had remembered that the fire had started in the furnace area. In the news he heard that some heavy machinery had tipped over, and it was too hot for a boom crane to pick up. Rysqo walked briskly to the next door, which led to some steps leading to a catwalk above him. Rysqo hurried up the steps. He had made it halfway to the other side of the catwalk when he heard his name being called.

"Rysqo, what was taking you so long? I was beginning to get very worried." Rysqo shrugged,

"What do you want me to do Venus? I am going to find my wife. Should I check in before I go to the bathroom as well?" Venus heard a spark of impatience in Rysqo's voice, so she kept quiet.

"Okay then, wait right there, I'm coming up. I thought I saw..."

Venus started for the stairs. Rysqo continued walking to the next room, ignoring Venus. Rysqo walked through to the next room. He saw that this room was well equipped with windows, across the full span of its ceiling. Rysqo was halfway across the catwalk again, when Venus called for him. Rysqo ignored her and continued walking. The sun's rays started to beam through the ceiling as it rose slowly into the sky.

Rysqo saw an array of shadows span across the floor. He looked up and quickly looked back down as more of the same assassins they had seen before came crashing through the glass ceiling. Rysqo covered his head. The ninjas rappelled to the end of the catwalk near Venus, and in front of Rysqo. Then three of them dropped to the floor below, in a room which seemed to hold some sort of chemicals in it.

Rysqo had suspected upon entering the room, that they had been flushed from their units at the time of the fire into these metal grates on the ground.

Rysqo stood up fully, to see a ninja about five feet away, fiddling with his line, trying to get loose. Rysqo ran at him and kicked him to the ground. The ninja behind Venus pushed her to the ground, and opened fire at Rysqo. Rysqo jumped off the catwalk reaching for one of the unoccupied lines. He made contact with it, and held tight. Rysqo swung out of harms way, and to the ground. Rysqo collided with the ground hard, and he rolled away.

He saw the men on the ground, reaching for their weapons, and running in his direction. It was now apparent to Rysqo, that they were both targets. Rysqo ducked behind one of the units, into the shadows, hidden from the sun's rays.

Venus laid chest down on the steel catwalk. She pushed herself up.

"Get down on your knees and face me. I want to look into your eyes when I kill you." The ninja man had the gun extended to the back of Venus' head. She complied and began to slowly turn around. The man backed up a little with caution.

"Those are not honorable weapons of combat." Venus said. The man laughed,

"Hey it gets the job done!" Venus was now totally facing him. He unlocked the chamber with his thumb. Venus closed her eyes as he slowly pulled the trigger. A smile that was hidden by the mask crossed his face. The chamber of the gun withdrew; click, click. He must have run out of ammo shooting at Rysqo. "Huh" the man said with total surprise.

Venus' eyes opened slowly. Now she had a smile on her face. The man saw her looking up, and he saw her expression. He quickly tossed his weapon to the ground, and reached for another. Venus grabbed his arm and pointed the gun at his stomach. He fell to the ground agonizing, dying slowly.

"You see; weapons of dishonor. You shall die by your own dishonorable acts. Your shame shall live with you throughout eternity."

Venus heard the gun shots below. She looked over the side of the catwalk. She saw the men firing rounds at what looked like nothing. Then she saw Rysqo. He was on the other side of the unit. The men all stopped firing. Then Rysqo came from behind the unit.

Venus ran to the steps to get to the bottom. Venus saw a man in front of her laying limp. It looked like he had broken his neck on impact.

Venus walked away from the man, she looked around for Rysqo. She found herself standing in front of the three men. They threw down their weapons. Venus knew that she would have to fight. They began walking towards her. Then one of them charged at her. She diverted his attacks and sent him to the ground. She finished the other two off in the same manner. She may have been mortal, but she still knew how to fight; due to training with her brother Strife.

Venus still could not find Rysqo. She decided to just continue walking. She proceeded through the doors in this room. She found Rysqo crouching down, watching something below. She crouched low next to him.

"You made it." Rysqo whispered. Venus did not answer.

"What…" Venus' speech was halted by Rysqo cupping his hand over her mouth. Rysqo pointed down over the rail of the catwalk they were crouching on.

Rysqo and Venus were watching Celerus, Deridus, and Disorium. They were talking about something outside of this room. They suspected that Tanya was inside of the room.

Rysqo started to move to his right towards the steps. The catwalk creaked. Rysqo stopped moving. Deridus, Disorium, and Celerus were all looking up now. They spotted Rysqo instantly. Rysqo felt the catwalk jerk again. He looked at Venus. Rysqo stood up and ran at Venus. He pushed her through the door, back into the other room. The catwalk gave way while Rysqo was standing. Rysqo jumped off before it smashed into the ground. He fell on his hands but held himself up, in an all fours position. He stood up quickly. As soon as Rysqo had stood up, he was greeted with a sucker punch from Celerus. Rysqo stumbled back, and grabbed his mouth. No blood, but Rysqo was angry. He looked up again. Celerus stood stiff readied for battle.

Rysqo did not see Deridus or Disorium. Rysqo was not concerned with their position though, because he knew that their powers were probably fully recharged by now, and they were no longer mortals. Rysqo was mortal, but he shared in their abilities. Rysqo knew that for once, he would have to use the abilities in battle. This should make things fair to an extent, and would make the fight easier for Rysqo. Rysqo was definitely ready, and he knew that these were kill or be killed battles.

Venus looked down, she took an estimate. She grabbed the ledge, and she swung her legs down. She let go and braced herself for the fall. She landed perfectly, as a trained gymnast would. She looked around and she saw that Rysqo and Celerus were about to engage in battle. She began to walk towards them to get a little closer. Deridus blocked her path.

"Hello Venus. Did you miss us?" Disorium came up behind her.

"...Because we missed you Venus!" Venus turned around, to look at Disorium. She looked at them both, back and forth, waiting for them to make their move. Disorium attacked her first. She dodged his attack and countered. Her hit did not do too much to stop him from his relent. Deridus tried to hit her, and she dodged his attack. Deridus' attack connected with Disorium. Deridus kicked at her, she knocked his leg down, and kicked him in the chest. He stumbled back, but was not hurt. They were both gathered on one side as she looked at them. All of the sudden they all heard a voice,

"That's enough" Recreanon came off of a wall. He had used his camouflage and was watching the whole scene. Recreanon grabbed Venus' arms. She could not do anything. They dragged her around the other side of the wreckage of the catwalk. "Let's wait until your little human friend finishes fighting" Recreanon said.

The three of them watched as Rysqo and Celerus prepared to fight.

Celerus became tired of waiting for Rysqo to make the first move. So he attacked Rysqo with a punch, and that was a mistake. Rysqo grabbed his arm and swung him to the ground. Celerus got to his feet and ran at Rysqo. As he attacked Rysqo, Rysqo defended himself. Rysqo noticed that his attacks were starting to speed up. Those who were watching on the side were in a daze. Their eyes could not keep up. Rysqo himself was beginning to get lost in the haze. Rysqo decided to end his opponent's raid.

Rysqo blocked a final time, and quickly saw an opening and exploited it. Celerus was struck directly in the solar plexus. The air rushed from his lungs, and he went down on one knee. Rysqo quickly looked back, to see the situation unfolding in his audience. Rysqo turned back to

Celerus. He walked up to him. Celerus did not look like he could continue to battle.

"Speed is not the only thing that will help you to win a battle." Rysqo kicked Celerus hard in the chest. Celerus fell backwards. Celerus was still gasping for air. He turned around on his stomach and began crawling towards the room. Rysqo walked up behind him and raised his leg. Rysqo brought his leg down, crushing his spine. Then Rysqo turned towards his spectators.

Deridus and Disorium immediately ran at Rysqo, whom was walking their direction. Deridus spun and tried to kick Rysqo in the face. Rysqo dipped back, and then he feinted forward kicking him in the inside back of his left knee. Deridus went down. Disorium tried to attack Rysqo as well. Rysqo delivered a two handed blow to his chest. Disorium flew backwards about ten feet. Deridus stood up, and he tried to sneak attack Rysqo from behind. Rysqo turned around, and grabbed his arm. He then hooked his leg around his arm, and kicked him in the side of his neck. He pushed his leg in further until it snapped. Deridus' body fell to the ground. Disorium rushed at Rysqo. Rysqo timed it perfectly. He stepped on Disorium's right knee, and then his shoulder, then he kicked him in the back of his head. The kick increased Disorium's momentum. He ran into a wall and fell to the ground. He turned around, as he tried to stand up with his body in a daze. Rysqo ran up to him again. This time he raised his leg to Disorium's chest. He back flipped off his chest while kicking him in the chin. Disorium's neck snapped back, like he was a bobble head doll. Disorium fell forward to his knees. He used his hands to try to slowly stand up. Rysqo walked up to him. Rysqo spun, while cocking his knee up, and aiming it for his temple. Rysqo landed the fatal knee blow. Disorium's body fell to the ground, not moving.

Rysqo started to walk over to Venus and Recreanon.

"Stay back Rysqo, I will kill her." Rysqo stood about seven feet away from Recreanon and Venus. Rysqo looked into Venus' eyes. She looked back into his. She saw his eye twitch. She softly nodded her head. Recreanon held her arms tightly at the wrist. Venus brought her arms in front of her, as far as she could. She leaned forward and pushed her buttocks into Recreanon. Just as she thought, he released his grip. Then Venus jolted her neck back, and head butted Recreanon. He grabbed his face with both of his hands. Rysqo got a small running start, and he delivered a jumping kick to Recreanon's chest. Recreanon stumbled backwards into the wreckage. Recreanon did not move after that, for a rusted appendix of the catwalk, penetrated his back and internal organs.

Rysqo and Venus headed for the door of the room. Rysqo went to open it, and when he did open it, he immediately saw the back of Tanya's head.

They had her tied up in a chair. She squirmed in the chair, "Rysqo…" Rysqo walked around to the front of her. A smile crossed his face. He untied the ropes. Tanya stood up and tightly embraced Rysqo. He hugged her back, and they kissed.

"Are you okay Tanya? They did not hurt you did they?" Tanya shook her head. She continued to hold him tight. "Where are they at now?" Tanya backed away from Rysqo a little bit, wiping tears from her face.

"I heard them in that room talking", she pointed to a door. Rysqo hugged her a final time.

"Venus stay here, I need you to watch Tanya. Do not let anything happen to her. Okay?" Venus nodded and Rysqo started to walk for the door.

Chapter 12: The Double Dragon

All things have their equal opposite. To rights, there are wrongs. To lies, there are truths. Life is an analogy of sorts; the yin and yang; opposing realities, opposing futures, opposing pasts, and presents. Good and evil. Like a two headed dragon. One of the heads represents good, the other represents evil; always in conflict with one another. Both knowing that doing harm to the other, will be in turn, doing harm to itself. So exists the balance of the universe. If the balance is disturbed, so disturbed is the flow of the universe. A world consumed infinitely by good or evil, is a world in which life shall not exist. A paradox of paradise to the human mind is that which would be sought for eternally, and sometimes gives peace. A paradox of paradise to the human touch is that which will be reached for eternally, and always brings pain...

The five members of The Collective waited inside of the room. Negroblatus looked at Strife, and he gave him a signal. They worked in unison.

"Sorcerer", Negroblatus shouted. Acumenus, as well as Coryphaeus and Euphor turned around. Negroblatus threw a knife directly at the forehead of Acumenus. It had penetrated his skull.

"What is this treachery?" Coryphaeus asked. Euphor ran at Negroblatus. Strife unsheathed his sword and decapitated him. His body fell to the ground. His head rolled away. Strife started to walk towards Coryphaeus. "You too..? You two blind fools, would dare to betray me? Then you shall both die!" Coryphaeus sent a blast of energy into the chest of Strife. Strife was killed instantly. "Now you shall see my true power Negroblatus, you fool. I knew not to trust you. I knew you would betray me. You should have known that you could not defeat me. There are no more of my men around, for you to turn against me. So what are you to do now traitor?" Negroblatus did not expect the speech from Coryphaeus. He wanted him to make his move.

"Then give me a fair fight. We will settle this for all eternity." Coryphaeus nodded,

"So be it." Then Negroblatus dashed at Coryphaeus, and drove his most trusted sword into his stomach. He pulled it upward, ripping through Coryphaeus' chest like it was butter.

"You are the fool, and you are the traitor." He walked out of the room.

~~~~~~

Rysqo put his hand on the doorknob. He started to twist it. Xavier bust through the door. Rysqo stepped back. Rysqo heard laughter behind him.

"Ha, ha, ha, fool" Tanya said. Then Rysqo looked back at Tanya. He saw her change into Compeerus. It was Compeerus all along. Rysqo wiped his mouth in disgust.

Suddenly Xavier snuck Rysqo, and kicked him through the window of the room. Rysqo flew about twenty feet.

Venus turned to see Compeerus laughing. She pushed herself away from him. She ran through the door and up to Rysqo. He was still down. Compeerus and Xavier exited the room, and walked slowly up to them. Venus looked up, and she nudged Rysqo continuously. It had no effect. Compeerus knocked Venus backwards, away from Rysqo.

"Leave him alone!" she screamed. Compeerus was still laughing. He picked up Rysqo by the lapel. He looked Rysqo in the face. Rysqo's eyes popped open. He kicked Compeerus back; hard in the stomach. Xavier hit Rysqo from behind. Rysqo stumbled forward, and turned around. He looked in the face of the man, whom was once his good friend. Rysqo knew that he would have to kill them both.

Xavier attacked Rysqo, as Compeerus did as well.

Venus knew she was too weak to help, and she also knew that Rysqo, was losing the battle, and he was in dire need of her help. She looked around, and then she saw something that could help kill them both.

Rysqo was getting pounded on. Their attacks were very swift, and they moved in unison. He ended up only blocking a few of their attacks, and landing none of his own. Rysqo held his ribs, as they walked slowly up to him. They stalked him like he was their prey.

Suddenly Compeerus looked down. He saw a sharp metal rod, sticking through his chest. He could not turn to see where it was coming from, because Venus held it very tight. Xavier turned around, and looked at him. Rysqo charged at Xavier. Xavier blocked his attack. Xavier and Rysqo battled hard. They held nothing back. Rysqo was losing, still weak from his previous battles. Xavier hit Rysqo with a punch combo. Rysqo grabbed his arm, and locked it up. Rysqo yelled and started pushing Xavier backwards. Xavier stumbled backwards, until he felt a sharp pain. Rysqo backed up away from Xavier. Xavier looked down, and then he looked at Rysqo.

"I'm sorry…" he said, but it was way too late. Rysqo walked over to him. He pulled Xavier from off the end of the metal rod, and he sat him down on the ground. Xavier reached in his pocket and took out the medallion. "Destroy it…please!" Rysqo took the medallion, and he looked at it. He then looked at Xavier.

"Where is Tanya?" Xavier pointed to the far side of the room to another door that looked like it led to a closet. Rysqo stood up. He handed the medallion to Venus. "Destroy this Venus", he said. Venus nodded. Rysqo started to walk for the room. Venus threw the medallion to the ground and it bounced like a metal ball. She pulled the rod fully through Compeerus, whom was long gone. She raised the rod over the medallion, and drove it down. The medallion slightly lit up, and it cracked through the middle, then it split. Xavier could feel the energy leave his body, he could feel the evil leave his heart, and he could feel his energy slowly diminishing.

Rysqo was about ten feet from the room now. He walked very slowly, for he could not remember the last time he had seen his wife, his real wife. He could not remember the last time he had held her in his arms. He could not remember the last time he felt the warmth of her body, the calmness of her voice. He could not remember the last time he had been in the paradise of her presence. He had not forgotten any of it though. He missed her dearly. The Collective was once again destroyed, Rysqo thought. He was a few steps away from experiencing his happiness once again. Rysqo had received his justice. Rysqo had received his final justice. Rysqo was now to receive his reward for once again saving everything. Rysqo reached for the knob.

"Rysqo..!" Rysqo heard Venus call him. Rysqo did not want to turn around. He knew that if he turned around there would be someone standing there waiting, ready to try to kill him. Rysqo was so tired of fighting. He was so tired of helping everyone else. Rysqo turned around slowly, expecting Venus to be ready to battle him. He rolled his eyes and put his hands up. When he focused in on her, about twenty feet from his position, he saw that she was not alone.

Negroblatus held his blade firmly at her neck. Negroblatus and Rysqo stared at each other from far away. Negroblatus threw his sword to the ground.

"Hello Rysqo, do you remember me?" Rysqo said nothing, he just stood stiff. "Ha, ha, you probably have no idea who I am. It is me Rysqo...Negroblatus, the Black Dragon." Rysqo still did not move. "You know, you used to be such a good kid. You could have had anything. I could have given you the world. I could have given you the universe." He started walking towards Rysqo. "You made one mistake though. You let your emotions, your sympathy, take over. You included yourself into the category of the mortals. I made you way more than mortal. I made you way more than immortal; and what did you do with my gift? You destroyed it, along with me. Rysqo.... I'm back! I have another gift for you Rysqo. This time, I will give you the gift of death; a gift that you should be very grateful for. No more pain or suffering. No more responsibilities. Think about it Rysqo. You can rest, while I take back my other gift." Rysqo was about five feet away now. "Rysqo, do the right thing!" Rysqo kicked Negroblatus in the chest. Negroblatus was not affected by it. He hit Rysqo back, and knocked him into the wall. Rysqo was dazed, as he slowly stood up. "And Rysqo, your lovely wife, oh I will take very good care of her." Rysqo clenched his fists. He swung at Negroblatus, whom locked up his arm. Negroblatus smiled into Rysqo's face. Rysqo gave him a knee to the groin. Negroblatus threw him across the room, near Venus. Negroblatus was in pain, as he slowly walked over to Rysqo. He reached Rysqo. "You don't have to thank me Rysqo, I understand..." he said as he delivered the final blow. As his hand was about to collide with Rysqo. He felt his sword drive through his stomach. He turned around to see Venus slowly backing away. He walked up to her and hit her hard with a grunt. She flew backwards near the room. He then turned around to finish off Rysqo, whom was still down, knocked out. He walked over to Rysqo, and prepared to finish him off. He picked up Rysqo with one hand, and looked at him. He smiled. Then a metal rod went through his chest. It had punctured his heart. He had one ounce of energy left, to see Xavier barely standing up behind him. Xavier's eyes rolled up into his head, and he fell to the ground. Then Negroblatus did as well.

Venus saw him die and she felt relieved. Venus ran to the room. She opened the door, and she saw Tanya, blindfolded and tied up. She untied Tanya. Tanya saw her and she asked where Rysqo was. Venus took her to see Rysqo.

Hours later, at Rysqo's house, Tanya waited along with Venus. Rysqo's eyes opened up, very slowly. He saw the blurred face of his wife, and he was relieved. Rysqo then spoke,

"Tanya, baby, I thought about it…and that vacation sounds like a good idea." Tanya smiled. Venus did as well. Damian ran into the room, and hugged his father. Rysqo smiled, finally he had his peace. It was over.

EPILOGUE

The funeral service had almost everyone emotional. It was the first time that Rysqo had attended a double funeral service. He paid his last respects to Hope and Xavier. He wanted to rebury Hope and give her a better funeral because he had new peace. His wife had a soft smile on her face, but she was not happy. Rysqo placed a white lotus on Hope's coffin, and a note on Xavier's.

He looked into his wife's eyes. He saw that everything was okay now. Rysqo formed a soft smile on his face as well, and squeezed his wife. Venus came up after them with Damian, Monica, and Michelle. They bowed their heads in respect. A tear streamed down Venus' face, and she felt a tug on her clothes. She looked down, at Damian. He handed her a tissue. She smiled and she wiped her face. She realized that though she had made some mistakes in the beginning, there were some very precious things left for her to save on Earth. She was grateful that she was given a second chance, and she was grateful to be forgiven.

Rysqo,

the

Black Dragon
Part 3

The Wheel of Destiny

INTRODUCTION

As we each follow life throughout it's definite course, preordained or not, we find ourselves plagued by the decisions we make. These decisions are sometimes made consciously, and sometimes inadvertently. In some bizarre cases though, individuals find reason, justified or not, to interfere in another's life, thus shifting the roads that one is damned to follow. If they do not damn themselves to walk these roads, they are in eternal unhappiness until they find their way back.

If a person walks down an unknown road, and is shot cold blooded, what justifies this? Nothing, no, nothing is far from the answer. In that split second, that minute chance of a change in decision; in the time between the sparks in the synapses linking, and the muscle in the shooter's finger contracting, to the time when the bullet actually leaves the barrel of the gun. The slightest chance that the direction of the gun was changed before the gun was triggered at all. What if another gun had gone off in the distance? The person remains shot in each scenario; the severity of the wound, the victim, and the gunman, all fates determined by that of one's destiny.

These are all decisions made from the outside, that might change one's life forever, and alter one's destiny. This stone thrown into the rushing river, this wrench hurled into the gears that turn the Wheel of Destiny, can all be tossed off course.

It is very difficult to keep on course in life, more so than to stray off a path. If a car rides down a road and strikes a stone, it's path may be slightly averted, but this all depends on the size of the stone, the size of the car, and who's driving.

Some argue that every person draws out their own destiny, writes their own book of fate. This just serves as a chapter in the book of one's legacy. This is a book that has existed for all eternity, its pages never singed or corrupted, and a book that is true to itself.

It is up to you though to decide how much of an impression you want to leave in this big book. Do you want to begin writing a one page essay, or would you like to begin a five hundred page novel? How much do you think you deserve? How much do you think you are worth? How much do you wish to be remembered, or do you wish to be a forgotten page in history; a page that existed nevertheless, but was forgotten; a page that sunlight might never illuminate again. You must look into yourself and decide, what you deserve, what you want for yourself. You mustn't sell yourself short or surround yourself with those whom sell themselves short, those whom have lost the battle with themselves. Those whom have been engulfed in negativity, or lack self-value, self-respect….integrity. Avoid those who have given up, or lost hope.

The stars are the limit, for they are vast. No definition can be assigned to the worth of a star. Nothing can be done to count all of the stars, for they are born, as dreams are born. They burn in our eyes, just as dreams burn in our minds. Also true with the concept of self value. You are what you make yourself. If you find yourself stuck, find a way out. As hard as it is sometimes to see the light, it is always there, glowing as the ember of hope, a divine destiny it follows too. Remember though, everything in the universe is included in this same Wheel of Destiny. Nothing is on the outside. Everything also has it's time. Trying to lengthen this time, struggling to preserve life, would be in turn serving a blow to shorten it. What can be done to change history other than to write it from the present and remember it? The paradox underlined by history, the paradox eternally unsolved.

PROLOGUE

The night was eerily cold and quiet. All of the city's sounds could be heard as vibrant echoes. The city streets were very wet from a rain shower earlier that day. The city streets were also virtually empty, except for a few areas near storefronts that were heavily congested with consumers looking to fill their material palate. They walked in a uniform motion. Each one of them seemed to be occupied with something else. They interacted, and spoke on cell phones. Cars extracted rain from the streets and into the air as they cruised on the open road. This part of the city did not usually see much action. This was the area which people had come to shop in on a regular basis, but it was usually quiet.

There was a sub-mall, concealed by store fronts and relative businesses. That was where most things had taken place in this city. Occasionally though, there was a bizarre crime or insane act committed that no one seemed to understand.

Sweat streaked down the young man's nose as his soaked hair repeatedly slapped him in the face as he ran. He panted heavily but he kept his pace steady. He came around the corner and he saw the shoppers. He ran towards them, pushing his way through, as they screamed, and reacted late, too preoccupied to mind his rude display. He ran into the street narrowly missing a car. He wiped his face and ran into the alley. He waited there, his back against the wall, panting. His body ached, and his mind was very weary. He sunk down until his buttocks were on the wet concrete. He whimpered and leaned his head back against the alley wall that was touching his back.

He then felt it again, that indisputable sensation that someone was watching him, following him. He closed his eyes and swallowed hard. He felt a tear streak down his right eye. He opened his eyes and he slowly turned to the left. He saw him standing there, watching and waiting. It was as if he enjoyed the chase. Then suddenly a motor vehicle passed in the street. The boy's eyes were still fixated on the man, but no, he had disappeared. The young man broke away from the wall and ran through the alley to his right. The alley had accumulated more water than the streets, and it was hard for the young man to keep his balance. He splashed his way through though.

He ran into another block of businesses. He turned left, and then right and he started to look left again, when in the corner of his eyes he saw them. Their eyes had met, and the chase was on again. He ran to his left diagonally across the street. He ran into a store and continued running until he reached the back of the store. The customers just looked at him. He paid them no mind. He ran up to the elevator and he pressed the button to go down. He had a keen view of the front of the store. He saw the goons enter. They looked around trying to locate him. He had lost them for a second.

The young men ran to the back of the store tracking his dirty wet prints. They saw that the elevator doors were about to close. They caught the elevator just in time to stick their arms in it and step inside. No one remained inside but regular customers.

"Damn", one of them exclaimed while striking the walls of the elevator with both hands. He had given them the slip. The elevator came to a stop at the bottom floor. He was now somewhere in the mall, a sly chameleon's playground. They each looked in a different direction. They backed up into a corner near the emergency exit. Suddenly the door opened, and the young man exited. He looked around, when all of their eyes met. He disappeared back into the escape. They grabbed the handle of the door and recommenced their chase.

The young man retreated back into an emergency exit. He thought that maybe he had lost them with his elevator dupe. He thought that maybe he had escaped them, and that it was over.

He ran down into the basement area, a restricted area. He hopped down the steps quickly as he heard the men up a few floors above come after him. He opened up the door leading to the outside, and he entered yet another alleyway. He ran to his right deeper into the dark moist alley. He looked back as he heard the door behind him open. Suddenly something knocked his head back, and he felt his feet leave the ground. The back of his head struck the ground hard.

He was clothes-lined. As he tried to look up he just saw the blurred image of the man.

The goons ran up to them. They looked down at him and they smiled.

"Finish him off quickly, and get rid of his body! We are running late!" the man ordered as he turned around and started to walk away. The man disappeared around the corner leading out of the alleyway, the way they had come from.

The young man had run so long, only to be captured. He hated himself for ever agreeing with them, and their wishes. When he first met

157

them, he knew that they were weird, a little scary even. He now wished that he would have followed his first instinct and walked away from them and their bizarre habits, their rituals, their trials, all of it.

They lifted him up and grabbed his neck. He thought maybe they would bite him, but instead, one of them pulled out a syringe and a medical vile. They loaded it with a clear substance. Then they tested the pressure squeezing some of the liquid out. They pulled his collar down, exposing his pale neck. The boy closed his eyes just hoping his death wouldn't be painful. He knew that they wouldn't want him to escape with knowledge of what they were doing, but he had no idea that they were going to kill him along with his secrets, their secrets. His heart was beating fast and hard. If they didn't hurry up, he would die of a cardiac episode before they could do as they pleased.

They other young men were excited, high on the thrill of taking his life.

"Just hold still, this will all be over soon."

"Yeah just keep your eyes closed." Then the boy holding the syringe looked to his right, towards the exit of the alley. He saw a dark figure standing there, just standing there. He tapped his friend and pointed. The third young man started walking towards him. The other two just continued with their objective. The figure still just stood there.

The young man walked slowly, but very confident. He pulled out a cigarette, and lit it up. He stuck it in his mouth, and he puffed away. He was about fifteen feet away, but he couldn't see a face or facial features. After two more steps, he stopped. He still couldn't see any face. He thought it was just because the alley was so dark.

It was a dark black alley. The only light in the alley was the light that came from behind the figure. The boy stood firm, cigarette in hand.

"Hey buddy, is there a problem?" There was no response. "Hey pal, I said, is there a problem." Still the figure made no response, not even a slight reaction.

The rest of them just looked on. The boy put the cigarette to his mouth and puffed it. The figure finally reacted. Slowly he reached for his back and grabbed the handle of the sword. Slowly he pulled it from the scabbard. The young man removed the cigarette from his lips.

"What the fuck" he said slowly. Suddenly he looked to his right. The cigarette smoke provided the outline for another figure. He backed up. He started to turn when he felt a sharp pain in his side. He looked down. There was a sword jutting out of his stomach. He felt his blood emptying into the alley. The other two turned to run away.

The young boy opened his eyes, and he heard a scream, then a muffled cough. He felt his arm being pulled. He was dragged around the corner where his capturers lay dead. They stripped him of his clothes.

They were looking at his body. He heard them say something while they were behind him. Suddenly everything went black.

Chapter 1: Power of mind

The river flows. The wise man is at one with nature.
The sun shines. The wise man is at one with nature.
The Earth turns. The wise man is at one with nature.
The fool speaks, and the wise man listens.

The man walked very slowly down the street; though it was more of a cruise than a walk. He was so sure that he could not be touched. He looked into the alleyway where he saw a horde of police activity. The man knew that something bad had happened, something bad enough to draw the attention of the very busy city police. Crime in the city had been on the increase. The overall mood had changed since **he** had disappeared. The mysterious young warrior whom was said to have went out during the great storm, and battled an extremely powerful evil presence, and was credited with saving everyone.

His name seemed to be fading. No one even remembered it in the city in which it became known. But criminals, they took advantage of people, their emotions, and their new outlook on life.

There were mysterious murders taking place all over the planet. They were unsolved, no suspects, no witnesses, no clues. After a while, police just categorized the crimes as copy cat murders. There was a small group that knew the truth though. I guess they could be called an organization. Their loyalty to each other, their resources, their prestige, was nothing short of admirable. All aspects of their organization were unknown to all except those whom were involved. Still though, no one knew who they were, or why they were around.

The man continued walking after a brief stare at the alley way he was in just hours prior to its congestion. "Wow", he thought, "They must have really done a number on that kid." A smile crossed his face as he once again disappeared into the shadows.

As samples were taken of the blood of each of the four victims, the detectives all were uneasy about taking on another one of the mystery cases. There was one detective though that seemed very anxious to take on the case.

He picked up pieces of the broken syringe and placed them into a plastic bag for evidence. He was a relatively fresh member in the squad. No one had disrespected him by calling him a rookie though. That title represented his level of skill in an almost ignorant matter. This kid was good, too good.

He crouched back down and searched each of the bodies. He had said nothing to anyone since he had been assigned to the case, but he seemed to show particular interest in this investigation. His partner stepped to the side to take some statements from the man who found the corpses. Two other detectives were standing against the wall talking. One of them smoked a cigarette, the other spoke. The detective still searched though. He pulled the collar down on one of the bodies. His eyes focused on the back of the neck of this young man. He took a photo. He searched the other two clothed bodies. He found their bullion to be on their arms.

He found what he was looking for; some way to link up these murders with the others. As he walked around to the naked body, the two detectives walked back around the corner. He immediately saw the marking on this young man's back as he lay face down.

Markings were on all the bodies of each of the cases. It was these markings, or symbols that meant something to the detective, but were a mystery to all else whom were on the case.

The detective wiped his forehead. Sweat ran down his face. It was not very warm outside though, in fact the air was pretty cool and humid. He saw what was happening. He saw what was to be his destiny. He let out a laugh of self doubt. He was on the edge, ready to jump, ready to plunge into his doom. He was sure that he would go out fighting though. He grabbed his left wrist and slid his cuff back revealing his watch. He was satisfied with the time, for he had no where to be, just another stab of anxiety. His watch slid down. Immediately his eyes locked on to it. They were fixed on his symbol, his commitment to the order. He concealed it quickly, and he took a deep breath. It was too late to change what he had done, but still he wondered.

Suddenly he felt a hand on his shoulder. He whipped around instantly. He saw his partner standing there with her hands up in defense.

"Whoa, calm down buddy! I just came for the evidence so I can drop it off at headquarters." He was relieved. His heart was now beating out of his chest. He abruptly handed it over to her. "Mark and Jimmy are over there having some smokes, you should head home, try to relax." He nodded his head.

As he drove down the highway, he kept his foot only on the accelerator. He just wanted to skip town, to get out of harms way. He knew that he had something in common with all of the victims. He had their same secret. He too was going to die with it. He looked in his rear view mirror, nothing. Just to be sure, he looked in his side view. As he resumed driving he felt it again, the uncommon feeling of being watched.

It was the same feeling all the victims of the mysterious murders had felt right before it happened. His eyes drifted from the road and they focused on his rear view mirror. Immediately he saw a black masked figure sitting in the back seat. He panicked and the car veered off of the road and into a wooded area. The man looked back into the mirror, gone.

He extended his right foot to the brake. He pressed the pedal in, there was no effect. He was going downhill, was it too steep to stop. He looked at his dash area. The brake fluid was low, virtually empty. He then knew what had happened. He let them get to him, and they had control. He also knew that it was now his time. His destiny was being fulfilled. He had no substantial part in the overall plan, for what they were trying to do had never been heard of.

He now came to terms with his death under the false terms that he was dying for a greater good. He saw the sky in front of him. In fact, he saw nothing but the sky. Then he closed his eyes.

The vehicle folded like an accordion upon impact, and it bounced into the air, somersaulting. It landed with a thud. The young detective had been killed instantly. The figure in black stood there. He brought his legs together, and touched the bridge of his nose with his index and middle fingers touching. He bowed his head.

It was a gesture done out of respect. Respect for the ignorant drawn into a war of certain magnitude that they could not begin to comprehend. A legendary war between good and evil fought for hundreds of thousands of years throughout the universe. Evil is a wicked being that always leaves trails behind for later generations to be tainted with. Good is the pillar of light that will shine forever, steadily getting brighter as the dark is pushed back. In the wars fought between these two armies though, the casualties are great, the risks are high, but the battles won are priceless.

<u>Chapter 2:</u> New weapons of war

To live in darkness is to live in seclusion...
To live in the light is to live weary of the dark...
To live in the shadows is to live aware of the light, but in the dark...
To live in twilight is to live a dream...but a definite impossibility.

The man walked forward very slowly. He was so sure that he was above all mortal reach, all living reach. He was deeply ignorant of the truth though. He was a middle-aged man, not too athletic, but he had a build. Just from first sight, there was an indiscernible sense that he looked at himself very highly. His chin was always held high, and he feared nothing, for he had yet to meet anything he should fear. As he walked back to his headquarters, he thought of one thing, his final test. He was hesitant to make the final step as it was done ceremonially. He wanted it to be special. He wanted to prepare for the change. Still, he had doubts that it would work. He only knew that he had taken all of the other steps, he had passed through all of the other trials, and he felt no different. He figured that he had come too far to turn back now. Nothing was going to stop him.

The ocean's gentle breeze completed the effect, with the assistance of the rippling of the waves, and the clean but not fresh smelling air. The sun's rays shot down on the umbrella. The serenity, the peace, the feeling of supreme satisfaction, it all put the man's mind to rest.

He released a sigh of contentment, and he closed his eyes. He lay there, thinking peacefully, living at one with himself and nature. He had achieved a level of meditation that is seldom reached. His mind was far from this peaceful place, in a place slightly more peaceful. He was rendered at the will of his imagination as he sunk deeper into his euphoria.

All he could see in his mind was darkness, and then it began to change. He saw one of his favorite things in nature, the clouds. He felt as if he was flying through them, it was so real, so seemingly tangible. Then his imagination shifted, and he was taken on another ride through one of his favorite natural occurrences. He saw the stars, the galaxy, a marvel he frequently saw himself captivated by. He zoomed through the galaxy as his conscious mind had seen it. Then he thought he heard a muffled sound. He listened more closely. It was his name, someone was calling his name. His mind twisted the situation, his subconscious reverted the truth. Suddenly he was transferred back to the sky scene. He was passing the clouds faster though. Then he broke through the ever surrounding moisture and saw he was on the path of a definite descent. Still he heard his name being called. "Rysqo" he heard in a pleading tone, a whining tone. Suddenly he hit the ground with a force that sent dust and dirt flying in all directions. He was in the middle of nowhere. No plant life, no vegetation, no human or animal life.

Flames circled around him in the distance, an approximate radius of one hundred feet all around him. Then he looked up into the once beautiful sky, and he gazed at the never ending darkness. It also seemed to be getting darker. Suddenly he heard a loud roaring sound. He spun around looking as the blare became louder. Suddenly, as if all at once the flames were put out, as massive waves overtook them with a great force. Rysqo had not known what to do as giant waves headed towards him from all directions. Rysqo disappeared into the waves as they collided with each other simultaneously.

Rysqo saw darkness again, and then his mind took him on another journey. He laid there wet on the grass. He heard the chirping of birds, but otherwise there was silence. He pushed himself up from the grass and stood up. He brushed himself off. He had no longer heard his name, he heard nothing. He heard a bird give a cry as it flew overhead. He looked up and was greeted with the sun's direct rays. He felt the earth rumbling up under him. He whirled around to see a swarm of black figures rushing at him. Then he turned the other way, to see many white figures rushing at him from the other direction. He was on a battle field. He was in the middle of a battle. "What side am I on..." he thought.

The two sides ran at each other and collided, but they were unarmed. They just fought, hand to hand, in an ostensibly fair battle. Each side seemed face to face. Then from behind the black side, and over the hills, more white figures emerged. They now had the advantage as they grew in numbers drastically. Rysqo watched as the black side was overtaken. He heard men scream and cry for help. Rysqo fixated his eye on one individual who was standing there facing him, dressed in black with his face covered. Suddenly white dressed figures came from all directions and knocked him down. He reached out for Rysqo whom now knew what side he was on as red dressed figures stood behind him. Rysqo heard the man's final scream, as his name was called, "Rysqo". The black figures start to retreat as Rysqo and his army of red people were left on the battlefield to deal with their apparent enemy. Then the white clothed people faced Rysqo and the red people. As Rysqo backed away, his followers did the same and the white colored people crept closer. Then a cliff appeared behind them. They were all trapped. The red colored people all began to call Rysqo's name, as if it was a chant.

Rysqo looked around, as he saw each of their faces all calling his name. Then he turned back towards the enemy and put his hands up. Then the colossal waves returned and washed them all away and headed for Rysqo.

Suddenly Rysqo awoke. His face was wet, and the sunshine was gone. It was replaced by dark clouds, and rain. His umbrella was gone, and his beach equipment was all gone.

"Rysqo...Rysqo! Get up! Rysqo I've been calling you for a long time. I already put the stuff in the car, come on Rysqo before it starts to come down harder." Rysqo shook his head and started to get up, his legs were soaked. "What a dream" he thought, "What a dream".

Chapter 3: The night's shade

To cast a shadow over the eyes of the holder of ultimate power is to contain, but not control it, to suppress not tame it. To guide this power into the light at the other end of the path is to not only give up this containment, but add to the strength.

R ysqo made his way up the stairs in the hotel. Tanya followed not too far behind him. She shielded her head with her hands and ran awkwardly. Rysqo rushed through the hallway down to his room. The rain shifted onto the terrace. Winds picked up and sent droplets splashing into Rysqo's face. They smacked into his left eye, and caused him to close it.

Rysqo reached into his pocket with his right hand, fumbling for his keys, while trying to hold their things in the other. Rysqo dropped his things and located the correct key. Access was granted finally. Tanya lunged into the room nearly knocking Rysqo off his feet as he picked up their things.

Rysqo entered the room wiping his face. His vision was still blurry, and he hated the taste of impure rain. Rysqo scanned the room trying to locate Tanya; but he saw nothing, no one. He walked into the bedroom area of the suite. Rysqo walked up behind Tanya, whom was fixated on an object on the bed. Rysqo walked up to her and squeezed her tightly when he looked past her and noticed the same object. A sword was penetrating the bed with a note attached to it. Rysqo grabbed the sword and pulled it out of the bed. He tossed it aside. He read the note. Rysqo took a deep breath. Rysqo closed his eyes, hoping that he would awaken from some other bizarre dream. Rysqo separated his eye lids slowly. He was still holding the note, and he was still standing there. Rysqo then turned to look at Tanya. She hadn't a clue what was going on.

Chapter 4: The Legendary One

The one has come. He has accepted his duties and he has fulfilled his birthright. The Prophecy as conjured by the blessed one has been rewritten. Destiny has had its way.

Now he must once again prove his majesty. The dark ones have returned. The mysterious ones have emerged. The victorious one has come back to defend all humanity once again. The war is fought differently this time though, and an alliance definitely must be made. Time is running out, for humanity, and for the living.

Rysqo's flight had gone smoothly. He had returned home, to his city of birth, and rebirth. Rysqo had made arrangements for Tanya and Damian so they would be far from harm. The harm of a battle he is once again leading.

Rysqo drove to his home with ease, though he was very tense. Tanya saw it on his face that he was not ready to return to his duties as the defender of all innocence. He was negligent of his responsibilities and had no desire to fight anymore. In their eyes the war had been fought and a victor had been decided. Tanya felt the peace in Rysqo's mind. She knew that he preferred this peaceful life, especially after what they had been through. She also knew that it was just a vacation, and Rysqo her husband, was still Rysqo, the Black Dragon. His responsibilities and priorities went far deeper than those dealing with fatherhood and marital issues. She knew this, and she accepted it. She remembered all that they had been through, and all that they expected. Though they had already seen more than they expected, she had an idea that it may not be over. Tanya saw Rysqo's lax attitude too. She knew he had to have expected more. She thought he was just moving on for her sake. Tanya felt a small warm feeling inside because of this. Her husband had given up so much for her, time after time. He had so much outside of his life with her though. She just wished she could do more for Rysqo than be his wife and lifetime partner.

Rysqo pulled up in front of his house and honked his horn and stepped out. The front door opened up, Damian stepped out with a suitcase. Rysqo met him halfway and relieved him of it. He placed the suitcase in the trunk. Damian returned to the house for another suitcase. Rysqo watched as he put it in the trunk. Rysqo returned to the driver's side door of his vehicle where Tanya had taken position. He gave her a kiss on the cheek. Damian hopped in the passenger side of the vehicle. Rysqo walked around to him and put his fist up Damian did the same, and they butted forearms. It was what he and Xavier used to do. No one spoke.

Tanya waved and pulled off. Rysqo turned and headed for his home. He waved to Monica whom was waiting to pull off. She had been babysitting Damian for the couple. Rysqo entered his home.

Rysqo turned on the television and switched to a news station to be updated on what was going on in the city. He wondered if he would learn some of the details as to the reason why he was contacted by the Wheels of Destiny. He had no idea who or what he was dealing with. Rysqo sensed the seriousness of their plea due to the message they had sent at the hotel. Rysqo was told that his services were needed, and that he would be contacted after he returned home. He had no idea when this would be. Rysqo did not like being on the long end of the stick. He felt threatened by the knowledge that these people had of him, and knew not what they wanted with him. Suddenly a news story caught his eye.

"This is a tragic day for law enforcement as detective John Donte Lamils' body was found in what appears to be a freak car accident. Not too many details are known in this case, at least, that is what police are telling us. What's that, I'm being told that detective Lamils was just working on a serious case, and had collected evidence that may have a great impact on the details of the crime that had taken place outside of the shopping center. Wow, once again a sad day for…" Rysqo switched the television off. He was satisfied that nothing was connected, just some freak accident by some punk reckless driving kid cop. Rysqo walked upstairs and to the master bedroom down the hall. Rysqo took off his shirt as he walked through the threshold, and tossed it towards the bed.

"It took you long enough Mr. Dauragon." Rysqo spun around to see a figure standing next to his door. Suddenly Rysqo felt a hand grab him from behind, as he turned to react, he was struck hard in the back of the head. Rysqo blacked out and fell to the ground.

"Bring him! It is time to get to work".

Chapter 5: The Dawning of an Eclipse

The sunrise starts the day, while the sunset ends the day.
An Eclipse is a blending of the two, a momentary end to the light, and a momentary addition to the dark.
To give a lesson partially, is to hold the full lesson as power over your student.
To continuously give the same lesson partially, is to hold the same power but gradually loose it.

"Wake him!" a man ordered.

"No…Not yet. I do not want the chosen one to see me. It is not meant to be, not here, not now." The younger man complied with the older man's wishes. He knew never to go against any of his requests. He waited until the elderly man had disappeared into the back of the room towards his lair.

"Okay, now wake him", the man ordered. The drones followed his orders. They gave Rysqo a whiff of some smelling salts. Rysqo had not responded. They reached down to try again. Rysqo grabbed one of their arms and twisted it so they fell to the ground next to him. He reached for the other one and they stepped back. Rysqo felt an intense pain in his head, and he fell on his stomach. He slowly pushed himself up into an all fours position. Rysqo felt a throbbing sensation in the back of his head. Rysqo rubbed the back of his head. He felt no abnormalities or disfigurement.

"The pain should leave you soon. We knew no other means of bringing you here."

Rysqo smiled and looked up at his apparent capture.

"Did you try asking?" Rysqo sarcastically questioned. The man did not respond.

"We mean you no harm. In fact, we are only here to keep you from that."

"Really; so who is this we you speak of, and what is your interest with me?" The man snapped his fingers. Suddenly it seemed as if the walls were moving and adding darkness to the already dark room. Black dressed figures started to come from the shadows. They were all around Rysqo. He couldn't even count all of them, but his guess was that there were at least fifty in the room. Rysqo stood up slowly, and he once again grabbed the back of his head. Rysqo was now in a state of amazement.

"We are the Wheels of Destiny. My name is Nightshade, and the Wheels of Destiny are under my command. Mr. Dauragon, we truly need your assistance. We all fight for the same thing. We are all on the same side in this war, and it is time that we work together." Nightshade could see that Rysqo was a bit lost, still amazed by their number.

"This way please Mr. Dauragon." Rysqo followed the man out past all the warriors. Nightshade guided Rysqo out of the room. He led Rysqo into a room not much smaller than the previous one. He led Rysqo to a long table dressed with food. He extended his arm as if giving Rysqo the go. Rysqo just took a seat though.

Nightshade walked up to a window and gazed out. He wrapped his arms around his back and clasped his hands. Nightshade pulled his face mask down, and re-clasps his hands. Rysqo could see that his hair was long, and in a ponytail.

"Everyone has their own beliefs and perceptions of the living, and of life. They have their own perceptions of death as well. Everyone has their own fears, and their own suspicions. Everyone knows something someone else doesn't know. Everyone also has the right to hold onto this knowledge. Everyone has the right to assume that someone else does know a little bit more or less than them as well. There is only one way to find out the truth though.

Knowledge is one of the most powerful weapons on this planet, and in the galaxy; knowledge of your enemies' advantages and disadvantages; knowledge of the past, present, and future; knowledge of the truth. To know the truth while others are still wondering, still guessing and hesitating to breach a wall holding them back from so much knowledge, or wisdom.

This knowledge is too sacred though to let everyone have access to. Some people can not handle this incredible weapon; the knowledge of the world's history and future, in perfect perspective.

Perspectives...there are too many to decide which one is credible. As history is written by different people, it is seen many different ways. There are many different accounts of what happened, happens, or is to happen, but only one truth. The truth and a truth are very different though. In their minds, they could be telling you their truth, involuntarily giving false information, false accounts of the truth. The truth cannot be combined with truths, for it will be tainted. In a room filled with doors, all exits, it is up to you which one you go through , you only have one choice. No matter what steps you take to get to this decision, no matter the logic you use, or your method; one choice, one chance. You cannot rewrite your history, or your life. The same goes with the truth. The truth and knowledge are similar though. Knowledge is constantly rewritten and updated to cohere with the truth. Bits and pieces are added throughout time. Still there is one truth, one real cluster of knowledge arranged to perfection. Think of it as a puzzle; the world's puzzle, the Earth's puzzle, the puzzle of time. To hold the accounts that fill this puzzle is to hold power. Power is controlled different ways though; sometimes concealed, sometimes flaunted. This power though, if given out to every individual, would in fact destroy the world. Rysqo, the knowledge of the truth...It can be rewritten! It has been rewritten. Thus the world has been changed or altered.

The Wheels of Destiny is an organization founded many thousands of years ago by a very wise old man by the name of Tevalian. Tevalian found out these truths a long time ago. He documented what he found in two accounts. Tevalian had believed what he had found was a power to be held with great responsibility, a responsibility too great for one man. So he entrusted a small group of young men with this knowledge to spread it out, but contain it. He told them only to share it with their families and pass it down generation after generation. Tevalian was reviewing his scriptures one day when he noticed that a small part of one was missing. This was the key to rewriting the truth. Tevalian remembered what it had included, the guidelines for attaining incredible power, and it was a power that could end the world.

This power was actually a translation of the believed worth of the knowledge. Tevalian saw that all the facts were not missing though. A warning still remained, and this was not good. The warning stated that the power was too much to exist in any galaxy. The holder of the power would be cast from all living beings, and existence.

No one would have expected that existence can be created and recreated by mortals time after time.

Tevalian quickly tried to determine the location of the scripture, but it was just too late. One of his associates had betrayed him. He was seeking ultimate power.

Tevalian then switched the priority of the group from protecting the people to insuring the knowledge did not get out of hand. Tevalian reviewed his scriptures searching for an answer to stopping this renegade. Tevalian read of a mysterious wheel placed somewhere on each planet that showed the destiny of the planet and its inhabitants. It said when the wheel stopped spinning; the fate of the world was in grave danger. Tevalian told his followers what they must do.

For years we have fought and protected the Wheel of Destiny, but it has stopped a couple of times and started up again. Rysqo, the Wheel of Destiny has stopped spinning again. Just as we have fought to protect the truth, the renegade and his followers have fought to put the truth out there. You see everyone would want their truth to be the truth, which is not possible. We search the world for any traces of his followers or descendants, and we eliminate the threat to the wheel, the Earth. We have had success in the past, but now after the last few years since you battled with The Collective, a product of the renegade's followers, the scripture has resurfaced.

An order has been created for the worshipping and experimenting of the script. This cult has reached out to young people worldwide especially. This is because somehow they are being contacted via the internet. With its nearly unlimited resources, this could spread very quickly. We are also suspecting that there are some who will be soon undergoing the process of attaining the power. If they succeed, and word gets out…that could spell the end for everything everywhere in the galaxy. Imagine an army of The Collective. Your past foes were just a sample of the secrets out there, a taste of the truth.

This problem must be contained. The world would be overcome so quickly that it would not have time to oust all of the fools. Imagine thousands of giant ticks biting into the Earth all at once, not giving it enough time to shake any off.

Rysqo time is running out, and we must do whatever it takes to get rid of this threat."

Rysqo looked at the man whom was still standing looking out of the window. It seemed as if he had told the story over and over or had it rehearsed. Rysqo then reached for a glass and poured himself some water out of a pitcher. He swallowed and his thirst was quenched.

"So, what do you want me to do?"

Chapter 6: A windless back

When the wind does not touch your back, but hits your face full speed, you are in front... but are you leading, shielding, or being sacrificed.

Rysqo was led to a small room with a large mirror and a bed. Rysqo looked over the room and located a box as he was instructed to do. The box was medium sized and square-shaped. Rysqo removed the lid of the box. He saw a black ninja suit like the ones that the other men were wearing. Rysqo grabbed it by the shoulders and lifted it up. It seemed to be a perfect fit.

As Rysqo lifted the uniform top higher and higher, he got a very awkward sensation. He had a flashback that came very suddenly. Rysqo saw the inside of the Divine Heights building with bullets streaming through its halls. He saw the black dressed figures fighting with the police enforcers. He saw the warehouse and the black dressed figures crashing through the ceiling. It all became too clear to Rysqo now. He was dealing with the same people, only now they were not after him. Rysqo began to think. He wondered if they were really after him before, or did they have some other purpose.

He now knew that they did not work with The Collective. He also knew that he was the product of one of the things that they were fighting. He was the product of haphazardly used power, forbidden power, false power. Rysqo looked at the mirror, and he became lost in his own eyes. He began to question their war. The war they have fought for centuries to no avail. Why had they requested his services? What difference would it make to hold off the evil for another couple of years? Rysqo dropped the top and began walking for the door. He reached for the knob when suddenly another flashback stunned him. He remembered his dream this time. He wondered what it had meant.

Rysqo sat down on the bed and plunged his face into his hands. Once again he was put into an awkward position, fighting someone else's war. Once again he falsely reassured himself that he was chosen, and no one else could do it.

178

Chapter 7: The chains of power

Witnesses to the legendary great power that holds the responsibilities that are so feared by the ordinary man learn to fear it's vessel or form when it is contained, or under control.
They see this controlling of the forbidden power as a threat to existence.
They find means of chaining down this power and making sure that it never is reached for.
They keep the power in check... but chains do weaken, and wills seldom break.

Rysqo finally emerged from the room in his new garb. His face as well as his feelings was covered. The other men looked at Rysqo and nodded their heads as if in acceptance. Nightshade was waiting in front of the door across the hall.

"Shall we begin" he asked as if Rysqo was in charge. Rysqo did not respond. He just shook his head.

As they walked through the halls, Rysqo observed their positioning throughout the halls. Their numbers were great but he questioned their skill level. A secret society trained to be an elite fighting force was something he seriously doubted was possible. Rysqo walked next to Nightshade, whom was taller than he.

Rysqo and Nightshade walked into a room filled with computers each with their own attendant. They walked up to the first attendant they saw. The man turned around to look up at the two.

"Now", he asked. Nightshade shook his head. Immediately, the man pressed the button. Rysqo watched as the computers in the room all reacted and went blank. The man's computer was the only one that had remained on. Rysqo looked at Nightshade for clarification. Nightshade smiled.

"…A virus. Our resources allowed us to move deep into the networking of the order. Our computer experts, or hackers as you would call them, are elite. We have disabled the servers for now, but we only have a couple of hours. You witnessed the other computers shutting down around us? They were logged on as members to the order. What you just saw, is what members are seeing worldwide. We have erased all traces of the order in their computers, and rebooted them. This is only step one, for we have about seven to eight hours before midnight."

Rysqo looked puzzled and was just about to ask Nightshade a question when he had it answered. "At midnight Rysqo, the believed leader of this cult order, the only man said to have passed nine trials, plans to undergo the final trial." Rysqo looked at Nightshade. "…Suicide! …To them it is self-sacrifice. It was to be broadcast via internet, but we have slowed them down. If word was spread that fast that the trials work, and that this was not just some punk order, the website would spread like the Macarena. Now we just have to go to their headquarters and take down the order."

"By take down you mean kill a bunch of innocent kids experimenting and trying to fit in", Rysqo jabbed.

"No by take down he means prevent a universal catastrophe, caused by children doing what they shouldn't be. They are not the innocents in this world."

Rysqo just looked at the man sitting at the computer. His job was done, and he had probably never even taken a life. He had no idea of his ignorant callousness, for it was all he knew. Rysqo knew the children were innocent, at least he knew they were as innocent as he was when he was in a similar position on the football field that day long ago. Having so many problems going on at the same time jumping into the first canyon you see. No matter the depth or consequence. These children accessing the internet though were innocent minded. The promise of power and the promise of brotherhood and devotion were attractive to them. The promise of safety and security in a cruel untamed world was comforting to them. Rysqo understood their feelings, because at one time he had felt it. He had felt lost and unwanted, like no one understood him.

What pained Rysqo now was that he knew what his dream represented. It represented a vision interpreted by his subconscious as colors that represented different levels of innocents. The black represented the Wheels of Destiny, innocent because they were not in the light. They were the killers in the shadows, for he was to be exposed. The white represented the members of the order, innocent because of there lack of malicious intent. The red represented those who were not involved, the families, the friends, all of humanity, animals, all of the uninformed. Their innocence need not be defined. All levels of innocence because of the sins of men eons earlier.

Evil is not created, it is found.

Chapter 8: Identity

A mirror allows you to see yourself, but it may not show who you are...

The heavy metal door opened very slowly as six men emerged. The two men in the front were draped in cloaks with hoods up. The two men in the back carried candles. In the middle there were two more men one in front of the other though, in a formation resembling a capital I.

The first man carried a pillow with a dagger on it. The second man walked very confidently with his head held high. They entered a very large room, and it was filled with many people, men and women of all ages, all different races and ethnicities. They all watched as the entourage proceeded to the center of the room. It seemed as if a stage had been set up. The first two men proceeded up the steps and took their position on the stage. The next man walked up and waited in the center. The next man did the same, standing side by side with the knife bearer. The remaining pair of men stopped at the steps of the stage. The men in the cloaks left the platform.

The man looked around the large room, almost in a trance. He reached for the dagger and pulled it from the pillow. The knife bearer then left the platform leaving the man there by himself. Suddenly the men already outside the platform lifted their candles to the apron of the platform. The flames spread around the platform instantly. The man watched as soon his vision was blocked by a wall of flames. He could see nothing but the bright red of the flames. He could feel nothing but the heat of the flames. He could hear the chants though. Through this wall of inferno, he could still hear them as they chanted. This was the part of the ritual in which you literally could not turn back.

He had almost forgotten what had to be done. He had almost let his one chance of absolute power slip through his fingers. He closed his eyes and raised his hands high above his head. Down they went as he plunged the dagger into his abdomen.

~~~~~~

Rysqo looked out of the side of the helicopter as they prepared to ascend. He fastened his seatbelt and took a deep breath. Nightshade and the others looked at him. Rysqo paid them no mind though. It was if they expected him to ride without being properly restrained. Nightshade had brought with him in the helicopter five whom he had considered the elite. There was Blaze, Chan, Vince, Rose, and Jade. Rysqo's eyebrows raised, he was confused.

"Okay, so you disabled their server, so what, but how do you know where to look for them? I mean this planet is pretty big. You don't expect to bump into them in the air do you?" Nightshade looked at Rysqo and smiled, and then he looked at his watch.

"Okay, it's go time, we have to get moving. It has probably already begun." On Nightshade's command the helicopter rose into the sky gaining altitude quickly as it propelled itself forward.

Rysqo looked at Nightshade, whom was raising his mask. The others did the same, so naturally Rysqo followed cue. They looked as if they were about to rob a bank. It was so ironic that they were wearing the garbs of evil to do good.

Rysqo peeked out of the helicopter again, when it hit him.

"What do you mean it has already begun?" Rysqo shouted.

Suddenly the sky became very dark. The helicopter jolted backwards awkwardly and stabilized.

"What was that?" Rysqo yelled. The others started to fumble with their equipment. Rysqo swallowed and leaned his head backwards. Then about thirty miles ahead in the northeast, a column of flames thrust into the sky. They all gazed at this bright beam as it spun in front of them. Then it exploded, sending a shockwave of fire in all directions for about a fifty mile radius. The flames collapsed upon the windshield of the helicopter, sending glass flying into the belly of this metal bird. The passengers all shielded their face. Rysqo watched as Blaze tossed the lines out of the side of the helicopter. He watched as they were yanked back and forth by the wind. Suddenly Rysqo noticed that they were no longer steady, but rolling into a death spiral. He looked to the cockpit area, and noticed that both of the pilots were slumped over. As he looked past them in the distance he saw a flurry of flashing lights and heard a clamor of sirens and alarms on the H.U.D.

"We must jump Mr. Dauragon, we are about to crash!" One by one they exited the screeching beast. Rysqo and Nightshade were the only ones left now. Rysqo unfastened himself, and made a leap from the side door. Rysqo balled himself up as he dropped. The wire was attached to a ring on his waist. The wire ripped through the ring quickly, as Rysqo could hear the whistling of the wind beside him everywhere. Rysqo opened his arms and legs as if he was a falling angel. He then realized that this was another wave of nostalgia. This was not the first time he had experienced this falling sensation, and it probably would not be the last. His dream was certainly coming true, right before his eyes. He didn't know whether to be worried or excited, for at least he knew what was coming next.

Chapter 9: Insertion

When placed in hostile situations we learn to adapt, creating a comfortable aura around ourselves.
We fall back into our instincts, and embrace a more primitive and reflexive way of thought.

A splinter is quick and usually not painful at first.
It sometimes slips in undetected.
Only when a splinter is recognized or extracted do you start to feel the pain.

Darkness surrounded him. It was a deep dark silence that was eerily soothing. His eyes were open, but still, he saw nothing but darkness. He glanced to the right, then left, nothing.

Was he awake? Was this another bizarre dream? Suddenly he heard a whistling sound. Moments later it shifted to a roar. It grew louder, closer, and then it moved all around him. Behind him, above him, circling him, then it stopped; so sudden, just as it began. Then in a flash of bright light he saw a glimmer of what looked like cold steel coming down on his head. It was if a sword was about to split him into two. Then he closed his eyes, hoping to ease the pain.

"Rysqo...Rysqo...Rysqo! You okay? He is not moving. I can't even tell if he is breathing." Blaze reached for Rysqo's neck to check for his pulse as the rest all stood around Rysqo's body.

"Stand aside", Nightshade commanded, as he extended his arm towards Rysqo's face. He waved his arm back and forth while holding a familiar set of smelling salts. Rysqo jerked forward, and shook his head. He wiped his eyes, and checked his head for gashes and blood. Then Rysqo looked around. He said nothing; he just stood up and brushed some dust and debris off of his body.

As Rysqo surveyed the landscape, he saw the damage was minor, though it did look like a battlefield. Most of the structures remained intact. There were patches of grass all around though that was aflame. Rysqo saw ashes everywhere, dust everywhere. He could only wonder how many people were hurt, and if he knew any of them. What a tragedy it would be to realize that someone he loved was hurt. Rysqo felt anger inside now, an anger that upset him like he had not felt for quite some time. His peace was interrupted; his life, halted; his destiny, steadily rolling along. Rysqo felt a burning rage inside himself. This sensation hurt him while at the same time aroused him.

Rysqo clenched his fists, and looked around, searching for an outlet, some poor soul to vent his emotions onto. None of these people were to blame though, although they did serve a role in this malefaction. This was all the aftermath of the sins of men eons before them. They were left to deal with their loose ends, their curses and secrets. Rysqo also realized that they were fighting for the same reason, though he did not want to classify himself in a group with them.

"Are we ready...I mean we are just standing around. Let's go enact some justice. That is our purpose, correct?" Nightshade smiled at the warrior's humor. "Where do we go now?" Rysqo asked.

"The path will reveal itself; we need not look for it. Searching for the uncertain will only prove to render us at the will of our expectations and imaginations. We shall walk in the direction of that pillar of light that we saw." Rysqo shook his head as he eagerly led the way.

Chapter 10: The blazing dragon of the rose garden

Ignorance leads one to question what they lack knowledge of, and how much everyone else knows. This can lead to over ambition or stereotypical interpretations of a world beyond your own. Respect for that of which you do not understand serves as the first stone being extracted from the wall that has kept you from understanding it. Willingness to accept and admit your own shortcomings can lead to a cure to them.

A dragon breathes fire and is a beast of true power. A dragon though inherently powerful and wise, lacks respect for all else in the realm. Roses are things of beauty when undisturbed, a marvel that displays nature's capabilities in full effect. Roses though, are misleading. Though they are beautiful, and peaceful, they have thorns.
A dragon knows only to hate that which it can not defeat or control.

Landing in a bed of roses, disrespectfully; pricked by multiple thorns at touchdown, the dragon lets out a roar. Peace is disrupted, and harmony broken. The dragon's pride hurt. Once again, its jaws open, this time to unleash waves of flames from its mouth. Then the roses ignite, one by one, their concord altered. The dragon was then overcome by its own flames as the blaze engulfed it, swallowing it up in its own misery.

Outnumbered they stood, about to enter what they presumed to be the origin of the pillar of flames they saw rise into the sky. Rysqo opened these broad metal doors. As they separated, a gust a wind was sent echoing out into the street. As it hissed pass their ears, they stared at each other.

Rysqo stepped into the building. It was nighttime, it was eerily dark, and it was quiet. The sounds of the city they had heard before seemed to be filtered from the building. There was nothing but darkness in this building as they stood in what had appeared to be some sort of lobby. Rysqo extended his hands and slowly proceeded through the room. An odor of barbeque did seem to fill this room. It was also blackened by stains that could only be made by carbon and smoke.

It was apparent to Rysqo that they were indeed in the right place. Blaze reached for his hip and freed a flare from a loop. He ignited the flare and waved it back and forth scanning the room. It was relatively small; charred and filled with debris. The only things that were in the room were a desk and pictures on the wall. Rysqo spotted a light switch mounted on a wall not to far to his right. He flickered the light switch, and got no response.

"C'mon, c'mon..." Rysqo exclaimed. Then they heard a surge, and the room was illuminated.

"Probably the back up generators kicking in..." Chan said.

Blaze threw down his flare and approached a painting. He stared at it, as it hung directly behind the desk. The symbol looked familiar to him for some reason. Then he realized that it was the symbol of the cult order. It was the marking that they had all shared.

"I see you are admiring the mark of Tevalian, or as I would like to call it, the mark of the devil." Nightshade approached Blaze from behind. "Let's just hope that we do not encounter too many of his followers that have that mark. It was said that if you had that mark you were a devoted follower of Tevalian, and one of the brethren. All of his followers believed that they were protected by him, as long as they were willing to sacrifice themselves at the time of his request, whenever it might be. Tevalian was a very powerful man during his time, but he was much feared, so feared that people misunderstood his purpose. He could predict things that were unbelievable, but some said that he made his predictions come true. A man of great power feared and revered. His followers were the worst types of all extremists, for they did more than sacrifice themselves for him, they would sacrifice others and stop at nothing to please him. He never did seem to be pleased though. Don't mistake him for an evil man either, just a misdirected soul that can't really be blamed for his actions. Throughout history though, The Wheels have respected that Tevalian's followers are the most extreme, because you must realize that we are his followers too, and we fight for a distinctive purpose as well." Blaze nodded, and walked away from the painting. He did not really care for Nightshade's lectures, but had respected his wisdom.

Rysqo paced the room scanning for some sort of imperfection that might lead to a trap door or switch. Success; he noticed that a floor panel he had stepped over seemed hollowed out. Rysqo cleared the area. They all walked up to him and waited to see what he would do next. Rysqo looked at them.

"This must be the way. Help me lift this panel." They all complied with his request except Nightshade, whom was not satisfied that this was the way. He went off on his own venture for an entrance. He turned around to face the painting again. Its size was captivating. Then he thought he had seen it ripple. As he leaned in to it, he noticed that it moved. Nightshade jerked himself through.

Rysqo turned around to see Nightshade disappear into the wall. The painting was nothing but highly detailed lattice work. Behind this entrance there was a long hallway. They had no choice but to follow it, for they did not see any other way to go. A chosen seven, embarking on what they knew would be a treacherous journey into enemy territory. They had entered without permission, and violated the secrecy of the order. They had many strikes against them already, and not one of them knew what to expect beyond the end of this hallway. Fear and uncertainty coursed through their veins and consumed their minds. As they reached the large doors at the end of the hallway, this sensation of fear grew stronger.

"Wait!" Rysqo ordered. "What can we expect behind those doors? I mean what are we fighting?" The others did not know how to respond to Rysqo's sudden question, so they turned to face Nightshade.

Nightshade looked down and shook his head. He was hesitant at answering any of Rysqo's questions, for it was easier to just keep him in the dark. He knew though, that it would be detrimental to hide any details or unknowns from the one person who was said to be their savior. He was the chosen one, yes, but how much could he do.

When the Wheel of Destiny had stopped spinning that meant for the universe the future was uncertain. It meant that the mortals must presently decide what fate would come about. Rysqo was indeed a valuable weapon in this battle, but he needed to be controlled. If he knew he was going up against a being of immeasurable power, something that has never been seen in such circumstances, he might lose task. What ever was behind those doors was a juggernaut. Nightshade edged his way up to Rysqo. He studied Rysqo's eyes. He saw that Rysqo's question was very sincere, and that he might not continue on if it was not answered.

"Tell me what difference does it make? All of you, what would it matter, if we were fighting a weak powerless being or an undefeatable one.

What would change? Would we not still be fighting to defend the defenseless? Would we not be fighting to defend peace, and uphold justice? Would we not be fighting to save what we care for? What difference does the opponent make? What value does the risk have? We are the chosen few. We are the one's that have no choice but to fight because we are chosen. We step into the unknown together, and we shall emerge together at the other end of the valley. We fight for a reason, the more we start to question this reason, the more victories our enemy has."

Everyone was silenced. It was really a shame the effect that Nightshade had on people. He possessed the ability to be so powerful using only words. Not many had seen him fight though, for all those that did died in battle next to him.

Rysqo was not fazed by his strong words. He asked a question, and he wanted an answer.

"This fight of yours Nightshade, is mine too, and theirs, it is everyone's. So I believe everyone has the right to know what we are going up against." Rysqo again waited for an answer. Nightshade answered the best he knew how to.

"I don't know…"

Chapter 11: Regret

As we try to find our place in life, we realize that it may not be known to others...
Generation after generation, there are some that stand out and take the reins of their brethren.
Day after day, there are some that take life for granted and try to separate this leadership from its obligation.
They hold the same power, the charismatic ability to lead others, but lack somewhere else, causing them to live lives of bitterness and regret, aware of what could have or possibly should have been.

Not many men have power, but everyone has strength...

Rysqo and the others were now ready. They were mentally prepared. Their questions had not been answered, but their imaginations and anxiety now took heed.

Jade and Chan pulled at the doors handles. As they separated, an even more powerful gust of warm air was sent surging through the threshold. Ashes were carried by this air and into the faces of the seven masked figures outside of the doors. Rysqo wiped his face and dusted himself off. The rest did the same as he led them into this room. It was charred and disfigured. The room looked very unstable and dilapidated.

As Rysqo walked forward he crunched many objects that were on the ground. He looked down, amazed to find that the ground was completely covered with skeletons and ashes. The many individuals that had died in this room apparently had their flesh burned completely off. Rysqo looked up to see the full moon through a gaping hole in the ceiling. Rysqo turned to face Nightshade and the others,

"Okay what now? I can't see a trace of anything. Whatever was supposed to be in here probably escaped through the ceiling…"

Nightshade looked up, and then looked left to right. He shook his head,

"No Rysqo, nothing escaped. Something was cast through there, by the planet. Do you understand that this means the trials were successful? Somewhere in the galaxy right now, a new being is born awakening to new power. Hopefully they will not realize the true extent just yet. It is truly up to them how powerful they will become. Decades ago, when Coryphaeus Apedien first completed his trials, and was cast away, he did not try to return to Earth. He created a planet of his own to rule. The Coryphaeus that you fought so long ago could have been a thousand times more powerful and a thousand times more dangerous. Mans' dreams create the power, so it can not be defined. One thing we must count on though is that we can somehow lure this being back to Earth, so we can destroy it."

Nightshade walked past Rysqo and up to the altar. Moonlight had shone directly onto it. The only thing inside of the room that was structurally intact was now before him. It was a glass case that housed the original scripture that had been passed down for years by the descendants of the renegade monk. He punched through the glass and grabbed it. "Okay, we are done here."

Chapter 12: Awaken

Sleep is a time of peace, undisturbed...
Sleep is a time of dreams, undisturbed...
But when reality blends with a dream, the result is a mind that runs wild
with possibilities.
To live and dream every day never tasting a thing of power always
thinking of what to do with it is more dangerous than waking up one
morning with everything...
To crave is natural, to have is fortunate, and to take is wrong...
But, to keep is even worse...

They walked slowly through the hallway, past the dark room, past the table with the food. Rysqo stopped to think where they were going, but the rest of them had not.

Rysqo followed Nightshade down a spiraling set of stairs deep into darkness. Then he opened the door. It was a beautiful room well lit, very colorful. The ceiling was clearly painted because it was sunny and bright. Clouds were full and it smelled like the outdoors. Rysqo was amazed that a room such as this could exist in this building. Suddenly Rysqo saw the ceiling change to stars, it was beautiful. He then realized that this corresponded to his dream as well. Nightshade stopped and turned around. He signaled his men, the five masked figures exited.

"He waits for you in here Rysqo. He probably already knows you are here. Be warned, that he sees all, knows all, feels all, and hears all. He is the one that originally requested your presence. We are just puppets to him. I serve him, as my father did as his father did, and all of my ancestors did. He is the one, the only one. So be careful not to harbor questions or thoughts from him. Rysqo I wish you luck in speaking with him, and I will see you when you emerge. And please give this to him." With that, Nightshade gave Rysqo the piece of the scripture and left his side.

Rysqo knocked on the door.

"Come in", he heard a voice say from the other side. Rysqo did as he was told. He was still so uneasy of everything that has taken place in the last couple of hours. Rysqo walked into a large round room. It had a huge bed in the center of it. Rysqo looked around, seeing nothing else in the room. "Have a seat" the voice said.

Rysqo looked down as a chair appeared before him. Rysqo was even more concerned now.

"With the last piece of the scripture returned to me, my strength will be at its max, and I will finally be able to rest." Rysqo was confused as he looked down at his hand that held the scripture. As Rysqo's eyes looked back up, he saw a very elderly man standing before him. He was very old, and very sickly looking Rysqo thought, forgetting what Nightshade had told him. Rysqo handed the piece to him. "Ah yes, finally" the man said while reaching for it. He reached into his garbs and pulled out what looked like the rest of the scripture. Rysqo's eyes opened wide, *could this be*.

Rysqo watched as the paper bound together and merged into one. Then the old man reached into his garbs again and pulled out a ball of fire. It was as if he was a magician. "I have just ended it all Rysqo. I will bring the one you seek to Earth and destroy the others that follow in his footsteps. I will purify this galaxy of all that which has plagued it for thousands of years. With my power restored, I can do this, though it should have been done thousands of years ago. Rysqo you have done well to make it here, you have done well for this planet. You wonder, about your dreams, you wonder about your purpose, you wonder about its purpose, and the purpose of purpose. Rysqo you wonder too much. I can answer any question you may have, or have ever thought of. No Rysqo, I will not harm you. Yes you are a being that was the result of all this negativity, but you are pure of heart, the purest of any other individual in this universe. You are the chosen one. You are destined to be endowed with my powers as they have surged through you for years. You are righteous, you are good. So I will spare you.

Rysqo, I am old though, I have existed for eons. I was man before I came across the truth so long ago. My time is here. For years I have fought, for years I have watched others fight. The time has come for me to step down. The Wheel of Destiny has been restored only to stop again, time after time. Rysqo, I have received all of my powers again, yet I can do nothing more in this war. I have seen the future to the extent of my powers, and I see my time must end here. The fate of the universe should never weigh down on one as it has done on me. I made the mistake of bringing this power into being, and for years it has kept me alive only to feel the pain of my actions. I witnessed death upon death for centuries. I am still not the most powerful being in this universe though. The one thing that has kept me here is love. Love for humanity, and love for life. I could have given up the war a long time ago, but I have seen it to the end. No more evil will be created through my mistakes, for now the ceremony can never be repeated again.

Rysqo I leave you here to fight the evil that still exists. You have suffered much since you first entered this war, and changed from an innocent into the chosen one. You are unable to live a normal life which has no impact on the outcome of the final battles. Rysqo you are the one, the only one that can save all living things, you are the secret to making and breaking destiny. The Wheel has no impact on you, for you are void. You are the one Earth warrior that will change everything.

I can do nothing more to help you though Rysqo. I will warn you though. Trusting your heart and love is the key to defeating any enemy. Never be consumed with hate, and be careful not to trust those whom are. Rysqo, Nightshade is unlike you. He is a very talented man, very crafty. He also is a traitor to all I have fought for. He knows the limits of my power, yet he still tests them. He works against me to aid in the destruction of this universe. He has no compassion for man, and he speaks of endless hate for the many living, sinning creatures of Earth. Rysqo he is lost, you must guide him. He knows what I have told you, for he anticipates it, and prepares for your destruction. He let me bring you here and inform you, because like me, he knows of your duty. He knew since the beginning, since the prophecy I scripted. He also knows that I will not be able to stop him. He knows that it is the end for me. He thinks that he will be able to complete his goal with you out of the picture, and of this I am unsure. Rysqo he means to destroy not only you but everything, including himself. This may seem impossible, but believe me, it is not. In my years of wisdom, I have found that there is a way. There is a process that can be started, and not stopped unless the ultimate Negroblatus is made. The name sounds familiar because Rysqo, Negroblatus means black sacrifice. A dark sacrifice is made to preserve the living one final time. It can only be made once, just as the process can only be started once. Eons ago men feared the apocalypse not knowing that with judgment day came no resolution. The process known only as The Forbidden is far more devastating to everything.

Rysqo, never before have you fought for a more important cause than this. The only thing that you can do is to wait until it begins. I am sure that you will know what to do when it begins. If you defeat them now before it begins, then you will surely have done nothing. Millions of years from now, the same events will take place minus me, and minus you, and nothing will be able to be done to save eternity. There are seven that wish to decide the fate for life, and in time you must grant them death."

Moments later Rysqo watched as the old man lay on his bed and died, knowing he had served his purpose, and would always be remembered. Rysqo was more focused now than ever in his life. Things had changed now, for him, for his family, and for all the living. One thing that did not change was his heart. He was eager to do his part now, for he knew just how important he was to everything. Rysqo bowed his head in silence now for Tevalian the keeper of The Wheel of Destiny.

EPILOGUE

Though Rysqo now knew of his true intent, Nightshade did not appear worried as he watched the door knob turn. He killed Acumenus years ago to start the chain reaction that made Rysqo realize his power. He knew everything Rysqo knew, and he knew more. He also knew how to start The Forbidden, and knew that he needed Rysqo for that as well.

Rysqo,

the

Black Dragon
Part 4

A Foretold Future

INTRODUCTION

The paradox of history; wise decisions made by wise men, shifting the future for later generations. The consequence of their actions, becoming the result they are left with, conjured by the worth of their words, the weight of their hand, the blessing of their presence. To live all days regarded highly as a saint, a savior, or to live revered and hated; the majesty of your name not displaying the arc of your wisdom. Your name in conversations, brightening faces, not causing similar frowns.

What a life to live the victim of a self determined act. To fall victim of a decision made many years in precession. To live plagued with gifts others dare not manifest, but would congratulate all good deeds that accompany it. Who could predict what every minute decision would produce.

A normal decision made by a normal man could weigh just as heavy on the balance of the universe as that of a wise man's.

All the components of consequence; no longer must you make wise and just decisions, but now you must live with the results.

PROLOGUE

He lay there, still in a crater he had just recently created. Upon impact he was knocked out. He returned through the atmosphere scorching hot, still disfigured from his first trip through. His flesh melted in certain spots to the bone. It was a miracle he was alive. Was he alive though?

The man had been burned severely in three separate instances recently, and stabbed himself in the stomach with a blade sharp enough to cut bones like butter. Still he lay motionless, with little life left in him. He knew that he was alive somehow. He knew that he was okay. He wondered how his final trial had gone, but he could not move. He could barely even breathe.

He felt no such strength that he had read about in the scriptures, no power. His mind and body were fatigued to a point past expiration. His limbs were bloody and burned. His body felt bad, and he wondered how he looked. Suddenly a mirror appeared before him. He was shocked that his thoughts were put immediately into action. It was then he realized that everything he had worked for over the past years had been well worth it.

He was successful; no he was more than successful, for he was a god. Alexander S. Gailor was no more. He would now call himself Genero.

Chapter 1: Manifest

Life is a gift given expected to be given again and again...this is love.
Life can be given expected to take life as well...this is hate.

Tanya sat with Damian as they watched the television program. He was so into it that he did not even notice his mother gasp and grab her chest. Tanya then grabbed her head. Damian then looked up at her. He had a puzzled look on his face. She walked out of the room, and towards the bathroom. She looked into the mirror as she turned the faucet on. She ran her hands through the water and up onto her face.

She felt strange, unlike she had ever felt before. She immediately thought about her husband. He was all she could think about. For some reason she felt that he was in danger, but there was no way for her to contact him. She had to know what was going on. She then left the bathroom and picked up the phone.

Venus walked towards the ringing phone in her apartment. She had picked up on mortal customs very well in a short time. She now lived by herself, and was doing well. She had almost reached the phone, when she had felt feint. She tried to grab the phone but her hand passed right through the table. She looked at her hands, they were translucent. Venus then looked towards the window as she watched herself fade away to nothing. The last thing she remembered was the bright sunny sky, it was so beautiful.

<u>Chapter2:</u> The Fortuned

Those whom are cavalier need not worry about pain, for they expect it.
There are also those that try to hide pain's effect on them.
It is hard to hide, and it will one day show…pain has no preferred victim,
for it falls upon some of most undeserving people…
Then there are also those that feel no pain because they have caused so
much…
The fortuned, are those that feel pain, but can move on past a downed time
in their life…
Everyone is not capable of doing this…

Tanya hung up the phone. There was no answer. She wondered if Venus too had felt the sudden jolt that she had just experienced. Tanya returned to the living room area next to Damian.

"Damian honey, I want you to stay here okay, I will be right back."

Tanya ran upstairs to search through her things. Monica and Michelle were both at work, and Tanya and Damian were still their guests. It had been one week now without word from Rysqo. Tanya had rarely seen times like this. She had not known if his mission was successful, she was curious as to if he was okay.

To be married to a man of such responsibilities is very tiresome on one's mind. Tanya spent twenty two hours of her days worrying, two hours wishing and hoping. Her life had become totally overtaken since her and Rysqo had been through so much together. Her love for him had never changed though. If he was to die, she knew not if she could love again. She had died once, and Rysqo proved his love to her by doing the same. This was before they had children, before they had greater responsibilities. Why could she not spend the rest of her days with him; Rysqo. She married Rysqo, not Rysqo, the Black Dragon. What a shame their relationship had become. She wondered if his love was still as strong. It was rare that they got to show it anymore. After all, they were soul mates right; destined to be together, fortunate to have found each other. The last time her husband had spent quality time with her was on the ride back from the trip. Rysqo was now, somewhere in the world, battling evil forces that would threaten to harm humanity. All the while, she sits at home waiting, for her husband, her love, to return. She knew that he needed her love and support, but she had no idea how much more he needed from her.

<u>Chapter 3:</u> Tomorrow's sunrise

Maybe tomorrow will never dawn,
Maybe tonight will never come,
Maybe the world is full of questions,
Maybe I could answer just one.

Tanya lifted her pen from her diary. The four line poem she had just written satisfied her. It summed up her feelings well. She wrote frequently in her diary, recording her thoughts. She planned to write a book one day, the book that housed all her feelings towards life and death, and everything in between. She thought that maybe she could do something productive. She took a deep breath and exhaled. Why did this happen to her? Then her eyes narrowed. What if Rysqo had never met her? Would things have changed for them? Would this evil have ever come? Would he ever have been endowed or chosen? It soon became clear to her, that she was not just some housewife to a hero. She too had played a part in the fate of the universe. Her children that she bore with Rysqo too, were important, only because she had them with Rysqo. She jumped up, and started to walk down the stairs. Damian was so obedient, still sitting there watching television. She looked at her watch, soon. She put on her coat and sat next to her son.

"Where are you going mommy? Can I come?"

"No sweetie, mommy has to go somewhere important. Your Aunties should be home soon." Just as she said that, Monica and Michelle walked through the door. They waved as Tanya rushed right past them. All they could do is look at each other.

<u>Chapter 4:</u> Becoming

When you start to understand your purpose in life, you realize that where you had searched before is a distant memory. To search is to fail, for some things find you.
The purpose of life is to live, search for another and you have failed...

Tanya pulled up to the small building and parked at one of it's sides. She had been here only once before. It was an experience she had tried to forget. It scared her tremendously. It was the day that Rysqo saved her and Monica in Mr. Long's store, she came here right afterwards. Monica had dragged her into the building that she thought was a hut…

"C'mon Tanya, stop being a wuss. We just survived a hair raising experience, we are lucky to be alive girl. We need to see this lady, because it might be the time to hit the lottery or something." Tanya shook her head,

"We aren't even old enough to play the lottery yet. Besides, I don't believe in mumbo jumbo. I wish I would pay someone to lie in my face." Monica smiled.

"Now you know that you are lucky, why try to hide it. Rysqo just happened to be walking through the back of the store. C'mon girl, think about. You love him, and he loves you. You two were meant to be together. It is a love that even death would respect."

Monica pushed her way into the door. The room was dark, barely lit. The air had many scents in it. They seemed foul to Tanya. Monica eagerly sat in the first chair. Tanya reluctantly sat next to her. She looked around and around. This place seemed eerie, but why, she did not believe in superstition. She did feel something though. A jolting pain echoed throughout her stomach.

"I think I am going to be sick", Tanya gurgled.

"What's wrong, you chickening out on me? Man I knew you were soft." Monica kept picking at her, knowing her friend did look ill.

"It's not that, it must be this smell or something." Tanya grabbed at her stomach. She was usually in pretty good health. For about a week though, she had felt slightly ill. Then a small middle aged woman emerged through a beaded threshold. She smiled while staring at Tanya whom did not even notice her yet. She waved at Monica.

"Who is your friend Monica?" Tanya looked up at the woman. She was dressed normally; she did not seem strange at all. Suddenly she felt relieved, but the nausea stayed with her. Monica got up and walked to the back, dragging the woman with her.

Tanya sat there alone in silence until moments later she heard cackling and loud talking. Monica came storming out with a smile on her face.

"Are you ready to go? I mean that is if you aren't going in there". Tanya thought maybe the lady had some water or medicine. She stood up and walked through the beads.

This room was even darker. Tanya saw that the woman had remained seated, even as she entered.

"Excuse me. You wouldn't happen to have any medicine would you? I need something for an upset stomach. Or do you have a bathroom around here?" The woman smiled, and pointed to her right. She watched as Tanya walked into the bathroom. Tanya turned on the faucet and ran her hands through and up to her face. Then she exited.

"Better?" Tanya responded by shaking her head. "I knew you would be. Besides, I wouldn't be responsible for giving you medicine in your condition." The woman continued smiling. Tanya looked at her. What did she mean condition? She did not want to engage in her mind games though, so she let it go. "Why don't you have a seat sweetie, chairs don't hurt, wonderful invention. I know you don't believe. Sometimes, the stuff I predict, I don't want to believe myself." Tanya sat down slowly.

"But I don't have any money on me…"

"Aw don't worry about that, think of it as congratulation, or a pre-graduation present from me. What is it, three more weeks" Tanya smiled,

"Four" The woman then smiled.

"You win some you lose some huh? Remember that. I bet you are wondering what I meant when I said condition. I mean you don't seem to know already, so I will have to say it. Tanya, you're pregnant."

Tanya's eyes opened wide. She didn't know if she could argue with the woman though, with the way she was feeling. The woman reached for Tanya's hands. She turned her palms upward. "I take it he isn't just any old guy either? He is special, special beyond words. Tanya honey, you have got a keeper. This young man is very important to you and this child, though it is sad to say that he can do nothing to protect the two of you. You and this child though, will form a bond that will be broken.

The two of you were destined to be together, and bear together. The stars do tell of the couple of lovers that would save them. Wonderful aren't they, the stars; so beautiful, and so bright. Surrounded by endless darkness, yet they still shine bright. You and he are stars as well. You must keep each other shining bright, adding fire to the other." Tanya was getting lost in the woman's words. She was stating everything about her and Rysqo.

"How could you possibly know all of this? Who are you?" Tanya was curious as to the whereabouts of the woman's wisdom.

"Me, I am no one, I never will be. I am here for you to see that you are someone. Time will continue on if I die, but you, you are needed; at least by him. He needs you more than you ever will know. You probably don't understand now though, but one day you will." Tanya stood up and backed out of the room. The woman sat there and watched, smiling.

Chapter 5: A Foretold Future

Past present and future are what we make it.
Then, now and soon, is how we see it.
But couldn't, didn't, and won't, just prove that you might or will...
To deny the inevitable truths by avoiding them is lying only to one's self...

Tanya walked through the small dark room into the darker room past the beads.

~~~~~~

She sat there, waiting for her to arrive. She knew she would be coming, for it was time for her to do her part. She looked well since the last time that she had seen her.

"You finally made it. Ah, and you have more pain. Rest assured, you are not pregnant again. Your days of bearing children with the one are over." Tanya sat down,

"What do you mean, over? Is Rysqo okay? Is there some way to reach him?"

"Ah, so the disbeliever has become the believer in need? Its funny isn't it, what time can reveal to a person? You never thought about coming back did you? I knew you would, I saw it. I see a lot of things about you. Tanya, Rysqo is fine for the moment, but he is in danger, his future is uncertain. No harm has come to him, but he suffers great pain. He needs you Tanya, but you can not be with him."

"Why are you contradicting yourself, you are making no sense?"

"Tanya, the end is coming, very soon. Rysqo can see it. He knows not what to do. You know not what to do. I can do nothing. There is darkness around you and him again. Remember I said you were stars. Rysqo must bring the light. He must save us from the darkness once more; only one more time will he save though. He will be free once his quest is over. Your wish shall come true. You will have a chance to be a normal family. Tanya, I warn you though, you think that you want normal, but you don't. It will cause you great pain in the end. Your love will be tested in the end, and you two shall suffer the same pain at the same time. It is the only way." Tanya shook her head, confused.

"I came here so you could clear things up, and I am going to leave, more confused".

"Tanya! Rysqo sacrificed himself once for this planet and saved it along with you and him. It can not be done again. He must choose what is more important, harming you, or saving everything including you. Tanya you must understand that the end is coming. There is but one way to stop it. There are two major sacrifices in this world, black and white. To save us, Rysqo must make the black sacrifice. To damn us someone will make the white sacrifice. The black must be made after the white in order for it to work. They are equally as devastating, but they conflict with one another, thus creating balance. This is the way it must be. With your love is the only way he can make the black sacrifice when the time comes." Tanya still was confused. Her suspicions were correct though, for Rysqo had needed her greatly.

EPILOGUE

Tanya exited the building, just as confused. He needed her, but she could not be with him. Tanya drove back to Monica's place, somewhere comfortable where she could think. The end, what will happen? What could she expect to see? Will Rysqo be able to save things again? Will good conquer evil? Will evil conquer good? What does the end mean?

Rysqo,

the

Black Dragon

Part 5

The Shadow

INTRODUCTION

To know one's self one must be alone. To be alone one must be unhappy. To be unhappy one must be willing to sacrifice. To sacrifice, you must be prepared to undergo any task. The great task at hand though far, far from any man's intellectual reach, is a task to be completed alone.

In every man's life, time is needed to find themselves. During the long stretch each man must overcome a period of time with themselves. They take time to review what they have accomplished. They take time re-evaluating their worth. Such a task could break a strong man's will, or erase the traces of a legend.

There is always more to be done, but the absence of the acceptance of results you produce, could drive one mad. No one can do everything there is to do in a lifetime, but everyone can dream. Some people live other peoples' dreams, some die trying. But everyone follows one fate. The chance that they could predetermine this fate is not likely.

To see your own fate is to live damned and constricted to the knowledge of the following second, waiting for each event to happen counting down every second, until the clock stops with its hands spelling your demise. The fortunes are to remain unturned, as the shadow valleys are to remain un-walked. Walk hand-in-hand with your past and present and meet your awaiting future.

PROLOGUE

"Something pulls me here, something is telling me to come here." The man floated into the building, disfigured. He was so horribly burned and injured. He was pulled to this building, but he knew not why. As he entered it, he lost all of his energy, and collapsed. It had been a long trip, across many miles of land and water. His powers were going to waste, he thought. What did he get himself into? He lay there in the darkened room, in the center of the floor. He remembered why in his dreams. He became Genero to help people. He wanted to do good. He didn't know how to go about it though. He now felt that maybe he had made some wrong decisions along the way. Many people were hurt so he could reach his goal. He now wondered was it worth the pain and suffering to bring peace and salvation. He hasn't even helped anyone, and he was about to die.

About twenty masked figures emerged from the walls to pick up the body of this man. They carried him through a large hallway and into a room. They put his body down gently, so not to wake him, and returned to the shadows, from which they emerged.

Chapter 1: The gauntlet

Finding the will to fight once it is lost is hard...
Finding an excuse to fight is easy...
Finding someone worth fighting with reason is the true test of a warrior...

R ysqo pushed his way through the door and into the next room. Rysqo made immediate eye contact with Nightshade. Nightshade smiled as he saw the fire in Rysqo's eyes burn brighter and brighter. Rysqo began to walk toward him. Nightshade raised his hand, and waved his finger back and forth warning Rysqo.

"Now is not the time...soon" Nightshade then snapped his fingers. Rysqo looked around as the walls started to ripple and move. One by one, masked figures emerged from the walls. Rysqo turned around to see they were behind him as well.

Nightshade signaled one of them to bring Rysqo to him. The ninja reached for Rysqo's shoulder. Rysqo turned into his hand and hit him in the stomach. Then he circled his arm around and locked it up. Rysqo then swung his body in a circle tossing the man aside. Nightshade signaled again. This time two ran at Rysqo. Rysqo jumped toward them with legs extended. He punched one in the face with his left hand, then right, then left. He then spun backwards delivering a back fist to the other. His necked whipped around. The first ninja swung at Rysqo. Rysqo blocked and countered while stepping to the side. The man went down. The other one ran at Rysqo. Rysqo dipped into him while delivering an elbow to his ribs.

"That is enough; I do not have time for this. Someone, bring me his head. That includes the five of you too!" Nightshade said while pointing at Blaze, Chan, Rose, Jade, and Vince. They nodded. Rysqo then started to run directly at Nightshade, using his speed ability. Nightshade smiled and disappeared into the shadows.

"What the..." Rysqo had no idea what Nightshade could do. Rysqo looked around at about twenty five opponents. He was outnumbered, and they appeared to keep on coming from out of nowhere. Every black wall appeared to be formed completely of Nightshade's followers. Rysqo ran for Tevalian's room and dove in.

<u>Chapter 2:</u> An Extreme Legend

The time has come for the one to fight like he has never fought before…
The passion to protect, the will to defend, the strength to uphold
The ability to make a difference…
He is alone, but he is looked after…

R ysqo backed away from the door. He waited for them to come, for he knew they would. He heard commotion on the other side of the door. Loud commotion, as if a fight was taking place on the other side. Then Rysqo readied himself as the knob began to turn.

Jade entered the room, followed by Blaze, Chan, Rose, and Vince. Jade put her hand up in a stop motion. She got on her knees.

"Rysqo, we mean you no harm. We have come to assist you. We are against what Nightshade is trying to do. Tevalian warned us what Nightshade would one day try this. That day has come Rysqo, for you have arrived. As we speak Nightshade is going to start the chain reaction of events that will start The Forbidden. We will take you to him."

Rysqo let his guard down.

"Take me there."

Chapter 3: Renzoku Toji

The term is used by The Wheels of Destiny and means last chance...
Many wonder, last chance at what, success, salvation...

The six of them walked slowly through the hallway towards the stairs. Rysqo saw that this building was built like a castle, much larger and more deceiving than he was led to believe. The stairs led deep down into the lower bowels of the building.

It was dark, damp and dark. No one even cast a shadow. With no light, Rysqo could barely see in front of him.

They made it to the bottom, an even darker area. Blaze walked up to a wall and hit a switch. The whole perimeter was immediately illuminated. Rysqo and the others walked in unison through this room. It was a long room.

"Keep your guard up!" Chan warned.

"His pet roams this area…" Blaze added. Rysqo knew not of what they spoke of, but he was ready. The lights started to flicker. Rysqo and the others saw this. They sped up. Behind them, one by one the lights went out on both sides of the room. They started to run. Rysqo kept up but he did not know why they were running.

"Stay away from the dark Rysqo!" Jade warned as they ran and ran.

Suddenly Rose tripped and slid forward. Rysqo almost stopped to turn around when Vince did as he tried to pick Rose up. Suddenly Rysqo heard a scream behind him. He continued running as he turned back to see Vince's body drop from the air. Rysqo could make out the silhouette of a flying creature. It swooped down upon Rose ripping her spirit from her body.

Rysqo turned back to see that about one hundred yards in front of him, there was a door. Jade reached it first, bursting through. Next Blaze ran through, then Rysqo, then Chan. She closed the door behind them. Rysqo was out of breath and hunched over.

"What was that" he managed to ask.

"That was The Shadow; the tortured spirit of a hungry phoenix that grants death to all that come in contact with it. Nightshade created it as his protector and as a protector for The Wheels of Destiny if we ever failed in our mission."

Rysqo was almost ready to move again when he saw the lights on the walls moving again.

"We must move" Jade said as she pushed Rysqo towards the next door. They fought their way through ninja after ninja, as they appeared repeatedly. They were so close.

Chapter 4: Wonder

Miracles happen so commonly that we do not even recognize them…
Life is one…
Living is another…
Saving a life is the most precious…

Rysqo pushed forward, as he saw Chan, Jade, and Blaze fall at his side. He fought and fought as he made it ever so close to the final run.

"Who are you" Genero asked. Nightshade smiled, but did not answer right away. Genero watched as he walked closer to him.

"I am a man, who is in need of you assistance." Genero was shocked that someone needed his help.

"How..." he asked. Nightshade rolled his eyes.

"You can help everyone at the same time. Only you can do it, with your abilities." Genero looked at him, how did he know? Nightshade smiled, "This is what you have to do."

Rysqo had almost made it to the final door when a ninja jumped in front of him. The man made quick motions with his hands as if challenging Rysqo. Rysqo walked up to him. They engaged in a fight. Rysqo defeated him quickly. As he started to walk forward again, many more appeared. Rysqo was starting to get annoyed. His attention was then adverted as he heard a roar behind him. Rysqo saw the ninjas backing up. He very slowly turned around. About twenty feet behind him was The Shadow. Rysqo was fed up. Anger consumed him and his mind was filled with the desire to cause pain. He started to walk towards it. The Shadow dove upwards and headed straight for Rysqo. Rysqo braced himself for impact as it collided with him. The force knocked Rysqo down on one knee. His shirt was ripped from his skin. Rysqo let out a roar of frustration, and stood up. The ninjas all stood there, puzzled. Rysqo turned around and faced them. He shook his arms, then his legs. Then he rotated his neck. He rolled his eyes then focused on his next victims. Rysqo was the chosen one, and the time had come. Rysqo looked around, no one had stepped forward, he had to initiate. Rysqo walked towards the door, and they made their move. The first attacked, Rysqo knocked him into a wall. The second, then third, and so on. Rysqo disabled them all, one by one, alone.

EPILOGUE

The stage is set for a battle like no other. Rysqo had been prepared to use his abilities on whatever he encountered next. He was ready and willing to fight anything. He was prepared for everything, or so he thought...

Rysqo,

the

Black Dragon

Part 6

The Forbidden

INTRODUCTION

This is a story about death. This story was not written to scare you, or make you take on some harsh actions. This story yields no response, no expectations, but respect. The respect of knowledge, the respect of opinion, the respect for the time and effort needed to write the book; the dedication and devotion to the series. To die un-respected, to die in vain, after living a lifetime of no worth, to be able to say that you did nothing, or not all that you wanted to do; to die dissatisfied with your life, your being. To cast away all it's worth and it's meaning.

To then say that you never lived is to speak the truth. Uncertain of your conscious being, maybe you did not live. Maybe you did not breathe the air of the Earth; maybe you never experienced the sensation of any thing on Earth. Maybe you never read this book...or maybe, just maybe you did, and you would like to forget it.

To accept death is not easy. We all know it can not be avoided, but to accept it...no. Some people fear death, fear speaking of it, fear thinking of it. Some people open their arms, for death to enter their lives. Should we question why? Is it our concern? Would our existence change sufficiently enough to care about anyone else's death? All questions answered at some time in life, though avoided. One thing is for sure though, death comes to everyone. Some expect it and some fall victim, the result is always the same, the end...

PROLOGUE

Tanya was sitting with Damian as he felt a breeze enter the room. Damian looked up to see how his mother was reacting. Almost as soon as he did though, she was gone. Damian jumped up and ran upstairs to find Monica and Michelle.

Tanya came to her senses in a round room. In the center was a dark pit. She looked up to see Nightshade holding a sword. He swung it down hard as she looked away.

Chapter 1: The Forbidden

The time has come…
Without love, a world is doomed to die in its own misery…

Rysqo entered the room. Nightshade held the body with both of his hands and tossed it into the pit.

"Rysqo, you made it. You are right on schedule too. You see, once I destroy her, it is unstoppable. I have already started the process."

Rysqo looked on the ground before Nightshade to see his wife. Tanya looked at Rysqo with fear in her eyes. She had just seen this man killed right before her. Rysqo started to walk toward Nightshade.

"Why are you doing this? What would cause a man to want to destroy everything?"

"I want the pain to end. I want everything to be done. This world is full off death, full of hate and anger. So many people don't deserve to live. So many people go through each day committing wrongs against one another. Animals are killing animals for food; the survival games that we live in. It must end.

Throughout the universe there is destruction, sin. I want to purify that which we have created. I want to correct the years of mistakes by man by erasing everything, here and now. I have seen all the evil this world has within it. I see no reason to let any life exist."

"You must not have seen too much of this world if all you see is the bad. This world is a terrible place and a great place. We live and die experiencing some of the most amazing things. I question those who see nothing but hate and I wonder if they have ever found love, or ever been hurt. When pain is all you seek, it is all you know. I know love, for I have questioned what love is. I can not explain it, yet I know I have found it. What you seek to do would be stealing this opportunity from everyone, everything that has never had a chance to experience it. Will you only be satisfied knowing that nothing exists? Men kill men thinking they do what is right. One of the worst things they could do, and yet they believe that it is right. You are no better, and you have no right to decide!"

Rysqo readied himself. Nightshade did the same, sword still in hand. Tanya crawled to a safer position in the room.

Nightshade charged at Rysqo. Rysqo dodged his first attack, then his second.

"When will you see that it is over? It can not be stopped. I have summoned The Forbidden, and soon it will arrive." Rysqo kicked Nightshade backwards. Nightshade stumbled and dropped his sword. He and Rysqo eyed it as it rolled. It rolled into the hole. Rysqo and Nightshade looked at each other. Nightshade charged at Rysqo with a barrage of punches. Rysqo used his speed to counter them one by one. "Men need not worry anymore about life, and need not fear death, for there will be no pain." Rysqo hit Nightshade again. Nightshade ran at Rysqo. Rysqo jumped and kicked. Nightshade ran right through his kick. Rysqo turned around to be hit in the face, sent backward. Nightshade kicked him in his ribs knocking him to the ground. Rysqo looked up as Nightshade was about to stomp on his face. Rysqo quickly disappeared into the ground and rose behind Nightshade. Nightshade whipped around. Rysqo was now on the attack, backing Nightshade into a wall. Rysqo was about to hit him when he collided with the wall and went through it. Rysqo dove through after him.

Tanya watched as they both disappeared into the wall opposite her. Moments later she saw Rysqo get knocked back through holding a long staff. He rolled forward up to her feet. Rysqo stood on one knee and faced her. He winked at her. Then she gasped. Nightshade brought his staff down above Rysqo's head. Rysqo blocked just in time. They fought with the staffs until Rysqo finally disarmed Nightshade, and they were tossed aside. Nightshade ran at Tanya as Rysqo swept him, and kicked him backward. Rysqo and Nightshade were now both breathing very hard.

"Well Nightshade, it doesn't look like The Forbidden to me!" Rysqo teased Nightshade, knowing he was already frustrated. Nightshade lowered his head, and charged at Rysqo. Rysqo stepped to the side and grabbed the back of his collar, pulling him backwards. Nightshade fell to his buttocks.

They fought more and more until Rysqo had enough. Nightshade swung one final time at Rysqo. Rysqo blocked and concentrated to land one more blow. He remembered all of his opponents, all of his friends, the words of the Black Dragon, the words of Tevalian, and his daughter. His hit landed, with a force that sent Nightshade flying. He hit the wall with a thud. Rysqo watched as he bounced off the wall. Rysqo walked up to his body as it lay there limp, motionless. Rysqo reached to turn him over, when Nightshade pulled out a dagger and cut Rysqo. Rysqo backed up, while grabbing his arm. Rysqo winced in pain, and then quickly healed it. Nightshade stood up, knife in hand.

"This ends here Rysqo. The end is now. I shall make the sacrifice." Nightshade drove the dagger into his stomach and fell to the ground.

Chapter 2: Rysqo, the Black Dragon

In the beginning, there was darkness in men's hearts.
The darkness came from not knowing, and not respecting the power of love.
One man saw this power and fought to hide it.
He failed as he too was overtaken by the dark as his one true love was lost to time.
Inside him there grew hate. This hate added to the darkness, and unleashed the power.
The actions and mistakes made led men to chase this power only to have their way with it, ignorant of their sins.
From this came more suffering and the planet could not withstand such losses of life at one time.
It banished those who would dare chase the forbidden power, and it created a being to end all existence.
Somehow one of the banished souls survived.
This soul already consumed with greed created an order of followers known as The Collective.
From this came a being, a being whose power was immeasurable, this was Black Dragon.
It marked a boy, the chosen one. Rysqo was his name.
Soon he saw his power, the ability to save all eternity and then there was light, a bright light that blinded all those that dared to hate.
Out of this light it came, a being more powerful, a being that was created to end all existence
This being now shall cast judgment through the will of one man.
Forces of life are affected by his existence, for he is in control of making the final decision.

R ysqo walked up to Tanya. He reached out to her and lifted her up.
"Are you okay?" She looked at herself.
"I think so. Is it over?"
"I don't know."
Rysqo and Tanya started to walk towards the door. Suddenly the ground began to shake and Rysqo held Tanya tightly. Everything went black.

Rysqo could see nothing. He was no longer holding Tanya. Rysqo looked around. There was endless darkness. Suddenly something began to appear in front of him. There was a faint light that grew stronger and stronger, until it was so bright it was hard for Rysqo to look into.

"Are you the one that is to decide?" Rysqo was forced to answer,

"Yes, I am Rysqo, the Black Dragon; who or what are you?" Rysqo stood stiff as he waited for his question to be answered.

"I am a question. Answer me Rysqo. Why do you fight? What is there to this world that would lead one on a journey such as yours, so full of pain, so full of suffering? Your unhappiness ails you as it brings others life. You have given, only to have to give again and again. Are all mortals like you? Do all things feel what you feel? What do you feel Rysqo? Are you angry now? Are you happy? To know that it is over, you should be relieved. Your story will be told never. Your name shall never be spoken again. You can rest. How do you feel?"

"How do I feel? It is not about rest, or how I feel. It is about right and wrong, good and bad."

"Do you feel that you can change things? Good and bad will always be Rysqo. There is little you can do. Something else drives you Rysqo, tell me, what is it?" Rysqo hesitated to answer, The Forbidden was right. Why did he fight? Why did he risk his life? Why did he give up so much, only to have accomplished nothing? Rysqo had justified his will to fight time and time again, but now, with the end here, why go on? He could rest, and let the damnations of every other living thing be washed away. It would be over. It would be the ultimate end to the legacy of creation. Rysqo would no longer be responsible for saving everything. He was tired of cleaning up the universe's mess.

Rysqo opened his mouth to say he did not know when he saw Tanya, laying behind the light. Rysqo then knew the answer to The Forbidden question.

"….Love", Rysqo softly said.

"…love. Would you justify years of fighting for love? Would you give up everything for love?"

"I have done it before!" Rysqo exclaimed.

"What you did before Rysqo, was sacrifice…If you truly believe in love, then you must be willing to give it up. You must be willing to do more than die, but live a dead life void of your love. You must give up your love so that everything else will exist. That is true love, to give it up at one end to preserve the being as a whole." Rysqo was shocked. Could he give up his love, with Tanya, just to save everything? Was it worth losing his one true love?

His soul mate lay there in a deep sleep as he prepared to decide her fate, and the fate of all existence. Why? I need to love, he thought. I need Tanya, he thought. One unhappy man in a world of love, is that a fair price to pay, he thought. Rysqo closed his eyes as a tear streaked down his face. The last time he cried, was when he lost Hope. Hope, he never wanted to loose her again. He never wanted to loose Tanya again, or have her loose him. He didn't care about being selfish. He didn't care about anything else. *"Rysqo, you must decide. Will you give up your love so that time will continue…? Will you make the black sacrifice?"* Rysqo wiped his face. He looked at Tanya, and remembered Tevalian's words. Rysqo closed his eyes again, and took a deep breath. The one thing he had always remembered since he heard it was *follow your heart*. With that thought Rysqo, the Black Dragon made his decision.

"…I can't, I love her too much…"

"Very well Rysqo, the Black Dragon, the pure of heart, goodbye"

Chapter 3: The End

When the real end comes,
We can be sure that there are those out there whom do believe in love, and would fight to preserve it.
Life is a precious gift, and death only teaches us to love more what we still have…
Time waits for no one as death overlooks no one,
Love is found by all those that welcome it with open arms,
In the end though, we all must give a little in order be sure that it will go on…
If we forget to pass on love, then we have forgotten all that we strive so hard for…

Rysqo, the Black Dragon. I knew him, having spoken with him once. He was different. He was pure. He made his decision through his true feelings, not what he thought was better. He did what he wanted, which was neither right nor wrong. He chose to keep love, rather than save a world full of love and hate. His love was so strong, that it cleared the darkness. The black sacrifice was made. He chose to give up everything so that he could love one last time. This is a lesson well taught to humanity. To be willing to give, and take when the time comes is something to remember. With all that plagues the planet Earth, there still exists a world of love, slowly fading away. The time will one day come when love may not be saved, but until then...cherish it, for you never know when the sun will set no more.

EPILOGUE

Rysqo walked with his son through the crowd of people. He waited in line for his check to be cashed, as he saw the bank teller look behind him over his shoulder.

"Excuse me sir hold on."

"Not a problem", he said.

The man turned around to see a middle aged man walking to the teller station next to him. He eyed him, he looked strange. The man turned to look at him. The man's teller asked the suspicious looking man,

"Can I help you with something sir? That teller is on a break." He looked at her, and walked closer.

"Yeah, fill this bag up now!" he commanded. The man pulled out a semi-automatic weapon. The man next to him saw the weapon and shielded his son.

"Get back Damian." the boy's father whispered. The gunman said,

"Empty it now." Damian's father raised his hands up and walked closer to the man. Damian looked on as if confused by what was taking place in front of his eyes.

"Don't do this." his father pleaded. The gunman pointed the gun at him,

"Shut up." Damian's father continued to try to talk him out of it.

"Look, my friend, it really is not worth…" he was interrupted.

"I said shut up." the gunman barked. Damian's father continued to talk. The gunman was filled with frustration.

"Why do you want to rob this bank? Don't you know that they will probably catch you anyway? You are risking losing it all for what, a little cash to get you moving? There is more to life than money my friend." The gunman started to cry. Tears streaked down his face.

"I know, I know…it's just…things are getting rough…I have got kids to feed and my wife she said he was going to leave me…" Rysqo felt sorry for the man now.

Three rounds entered the man's chest. His body dropped slowly to the ground. The security guard holstered his weapon and walked over to Rysqo.

"You okay? You did some fancy talking there son. You ever thought about going into law enforcement?" Rysqo grabbed Damian's hand.

"No, your job is dangerous. I lost a friend to security once and I have a wife and son whom I love. I can't take any risks like that."

Rysqo and Damian walked out of the bank to Tanya whom was waiting in the car.

"Rysqo what just happened in there, I heard gunshots?" Rysqo started up his car,

"Nothing, just another confused man not knowing what he had, getting what he thought he wanted."

Rysqo sped off into the traffic, rolling up his windows to avoid hearing the road rage comments, or loud music, and boisterous noise. Now was the time for him to be with his family, Rysqo Dauragon's family.

AFTERWARDS

Rysqo raised the pen from the paper. He was satisfied that he had completed his point. He read his letter silently to himself.

Dear Xavier,

My friend, I forgive you.

~Rysqo

The End